Destroying the

BIKER

CASSIE
ALEXANDRA

Destroying the Biker

Cover designed by Kellie Dennis at Book Cover By Design
Cover model – Gus Caleb Smyrnios
Photographer – CJC Photography

ONE

AVA

"**A**CTION!" THE DIRECTOR called.

Adrenaline on fire, I shifted my foot from the brake to the accelerator of the pickup and took off down HWY 95. Reaching the first marker, I turned the wheel toward desert terrain, feeling every bump all the way through to my teeth. Checking the rearview mirror, I noticed Chuck Donovan, the other stunt driver, gathering speed behind me in the black SUV. I mentally prepared myself for what was to come next.

You've got this, I told myself, trying not to think of the crash that had happened on the set the day before. There'd been a chase scene down *Flamingo Road*. Another stunt driver had miscalculated a turn and was now dealing with a spinal injury. If that wasn't bad enough, two weeks prior, one of the Special Effects techs had lost a couple of fingers in an explosion. Being that I was slightly superstitious — okay *very* superstitious — my inner alarm was screaming that something else was bound to happen, because *everyone* knew… bad things happened in threes.

I quickly touched the lucky crucifix hanging from my neck, the one my foster mother, Millie, had given me the day she signed the papers to legally adopting me. Millie told me that if I believed in what it represented, it would lead me down the right path and keep me safe. Although I wasn't a religious person, I had to admit, life had gotten easier. Especially compared to the hellish childhood I'd endured prior to Millie. A childhood that still had me visiting a therapist once a month.

Chuck gunned it and was next to me as we raced through some of the shittiest territory imaginable. Bracing myself for impact, I clenched my teeth as he slammed the side of his vehicle into mine.

The pickup fishtailed. I quickly regained control and waited for him to hit me again, which he did. In turn, I hit the gas and turned the wheel sharply to the left, rolling the pickup onto its side.

"Cut!" the director yelled through his megaphone.

Hoping this take would stick, I waited until the signal came for me to get out of the vehicle.

"Great job, Rhodes," Ben, the assistant director, said after I crawled out of the pickup and removed my helmet. "That shot was good." He looked me up and down. "What about you? All in one piece?"

"Yeah, I feel fine. What about that other scene, Ben?" I set the helmet down on the sand and removed my sunglasses. "The gas station explosion? We still on for that one too, or are they shooting it tomorrow?"

"Tomorrow," he said, watching me clean the dust from my glasses. "Go and take the rest of the evening off." He checked his clipboard. "Just be back around eight a.m."

I sighed in relief.

It had been a long day of retakes and I was starting to get a headache. A cold bottle of beer and some Chipotle sounded like heaven at the moment.

"Sounds good. See you tomorrow."

Ben patted me on the back. "Have to say, I'm impressed with your work. You do your job and don't complain. It's a nice change from some of the people we've hired in the past."

I grinned. "Thanks for giving me a chance."

Although I'd done a lot of other jobs, most of them had been low-budget commercials and movies. This one was definitely a much higher caliber, as was the pay.

He winked. "No problem."

I left the set, still feeling pretty good about Ben's compliment, and changed out of costume in one of the trailers. As I headed toward the red Kawasaki Ninja I'd rented during my stay in Vegas, I ran into Hunter Calloway, who was the lead actor in the movie being filmed. It was about a CIA agent who'd lost his memory and was being hunted down by other agents he'd double-crossed. I was his co-star's stunt-double for the movie, an actress named Valerie James, who didn't do action or nude scenes. I did both, mainly because it paid very well and, frankly, modesty was something I'd lost a long time ago. Hunter was in his late forties, handsome, but also an arrogant pig with an ego the size of Texas.

"Ava, hold up," he said, as I pretended not to see him.

Grumbling under my breath, I turned around and curled my lips back into a smile. "What's up, Hunter?"

He jogged up to me. "I'm done filming for the day and was wondering if you'd like to join me for dinner?"

I took in Hunter's fake orange tan, and had to bite my tongue to keep from commenting on it. "I wish I could. I'm having dinner with some friends. Thank you, though."

"Maybe next time?" he asked, looking disappointed. "I'll take you somewhere nice."

I don't know why... but that statement irritated me. Probably because I couldn't stand the prick. We'd recently had an intimate scene, and although he was supposed to have worn a penis-sock during the shoot, Hunter had "forgotten" to put it on. I'd ignored his arousal completely, mainly because he didn't even apologize for it. In fact, I could tell by the way he'd been looking at me that I was supposed to have been impressed.

"Honestly, I don't think it's a good idea. Unless, we're going to dinner as a group."

His forehead wrinkled. "Why?"

"I think it's important to keep a platonic relationship when you're working with someone. It's a rule I have."

"It's just dinner between some friends," he replied. "Nothing romantic."

I raised my eyebrows. "So, it wouldn't just be the two of

6

us?"

"Look, if you don't want to have dinner, fine. I was seriously just trying to be a nice guy," he said gruffly.

I wondered if I'd been too quick to judge him. I normally had a hard time trusting anyone, and many times, looked for the bad instead of the good in people.

Hell, maybe I'd even been wrong about the missing penis-sock? It was quite possible he'd really forgotten to bring it.

Feeling a little foolish, I apologized for jumping to conclusions and thanked him again for the offer.

"Another time then?" he asked, smiling again.

I nodded. "Yeah. Of course."

We said goodbye and then I headed to my motorcycle. I started the engine, pulled my hair back, and slipped the helmet on. A few seconds later, I was on the road, leaving a day's worth of stress and anxiety in my dust as I drove back toward Vegas.

AN HOUR LATER, I walked into the bungalow the studio had rented for me, a bag of Chipotle in one hand and a six pack of Michelob Ultra in the other. After putting everything down on the kitchen table, I checked my cell phone, which had been vibrating in my pocket on the ride back. Seeing that I had a voicemail from Millie, I played it right away.

"Ava," she said in a somber voice. "I have some news for you about your birth-mother, Sheila. Please, call me when you get a moment."

The message caused a lump in my throat. I hadn't seen Sheila in almost twenty years and the unexpected rush of emotions surprised me. She'd been a junkie, which was why Social Services had taken me away from her in the first place. Instead of trying to clean up and get me back, she'd disappeared, leaving me in a system even more dangerous than living with her.

Dialing Millie, I thought about my older half-brother, Andrew, and wondered if she'd learned anything about him. When I was little, he'd lived with his old man and had visited us every other weekend, until one morning there'd been some kind of argument between Sheila and him. I couldn't even recall what it had been about, but afterward, she wouldn't let him come over anymore. It had broken my heart. I'd *loved* my older brother. He'd been sweet, caring, and closer to me than anyone else in the world. I still remembered the days when Sheila had been too high to do anything but stare at the wall. He'd read to me, make us both pancakes, and sometimes take me into town for pizza or ice cream. He even bought me my first pedal bike and taught me how to ride it.

After their big fight, I asked Sheila why he couldn't come around anymore and she'd said that he was hanging out with some scary men and didn't want him bringing danger around. Back then, I didn't understand the irony of her words. I only understood that she'd taken someone I'd loved away from me. I could remember crying for days, wishing that he'd return. Unfortunately, he never did. But, he did send some letters and promised that one day we'd hang out again. Unfortunately, that never happened, either.

"Hi, Mom," I said to Millie when she answered.

She cleared her throat. "Hi, Ava. How's the movie coming along?"

"We're almost finished."

"Good. I saw that one of the other stuntmen had gotten hurt the other day. I wanted to call you, but I know how busy you are."

"It's okay. Call me whenever you want," I told her. It was a familiar conversation. Millie was always so concerned about disturbing or troubling other people. Sometimes, I thought she was almost *too* considerate. Of course, it was that same kindness that just might have saved me from following in

8

Sheila's footsteps. She'd used drugs to cope with her demons and... I'd started smoking pot and drinking at eleven. The worst part was that the drugs and alcohol had been introduced to me by a sicko who'd wanted me compliant so he could have his way with me. And... he had. Unfortunately, he hadn't been the first.

Millie took me in at thirteen after I'd run away from several other foster homes. Hell, I'd been mad at the world and had been acting out because it had given me some sense of control, especially after the abuse I'd suffered in a system which was supposed to have protected me. I could still remember how angry and defiant I'd been when I'd first walked into her living room. Fortunately, she'd seen beyond that and had been my light at the end of a long, and terrifying tunnel. Millie had been a miracle, and I knew that if it wasn't for her love and support, my life would have been over before it had barely begun.

She sighed. "About your mother —"

"*You're* my mother," I corrected.

"Okay, about *Sheila*," she said, knowing well enough not to argue with me on the matter. "I'm so sorry to tell you this, sweetie, but... I found out that she died yesterday. I guess she had lung cancer. I'm so sorry, Ava."

My legs felt like they were going to give way as images of my childhood flashed before my eyes. There hadn't been many good ones, but there'd been some. Like the time I'd started kindergarten. She'd taken me shopping for school supplies and new clothing, making it a very rare and special day. Then seeing her watch me get onto the bus. I still remembered the tears in her eyes as she waved and smiled at me. I knew Sheila had loved me in her own way, even though in the end, she'd broken my heart. She'd never been an intentionally cruel or hurtful person. Just a weak individual who'd disappointed me, and probably herself because she'd

9

loved her high more than her children or herself. At least that's what my therapist told me.

"How did you find out?" I asked, trying not to sound upset as I sat down on the sofa.

"I received a phone call from a man named Dwayne Bordellini. He claimed to be your half-brother's father."

"Yes," I said, recalling the name and face of Andrew's father. I remembered one time when he'd pulled up to our trailer riding a motorcycle. I'd thought he looked scary, with his thick muscles and tattoos. He'd been really nice, though, and even asked if I wanted to take a ride on his bike. I'd wanted to badly, but Sheila hadn't allowed it. "Yeah, that's him. Did he mention if he's heard from Andrew?"

"I didn't ask. I'm sorry."

I'd tried reaching out to Dwayne a couple of years ago to see if he knew where my brother was. Unfortunately, they'd had some kind of falling out and he had no idea where Andrew had disappeared to. The only thing he knew was that Andrew had connected with some outlaw biker clubs. They'd argued about it and it had been the last he'd heard of his son.

"Anyway, he left me a number for you to call him back at." She gave it to me and I wrote it down.

"Thanks, Mom."

"I'm sure there's going to be a funeral. If you'd like me to go with you, I will," she offered.

"I'll let you know. I might not be able to even make it," I replied, my chest heavy. The truth was, I didn't know if I could handle seeing my birthmother after all of these years. Especially in a casket.

"I think it would be good for you to go," she said. "You might regret it later if you don't. In fact, I know you, Ava. You will."

"Maybe," I mumbled, my eyes getting misty.

"I hate to do this, but Jan just pulled up. You remember

10

her, don't you? My friend from church? Anyway, we're going to play Bingo at the Supper Club. I'll be home in a couple hours if you want to talk some more."

"I'll be fine," I said, wiping a couple of tears from under my lashes. "I'll definitely let you know if I'm going to the funeral, though."

"Okay. I love you, sweetie. Call me when you're free and let me know what's happening."

"I will. I love you, too."

TWO

AVA

I FINISHED MY Chipotle rice bowl, showered, and put on a pair of black leggings and a hot pink tank top, intending to go for a run. Strangely enough, I needed a shower to help invigorate me before any workout. Otherwise, I never found the energy, only excuses not to instead.

I pulled my light-brown hair back into a ponytail and stared into the mirror. It's been said that I closely resembled Jessica Alba, but personally I couldn't see it. Sure, we had similar bone structure, brown eyes, and lips, but below the neck, I looked more like a Kardashian. *Especially* in the hip department. Another reason I had to stay on top of my exercise regime. Of course, I liked to joke that an ass like mine was perfect for a stuntwoman to help cushion the falls. But, it was still a lot of work to keep it from bouncing back on its own.

Yawning, I put some moisturizer on my face and walked into the living room to call Dwayne. He answered on the second ring.

"Hi, Dwayne. It's me, Ava. I heard the news."

"Sorry for your loss," he replied in that gravelly voice of his. I could hear him light up a cigarette and then take a long drag. "Such a waste."

I wanted to say that my loss happened a long time ago, but he already knew that. "Yeah."

Dwayne let out a ragged sigh. "You know, it might not mean a lot to you now, but your mother loved you."

"Just not enough to get help," I said wryly.

"She tried a few times to clean herself up and get you back. She just wasn't strong enough to resist her drug habit. What she needed was to enter a treatment center, but refused to. She always thought they were too expensive."

I laughed harshly. "And heroin wasn't?"

"I know. You're preaching to the choir, darlin'. I'm with you. One of the reasons why we split up all those years ago was because of drugs. Of course, she didn't hit the hard stuff until after you were born."

"Great. I guess I was the catalyst for that, huh?"

"Not you. Your father taking off on her is what did it. He was such a jackass. Sorry, Ava."

"No need to apologize. I never met the guy." All I knew about my old man was that she'd met him while working at a casino. My mother had been a card dealer, back before her addictions, and he'd been a customer. After winning a few big hands, he asked her out. Knowing it was against the casino's rules, she declined, but then ran into him a week later at a local mall. That time he'd been able to talk her into dinner and then romanced her until she fell in love with him and eventually became pregnant. Unfortunately, she learned later that he'd been only using her to try and win big at the casino. After finding out that she was carrying his child, he admitted that he was already married with a family of his own and asked her to get an abortion. She refused and he walked out of her life. It had been a devastating blow.

"I met him," he admitted. "I worked on his car once when it broke down."

"Really? Nobody ever mentioned that," I replied.

I remembered something about Dwayne's family owning an auto body shop, and how he'd wanted Andrew to take over the business one day.

"It wasn't anything we wanted to talk about, you know?"

"Yeah." If memory served me correctly, Dwayne and Sheila had always been pretty civil to each other, for the most part.

"Anyway, the funeral is next Friday. I'll get you the address here in a second. It's in the kitchen. Hold on."

I grabbed a notepad and a pen. "Who's paying for it? Andrew?"

"Not him, I'll tell you that. I was able to locate an old

friend of Andrew's and he gave me his phone number. I've left him several messages, but he hasn't returned my calls."

"You told him about Sheila?"

"Of course. I know he's pissed off at both of us, but the least he could do is call me back."

"If he doesn't, hopefully he'll at least show up at the funeral," I answered.

The Andrew I remembered had been stubborn, but he'd also had a heart. I couldn't imagine that after finding out about his mother dying he wouldn't at least attend the funeral, no matter how angry he'd been.

"Let's hope he does attend," he replied in a tired voice. "I'd like to smooth things over with him, too. Life's too short to hold grudges. He's an adult. If he wants to hang out with one-percenters, that's his prerogative. I'll accept it, I guess. I just want my son back."

"What's a one-percenter?"

"It refers to illegal motorcycle clubs. Ninety-nine percent of clubs are law-abiding citizens. The one-percenters take the law into their own hands."

"Oh."

We talked a little longer and then he gave me the information about the funeral.

"You never did mention who's paying for it," I said, thinking that if needed, I could chip in.

"I am."

His answer surprised me.

"*You*? Why?" I asked.

"As pissed off as I was at the woman, I always had a soft spot for her. Hell, she was the mother of my child." He let out a weary sigh. "Whom we both obviously disappointed. Anyway, someone's got to bury her. She may not have lived with a lot of dignity, but I'm going to make sure she gets buried with some."

15

My heart warmed at the gesture, and his words made my eyes misty. "That's very nice of you." I replied quietly.

He chuckled. "Do me a favor, though, don't go tellin' folks I'm footin' the bill. Being 'nice' isn't a good trait in my line of work."

"And what is it that you do?"

"I'm a debt collector," he replied.

I suddenly remembered the last conversation my mother had with Andrew before he stopped coming over. They'd been talking about how Dwayne worked for the mob.

"Now you're following in your father's footsteps. What in the world are you thinking by hanging out with a gang of criminals?"

"They're not a gang and they're not criminals!" he'd replied angrily. *"It's a club and those guys are my friends. They've got their shit together and are going to help me get mine."*

"Don't worry. I won't say a word," I replied. It wasn't any of my business and I was relieved that he'd volunteered to pay for her funeral anyway. "If you want any money —"

"Keep it, Ava. I appreciate the offer, but it's all paid for."

"Well, thank you."

"No problem. Hey, would you like Andrew's phone number?"

"Yeah, sure," I said, grabbing the pen again.

"Maybe he'll talk to you," he mumbled after giving it to me.

"I'd like to think that he would, but it's been so long."

"He always loved you. If anyone can get him to talk, it will be you."

I smiled.

Dwayne sighed. "Well, I guess I'll see you on Friday. Unless, you want to get together beforehand and have dinner or something."

"I'm in Vegas right now in the middle of a shoot. I probably won't be back until the day of the funeral."

"That's right. Millie said you were a stuntwoman. That must be pretty exciting work."

"It can be."

"You ever get hurt?"

"Not yet," I muttered, knocking on the wooden sofa table lightly for luck. My superstitious nature hated when people asked that question. It was a sure way to jinx someone.

"That's good. Oh, my pizza is done. I gotta go. See you soon?"

"Yeah."

We hung up and I called the number he gave me. Unfortunately, Andrew didn't answer and he used an impersonal, automated voicemail greeting, so I couldn't even be certain if we had the right number.

"Hi, Andrew. It's Ava. Your sister," I said, laughing nervously. "Surprise, huh? It's been such a long time. Too long. Anyway, I would really like to talk to you, so please call me back."

I left him my phone number and then hung up, hoping he'd call me back. There was a lot I wanted to say, like how much he'd meant to me, especially during the darkest times of my life. Even just the memory of his smile had given me comfort when I'd needed it the most. He was all I had left of my childhood; the best part of it. I honestly didn't care if he went to the funeral. I just wanted to see him again and hoped he felt the same.

THREE

AVA

A LOUD KNOCK on the door jolted me awake. I'd fallen asleep reading a book about World War II, which always fascinated me. My biological mother's ancestors, who'd been Jewish, had escaped East Berlin and somehow managed to move to America and start over. From what I'd learned, they were now all gone and my last living relatives had been my mother and Andrew. Still, I had to wonder if I had others still living in Germany. I'd been thinking about having my DNA tested through an online ancestry company and decided that as soon as I was done with the movie, I'd look into it.

Getting out of the recliner, I set the book down and headed over to the front door, wondering who could be visiting me. Nobody had called or sent a message, and unexpected visitors annoyed the hell out of me. Unsure if I should even answer the door, I peeked through the peephole and swore under my breath when I saw who it was.

Hunter Calloway.

Trying not to lose my cool, I unlocked the door and faced him. "Hunter, what are you doing here?"

Hunter, who was dressed in a pair of black slacks and a Tommy Bahama shirt, grinned. "I received your message. I'm glad you changed your mind." He held up a paper bag. "I brought over a bottle of Cristal."

I stared at him in confusion. "What message?"

His smile faltered. "Didn't you text me?"

"No."

He pulled out his phone and showed me the message he'd received.

I changed my mind about dinner. Let's just make it the two of us. Wendy has my address.

Wendy was his personal assistant and definitely did not

19

have my phone number. At least not that I was aware of.

"Let me see that," I said, grabbing his cell to get a closer look. I checked the phone number the text came from and it wasn't mine. "I think you have me confused with someone else." I handed it back to him. "That's definitely not my phone number."

He looked embarrassed. "You're kidding? I am so sorry. Hmm... I guess I don't know who sent me it either then. You're the only person who has ever turned me down for dinner, so I assumed it was you."

"You obviously made a mistake. You should have asked."

"You're right. I was just so elated to think you wanted to share a meal with an old goat like me," he replied and looked away. "Damn, I feel like a stupid fool."

"Don't be so hard on yourself. Mistakes happen," I said, wondering again if maybe I was being too critical about the man. He honestly looked embarrassed about the ordeal.

"Well, I'll get out of your hair. Sorry, again."

"No problem." I began closing the door. "I'll see you tomorrow."

"Wait." He put his hand up, preventing the door from shutting.

"Yes?"

He pulled the bottle of Cristal out of the bag. "Here, I usually don't drink champagne; too much of it gives me heartburn. Why don't you keep it? After working so hard today, I bet you could use a glass to unwind."

"No, I couldn't take that," I said, staring at the high-priced bottle. Admittedly, it did look appealing and I was sure he'd spent a good deal on the champagne. "Save it for another day."

He glanced at the bottle and then back to me. He grinned. "Hey, I know... why don't we just share a quick glass

20

together and then I'll be on my way? Otherwise, I can almost guarantee that it will go to waste."

I sighed and relented. Hunter looked so hopeful that I didn't have the heart to send him away.

"Okay." I stepped back. "Come on in."

"Excellent." He stepped into the house, smelling as if he'd bathed in aftershave. The scent was so overpowering, it started giving me another headache. I backed away as he looked around the living room. "Nice place, by the way. Is it yours?"

"No. It's just a rental," I replied, walking around him toward the kitchen. "What about you? Where are you holed up?"

"The MGM Grand. I always stay there."

"Nice. Come on into the kitchen."

Hunter followed me.

"I can take that," I said, when we were both by the center island.

He handed me the bottle.

"I guess I should have known something wasn't right when you answered the door in your yoga outfit. Not that you look bad," he mused. "You just look settled in for the evening."

I looked down at my attire. "I was actually thinking about going for a jog soon."

"It's getting dark outside," he said, walking around the kitchen island to where I stood by the sink. "That's kind of dangerous for an attractive woman like yourself, don't you think?"

I shrugged. "I can handle myself."

"That's right, you've had some martial arts training, right?" he said, leaning back against the counter to watch as I reached up toward the champagne glasses. Unfortunately, they were just out of my reach.

"Among other things," I murmured, irritated that I couldn't get to the flutes. I was just about to ask for Hunter's assistance, when he moved up behind me.

"Here, let me help you with those."

"Oh. Okay," I replied, thinking he was a little too close for comfort.

He reached up and grabbed two glasses. I could feel his warm breath in my hair, which made me grip the counter tightly in annoyance. "By the way, you smell lovely," he said near my ear. "I noticed that when we were filming, too."

"Thanks," I replied tightly.

He backed away and then watched as I removed the cellophane from the bottle and popped the cork.

"Impressive," he said as I began to pour the bubbly into the champagne flutes. "You look like a pro. Do you drink champagne often?"

"No. I do enjoy a glass of wine now and again, though," I replied.

"Really? You'll have to come and visit my wine cellar at my place on Martha's Vineyard. What's your fancy? Red or white?"

"I don't know, really. I do prefer a sweeter wine that's not too heavy." I shrugged. "I mean… I'm not a true connoisseur. I just like a glass once in a while."

Watching me pour the champagne, he grinned. "I used to be strictly a beer drinker until someone educated me on wine. I'm not exactly a wine aficionado, but I know now what I like and what I won't like. I also know what pairs good with different types of food."

"What kind of wine do you prefer?"

"Usually you'll find me with a Cabernet Sauvignon, when I'm in the mood. Admittedly, I have a bit of a sweet tooth as well, so when I'm not drinking wine, you'll find me with a rum and Coke."

"Ah." I pushed his glass toward him. "Thanks again for sharing your champagne. I have a feeling after this, I'll be going to bed instead of hitting the pavement."

"You mean jogging?"

I nodded.

He picked up his glass. "Good, because I still don't feel comfortable knowing that you'd be out in the dark, especially dressed like that," Hunter replied, his gaze sweeping over my outfit again.

"Eh," I waved a dismissive hand, "I can take care of myself," I repeated.

"You sure don't lack courage, that's for sure. Let's toast, shall we? To new friends?" he said, holding his glass up.

"To new friends," I said, clinking my glass against his.

We both took a sip of champagne and then his stomach growled.

"Pardon me," he said, looking embarrassed.

"No, I'm sorry. I don't have anything in the refrigerator, otherwise I'd make you something."

"We could go out and grab a bite to eat," he suggested.

"I already had dinner. Anyway, it's getting late." I glanced at the clock on the microwave. "We both have to be on the set early tomorrow, I'm sure."

"I don't have to be there until noon."

"Lucky you." I snorted.

"I bet if you wanted to go in late, I could talk to the director," he said, taking another sip of champagne.

"I don't need to go in later. Besides, it wouldn't be fair to the others."

He stared at me. "God, you have the most beautiful eyes. I bet you hear that all the time though, don't you?"

Crap, here we go…

"Thank you," I said, stiffening up.

"You don't like it when someone compliments you, do

you?"

I looked over at the clock again. "Wow, is it really nine o'clock already?"

Amused, he chuckled. "Okay, I get it. You're not into me. It's too bad because I think we could be good for each other."

I folded my arms across my chest. "Is that right?"

"Yeah. I could help further your career and... well, how could you not be good for me? You're young and beautiful — and obviously talented." He added that last part as if it would make his compliments less creepy.

I laughed harshly. At least he was honest. "Hunter, my career is perfect, thank you very much."

He took another sip of champagne. "We all know how quickly things change in this industry. One moment everyone wants you. The next, you're struggling to find work."

"I've been pretty fortunate in that department."

"And why do you think that is?" he asked with a sly grin.

I lifted my chin. "Because I'm good at what I do."

"True, but there are dozens of other stuntwomen, with much more experience, vying for movies like this. You are relatively new to the industry. The fact that you were able to hook this movie must have surprised you."

I didn't know what he was getting at, but something in his eyes made my stomach twist. It was certainly true that I'd struck gold in getting hired for the movie, but I hadn't thought it was exactly a miracle. It definitely wasn't my first gig, but obviously the best so far.

"Maybe a little. What are you getting at?" I asked, frowning.

"I visited the set of your last movie. Do you remember?"

"I think someone might have mentioned it to me."

He smiled. "You were in the middle of a shoot when I showed up. The moment I saw you, I thought you'd be great for this film. Hell, from a distance you could even pass for

24

Valerie, although I must say you're much prettier."

"Are you trying to tell me that you're the reason I was hired for this film?" I replied, angry at the idea. Especially the way he was putting it out there.

His smile widened. "Let's just say... the director and I are good friends."

Trying to keep my cool, I tossed back the rest of the champagne and set the glass in the sink. "While I appreciate that you may have been involved with me getting hired, I hope you're not insinuating that I *owe* you anything for it."

His eyes turned cool. "It wasn't easy talking the director into using someone he'd never heard of."

So I'd been right about him from the very beginning. He was an arrogant, self-serving ass. It reminded me of the shit I'd been exposed to in foster care. One person in particular had used a similar tactic to sexually abuse me. I'd been vulnerable back then—but I wasn't anymore.

I pointed toward the front door. "Get out."

Hunter's eyes widened in shock. "What?"

I picked up the champagne bottle and shoved it at him. "I see right through you, Hunter, and the hell if I'm going to let you bully me into whatever it is you came here for."

He tried backtracking. "I think there's been a misunderstanding. A mistake—"

"I agree. The mistake was that I let you in here, thinking maybe I was wrong about you. I should have known better."

He tried reaching out to touch my arm. "Listen, I'm sorry if—"

I slapped his hand away. "Touch me and you'll really know what 'sorry' is, you piece of shit."

Hunter's face turned red. "You're crazy," he said, walking around the island toward the door. "Maybe even too crazy to be in this movie."

I knew a threat when I heard it. "I've got one word for

25

you, Hunter: Borgenstein."

He stopped in his tracks and turned around.

I smiled. Harold Borgenstein was a famous movie producer who was currently being sued by dozens of actresses for sexual harassment. I'd never met him myself, but everyone in the business knew that the accusations were true. It was also a scandal that nobody wanted to find themselves in, guilty or not. Something told me I wasn't the only woman Hunter had tried pressuring into sex, and it certainly wouldn't be that difficult to find other victims.

"Excuse me?"

"Don't fuck with me or my career, Hunter. You'll regret it."

He walked toward me with a sneer. "Listen here, bitch. You've got nothing on me. *Nothing*. I could make one phone call right now and get you kicked off of the set faster than you can pat yourself on the back for being a stupid, mouthy cunt."

I clenched my hands into fists, ready to wipe the ugly smile from his face. "Excuse—"

He went on. "In fact, I have so many friends in this business, some who could actually make you disappear, so it would be in your best interest to be nice to me," he said, setting the bottle back down on the counter with a little too much force.

I gasped. "Are you threatening me with *murder*?"

"Your words. Not mine," he replied. Hunter moved closer to me until I was backed up against the counter. "Look, this is obviously getting out of hand. I didn't come here to fight."

"Fuck you. I know exactly what you came here for," I said between clenched teeth.

He tilted his head and smiled. "You're so beautiful. Probably the most beautiful woman I've ever seen. Especially when you're angry." Before I could reply, he leaned forward

26

and tried kissing me.

Horrified, I shoved him away from me. The way he was trying to manipulate me brought back so many terrible memories. "If you don't get out of my house right now, I'm calling the police."

"Ava—"

I tried moving around him but he blocked me and smirked. "Last chance to keep your career."

Having had enough, I punched him in the jaw.

Gasping, he stumbled slightly and then grabbed me by the ponytail, jerking my head back.

"You bitch," he growled, crushing his mouth against mine and roughly fondling my breasts.

Crying out, I bit his lip, drawing blood. He swore and released me, but not before I kneed him between the legs.

Hunter howled in pain and leaned forward clutching his balls. "Fuck!"

I raced over to the butcher block and pulled out the largest knife. I turned around and held it up in front of me. "Get the hell out of here!"

Still hunched over, he glared at me and backed away. "Your career is finished, you cheap, trashy cunt!"

Now I was triggered. "You forgot psycho!" I snarled, moving toward him.

Hunter's eyes widened. He turned and bolted out of the kitchen. I followed him until I knew he was out of the house and locked the deadbolt. Turning around, I leaned against the door, trembling. When I heard his car pull away, I slid to the floor and began to sob.

FOUR

AVA

THE NEXT MORNING when my alarm went off, it was a struggle to get moving. I'd had a hell of a time falling asleep after stewing about Hunter all night. I'd even considered calling the cops, but in the end knew it would have been his word against mine. Not only was he famous, but he had money and the kind of power that really *could* get me killed. I decided that the best thing to do was return to the set, finish up the last couple of scenes I'd been hired to do, and never work on another movie with Hunter.

After rolling out of bed, I forced myself into the shower and then made myself a container of coffee to take with me. As I was adding cream, my cell phone rang. Hoping it was Andrew, I quickly grabbed it and answered.

"Ava? It's Ben Jones."

Realizing that it was the assistant director, my stomach clenched as Hunter's threats resurfaced. "Oh, hey, Ben. What's up?"

"How's it going?"

I could tell by the sound of his voice that he had bad news for me.

"Fine. I certainly wasn't expecting a call from you so early. Is anything wrong?" I asked, my blood boiling with anger. Last night, Hunter had gotten under my skin and I'd felt vulnerable and weak. Today, I wanted to attach a chain to his neck and the other end of it to my motorcycle and drag him across the desert, naked.

"Actually," he cleared his throat, "I hate to be the one to break the news, but we're not going to be needing you today."

"And why is that?" I asked, clenching my teeth.

"The actress has decided she's going to do her own stunts."

Now that surprised me. Valerie was afraid of breaking a nail, let alone her neck. It definitely didn't sound like her.

29

"What? Seriously?"

"Yeah. The gas station scene will be easy for her, especially since we made a couple of changes, and then the last love scene, she's going to do it. We've decided to not make her fully nude, so she's okay with it."

I wouldn't have questioned the change had Hunter not made his threats the night before.

I began pacing across the floor. "Does this have anything to do with Hunter?"

"Hunter Calloway? No. Not at all."

I rolled my eyes. Ben was a horrible liar. "I'm sorry, but I don't buy it. And by the way, my contract states—"

"Relax, Ava. You're still getting paid what we promised," he said quickly. "Your contract still stands. It's just that you don't have to do all the work now. You should actually be relieved."

He was right, I should have been, but I wasn't. Hunter had pushed his weight around and that irritated the fuck out of me.

"Ava?"

"I'm here." I wanted to tell him all about Hunter and his threats, but somehow I knew it would fall on deaf ears. Hell, even worse, he wouldn't offer me any support, after all… Hunter *was* the star of the show and his name sold millions of movie tickets. At least I could go to the funeral now without missing any work.

"I thought you'd be happy. You *should* be happy."

"Yeah, I know." I sighed. "Thank you for calling me so I didn't have to waste time driving in."

"No problem, and if there's anything you need, call me, okay?"

"Sure. Thanks, Ben."

"You're welcome."

I was about to tell him to call me if Valerie changed her

mind, but he hung up before I could get the words out. I pictured Hunter, grinning smugly, and hoped to hell that one day someone would put the bastard in his place.

FIVE

AVA

Cassie Alexandra

LATER THAT DAY, I returned the motorcycle to the rental company, and took the first flight back to my condo in Miami. After walking through the door, I called my mother and left a message, letting her know I'd returned. I then attempted to call Andrew again, but there was still no answer. I began to wonder if he'd chosen to avoid me as well. It was a sad thought, although I didn't know what kind of life he had now, and the fact that he was mixed in with an outlaw biker club spoke volumes. It was very possible he'd changed and wasn't the sweet guy I used to know. I hoped I was wrong, but life could do a number on an individual. I knew that more than anyone.

Later that evening, Mom called and asked if I wanted her to go with me to the funeral. I knew she wanted to support me, but for some reason, I wanted to keep my past and present separate. I guess part of me was worried that something might change between us when Millie saw my mother. It was probably a silly notion, but I couldn't seem to shake it.

"No, I'm just going by myself. Thank you, though."

"Are you sure?"

"Yes. If I change my mind, I'll let you know. We should get together, though."

"Yes. I would like that."

We arranged to have lunch later in the week and then talked about the movie.

"So, why did they let you leave early?" she asked.

I thought about shielding her from what happened, but decided to tell her the truth. When I was finished, she was furious.

"You should have called the police on that jerk," she said angrily.

"I know. With my luck, they would have arrested me for punching him in the chin," I mused, looking down at my

33

knuckles. They were actually still a little sore from hitting him.

"Do you think he has the power to keep you from getting other stunt jobs?"

"Honestly, I don't know," I replied. "I'm hoping he forgets about it."

"You should report him to someone," she said. "Especially if he's threatening to blackball you like that. You know, there's a woman at church who used to work in the media. She was a reporter. I bet she could talk to someone for you and set up an interview, I'd be happy to talk to her if you'd like."

"Thanks, Mom. I'd rather just put this behind me. I mean, if I have problems getting jobs down the line, I might take you up on it then."

"I hope so. He sounds like a real creep. I'm not watching any of his movies anymore," she said angrily.

I smiled.

"Are you sure you're okay?" she asked.

"I'm fine," I replied. "Really."

"Have you heard from Andrew yet?"

"Unfortunately, no."

"Maybe something happened to him? He is mixed up with some dangerous people."

The same thought had crossed my mind. "I hope not."

"I have to go. My show is almost on. Call me tomorrow?"

I told her I would and then we hung up.

My thoughts returned to Andrew. Had he fallen into harm's way?

My gut was telling me that something might indeed wrong. I decided that if he didn't return any of my calls by the following week, I'd consult with a private investigator to see if he could help locate Andrew. At the very least, I wanted to make sure he was alive and doing okay, even if he didn't want a relationship with me.

AVA

Cassie Alexandra

I ARRIVED A few minutes early to Sheila's visitation on Wednesday. As I entered the church, I found myself face-to-face with Dwayne, who was standing just inside of the double-doors wearing a dark gray suit.

"Ava?" he said, staring at me with wide eyes.

I managed a smile and nodded.

"Wow, look at you," he said, looking me up and down with a sad smile. "You've changed a lot and yet, I still see that sweet little girl Andrew used to brag about."

"Thank you," I replied, noticing that he'd aged pretty roughly. There were deep lines and crevices along his face, especially around the lip area, and there were bags under his eyes. He looked haggard and rough. "So, he bragged about me?"

"Of course. You know how big brothers are. He used to talk about you all the time."

I smiled sadly.

He looked at the doorway, his eyebrows knotted together. "He didn't call you, huh?"

"No. Unfortunately."

Dwayne let out a ragged sigh. "That's too bad. It's early, though. He might still show up here."

As much as I wanted him to, my intuition was telling me that we wouldn't be seeing Andrew at the funeral or anytime soon.

"Come on," he said, offering his arm. "I'll walk you over."

Taking a deep breath, I slid my arm through his and we walked together up to the casket. Sadly, the church was almost empty, with only a couple of older people sitting in pews. They stared at me curiously as we moved past them and I had to wonder who they were as well. As far as I knew, my mother didn't have any living relatives.

When we reached the casket and I saw her, all of the

37

mental anguish I'd undergone as a child hit me at once, and my eyes filled with tears.

"It's okay," Dwayne whispered, patting my hand.

Trying to keep my composure, I stared at the woman who'd given birth to me. Although she had to have been only in her mid-fifties, she looked like a frail, gaunt, old woman. One I barely recognized. The drug abuse had definitely taken its toll on her, and it surprised me she'd made it as long as she had.

"Hello, are you the daughter?" asked the minister, approaching us from the side of the chapel. He was a gray-haired man with kind eyes and a sympathetic smile.

I nodded.

He offered his condolences and then told me he'd been with her when she'd passed away.

I stared at him in surprise. "Really?"

"Yes. She'd been coming to my church for the last couple of months, trying to make her peace with God before her time came," he replied softly.

"Did she die *here*?" I asked, confused.

"No. She died in hospice," he said. "In a care facility."

"Oh," I replied.

"Sorry, Pastor. We didn't even know she'd been in hospice," Dwayne said, looking troubled. "Of course, the cancer had been a surprise, too. She never mentioned it."

He nodded. "I know. I asked her a couple of weeks ago if she wanted me to gather her family to be with her at the end, but she refused."

His words stung. "I guess nobody should be surprised by that," I said bitterly.

"Sheila was ashamed and didn't want to burden anyone with what she was going through," he explained. "Especially you. She knew how badly she'd hurt you and didn't think it would have been fair to walk back into your life as a dying woman."

I nodded.

"She wanted me to give you this, though," he said, holding out an envelope with my name on it.

I stared at it.

"Go ahead. Take it," Dwayne urged.

Swallowing, I took the envelope, folded it, and stuck it into my purse. "I'll read it later."

He nodded.

"Was there one for Andrew, too?" I asked.

"Your brother?" the pastor replied, looking confused. "No. She told me he'd died recently."

I felt like someone had punched me in the gut.

"What?" Dwayne and I asked in unison.

The pastor's eyes widened. "I'm so sorry. I feel terrible. You didn't know?"

"No," Dwayne replied in a hoarse voice, his face stricken with grief. "Died? Why... h-how did he die?"

"Sheila told me she found out about it on the news. He was... he was killed," the pastor replied, looking horrified to have to be the one relaying the information. "In Minnesota, last summer."

Dwayne and I both started asking questions at once.

"Look, I don't know much about it. I'm sorry," he said. "Just what I told you."

"Does anyone know who killed him?" I asked, heartbroken.

"She never said," he repeated. "I'm sure you can find something about it online or get ahold of someone in law enforcement for the information. She didn't really want to talk about it with me too much. It really devastated her."

"I just can't believe I'm finding out about this now. She could have at least told me," said Dwayne who was already on his phone, trying to look up information on the Internet.

After a few seconds, he moaned. "Oh, no. Dear God..."

"What is it?" I asked, moving closer to him. I looked down at his phone and my stomach dropped at the gut-wrenching headlines.

Blood Angel Killed Trying to Assault Local Woman

We read the article, which didn't make a lot of sense. Apparently, Andrew Bordellini, who they were referring to as "Blade", had been shot after trying to attack some woman in East Bethel, Minnesota. After reading more into the article, it appeared that the woman was associated with the Gold Vipers, a rival club with a shady past.

"See? This is why I warned him about getting involved with outlaw biker clubs! Obviously, these Gold Vipers had him killed and set it up to look like he was at fault," Dwayne said angrily.

"You think so?" I asked, stunned.

"Hell, yeah. Especially these Gold Vipers. I've seen them in the news more than once and I know damn well that they assassinated him. It's what those fuckers do." He glanced at the pastor, who'd been observing us silently. "Excuse my language. Andrew was my son."

The man nodded and put a hand on his shoulder. "I'm sorry for your loss."

Blinking back tears, Dwayne nodded and put his phone away. "Thank you. I need to get out of here. I'm sorry."

"In times like this, a church might be the best place for you," replied the pastor gently.

"Right now, the best place for me to be is at home, alone, with a bottle of Jack," he muttered and looked at me. "I'm sorry, Ava. I know this is hard on you, too. I just... I need some time by myself."

I felt sick to my stomach and could only imagine what he was going through.

He hugged me and then quickly left the church.

As much as I understood him wanting to be alone, I felt the opposite and wished I'd allowed Millie to join me. I felt as if I was barely holding it together as memories washed over me. Losing Sheila had been bad enough. Knowing I would never get the chance to see my brother again was devastating.

"Would you like to sit down and talk about your brother?" the pastor asked kindly.

I knew his intentions were good, but I suddenly felt a strong desire to find out exactly who was responsible for Andrew's death and bring those people to justice. My brother might have made some bad decisions in his life, but deep down, I knew he wasn't the monster the media was making him out to be. The guy I remembered wasn't the kind of person who went around assaulting women, and the only thing that made sense was what Dwayne had said about Andrew being set up and murdered.

Pulling myself together, I shook my head. "Thank you, but I'm fine," I said, my determination to right a wrong making me stronger. "When does the service start?"

"In twenty minutes," he replied, still looking concerned. "Are you sure you wouldn't like some private counseling?"

"I appreciate the offer, but I'll be fine."

"Okay." He looked at his watch again. "If you'll excuse me, I'll be back shortly. I'm going to change into my robes."

"Of course," I replied.

He stepped away and I looked around the church, not exactly surprised that more people weren't filing in the doorway to pay any last respects. It was actually pretty depressing. But then again, Sheila had alienated herself from most everyone. She either pushed everyone away or simply abandoned them. Although I was still hurt by how she'd failed as a parent, I took a deep breath and told myself to let go of the grudge I'd been holding for so long. She was to blame for me ending up in foster care, but Sheila had been fighting her own demons. I just hoped that in death, she finally found some kind of peace.

Remembering the letter, I walked over and sat down at one of the pews. I opened it up and began reading it.

My Dearest Ava,

What I wouldn't do to be able to reach back in time and make things right. I don't expect you to ever forgive me for how much I failed you. I made so many terrible choices and I can't tell you how many times I wanted to try and fix things between us. It wasn't just shame that stopped me though. I was afraid that I'd hurt you again because of my weaknesses. I want you to know that I never stopped loving you or Andrew. Whenever I'd try and get straight, I would think about my screw-ups and what I should have done. Instead of doing the right thing, I'd only get high again to try and forget what a shitty mom I was.

I'm sorry, Ava. I truly am. I hope that you make better choices in life than me and will always fight for the ones you love.

She didn't sign the letter I noticed, but there was a key taped to the paper. I stuffed both items into the envelope and walked back over to the casket. My heart felt heavier than ever as I stared down at her. "It's okay. I forgive you," I whispered, feeling a weight lift off my shoulders. The letter couldn't really make up for the horror I'd gone through in foster care, but to know she'd owned up to her screw-ups made me feel better.

SEVEN

AVA

AFTER THE FUNERAL, I asked the pastor if he knew anything about the key in the envelope.

"It's for her trailer home," he said and gave me the address. "She wanted you to have it."

I thanked him and then said goodbye.

"Aren't you going out to the cemetery while we lay her to rest?" he asked.

"No," I replied, unable to take any more sadness for one day. "Where is she being buried? I'll stop by another time."

He told me and then invited me to church the following weekend. I told him that church wasn't my thing, but if it ever changed, I'd let him know.

"I hope you do. Peace be with you," he said, staring at me with concern.

"Thank you. You, too."

THIRTY MINUTES LATER, I stood outside of what was apparently my mother's run-down, dilapidated trailer. The grass needed to be mowed, and the exterior of the home was shot to hell. I had no idea what I was going to do with the place and decided to see if I could donate it somehow.

Expecting it to be just as shitty on the inside, I was surprised to find that it was clean and had some nice furnishings. Dropping the keys on the kitchen counter, I looked around for a while and that's when I found a stack of brief letters from Andrew. They were in an empty milk crate in her bedroom. Intrigued, I started going through them and noticed that he'd been sending her money in the form of cashier's checks. I stared at the stubs, surprised of the amounts. Some were over one-thousand dollars. Unfortunately, there wasn't a whole lot of information in the letters about his personal life and I couldn't find a return address. As I sorted through each of them, I wondered if it was because he hadn't wanted to be found.

Sighing, I glanced over to the other side of the bedroom and saw a picture of me when I was a child sitting on her nightstand. I walked over for a closer look and noticed a Valentine's Day card I'd made for her back in elementary school lying next to it. I picked it up and grew teary-eyed again as I remembered making it for her. I'd been in first or second grade and so proud of the card. When I'd given it to her, she hugged me and started to cry. When I asked her what was wrong, she'd told me that I was the best daughter in the world and that she didn't deserve me.

I lay down on the bed and put the card against my heart. Closing my eyes, I stayed there for a while, feeling a hailstorm of sorrow for both my mother and now my older brother. Life had been so unfair for both of them, and although I'd lived in my own kind of hell, I'd been able to rise above it, for the most part. Now, more than ever, I was so grateful that I had Millie in my life.

Suddenly, my cell phone began to ring. I picked it up and noticed it was Dwayne.

"I'm sorry for leaving you like that," he said, his words slurred. "I shouldn't have done that to you. It was shitty."

"It's okay."

"No. Everyone's always abandoning you. It's not right." He let out a ragged breath. "I just… I just can't believe he's gone. My son," he said, his voice cracking. "My… my boy."

"I know," I replied, heartbroken, too. "It's not fair. Something needs to be done. Those people can't get away with what they did. Is there anything we can do?"

He blew his nose. "Sorry," he said, sniffling. "And no. Nothing legal, at least."

"Are you sure? Maybe we can find a lawyer or something? Someone who can do some digging?"

"You have no idea who we're dealing with," he said. "These guys are outlaws. They live by their own rules and do

45

whatever the fuck they want, *whenever* the fuck they want. They're evil, Ava. I'm telling you…"

"So, we're just supposed to forget about it?" I asked in disbelief.

"Hell no. I'm not," he replied.

"What are you going to do?"

"Find out who framed and had him killed — and return the favor."

I was stunned into silence.

He took a drink of something. "Yep. An eye-for-an-eye," he slurred. "The people responsible for this are drug-dealing, cold-blooded murderers anyway. They're the kind of guys who turn people like your mother into heroin and crack addicts."

My blood began to boil as he went on, talking about the type of monsters associated with the Gold Vipers and how awful they were.

"They're involved with everything. Prostitution. Pornography. Child trafficking. I could go on and on. Hell, I'd love to go vigilante on all of their asses," Dwayne muttered. "The cops are worthless."

"How do you know all of this about them?"

"Because the guys I work for aren't exactly angels themselves. But, I tell you what… they're not as bad as who we're dealing with. Not by a longshot."

"Is there something I can do to help?" I asked in a solemn voice.

He grunted. "You? No way. You can't get involved. It's too dangerous."

"I'm not afraid," I said, meaning it. The more he talked about revenge, the more my stomach burned for it too. They couldn't get away what they'd done to Andrew. "He was my brother."

"I know but you're… you're just a girl."

"I'm a woman," I corrected. "And one who knows a few things."

He groaned. "I… I shouldn't be saying this stuff, especially on the phone. I gotta go, Ava."

"Wait, give me your address. I'm going to stop by tomorrow, if you don't mind."

"I'll text you," he said and then hung up.

I put my phone away, snooped around my mom's trailer a little while longer, and then packed a few things I wanted to take with me. I still didn't know exactly what I was going to do with the trailer, but knew I wouldn't be keeping it. I decided I'd return the following day and look through her financials to see if she had a mortgage or owed any money on the place. Then I'd go from there.

AN HOUR LATER, I returned to my condo and called Millie. We talked about the funeral and then confirmed our lunch plans again. Afterward, I took a shower, watched some television, and then lay in bed thinking about my conversation with Dwayne. The more I thought about his plan for revenge, the more I wanted to be part of it. Just like me, Andrew and been used by deviants and assholes. Ones who definitely deserved a bullet and a shovel.

Sighing, I decided that no matter what Dwayne said the next morning, I *was* going to get involved. Whether he liked it or not.

EIGHT

AVA

I WOKE UP to the sound of my phone ringing early the next morning. It wasn't a number I recognized, and the sun hadn't yet risen, which meant it wasn't a telemarketer. Curious, I reached over and picked it up from my nightstand.

"Hello?" I mumbled, closing my eyes again.

"Is this Ava Rhodes?" a male voice asked.

"Yes. Who's this?"

"My name is Doctor Farrah and I'm calling from St. Mark's Hospital. I'm sorry to call you so early, but there's been an accident involving a friend of yours. Now, he's in stable condition—"

"Who are you calling about?"

"Dwayne Bordellini. He asked us to call you."

His words sent my heart racing. "Is he okay?" I asked, fully awake now.

"Yes. He suffered a head injury, but we were able to operate quickly enough. All in all, I think his prognosis is very good. He just needs to stay in the hospital for a few days. He also has a broken arm and some bruised ribs."

I sighed in relief and then asked about the head injury.

"Nothing major. There was a little internal bleeding, but we managed to stop it. You should probably know that Mr. Bordellini admitted to being under the influence of alcohol, which resulted in the crash. Obviously, he'll have to answer to the police when he's able to. Fortunately, there wasn't another vehicle involved. Just a tree," he said with a smile in his voice.

That definitely meant a DUI. I groaned. "Can I come see him?"

"Of course."

"St. Mark's, you said?"

"Yes. He's sleeping, so don't feel you have to rush. He'll be fine. He just needs to rest."

"Okay." I thanked him and hung up.

A COUPLE HOURS later, I walked into Dwayne's hospital room and winced when I saw the bandages around his head and arm. He was still sleeping, so I sat down next to him and stayed there until a nurse came to check his vitals. As she was finishing, he woke up, and that's when he noticed me.

"Hey," he mumbled, trying to keep his eyes open. "They called you, huh?"

"Yes," I replied as the nurse smiled and stepped out of the room. "How are you feeling?"

"Like shit."

"I bet. So..."

"I know. I fucked up. Badly. Do you know what happened to my car?"

"No. I don't have any idea. I just heard that you hit a tree."

He was quiet for a few seconds and then sighed. "So, nobody but me was hurt?"

"Sounds that way."

Before he could say anything else, an attractive Middle Eastern man, wearing blue scrubs, stepped into the room with a clipboard.

"Hello, my name is Dr. Farrah," he said, smiling at me and then at Dwayne. "I see you're awake."

"Unfortunately," Dwayne replied. "My head hurts like a son-of-a-bitch."

"I imagine it does. "He looked at me. "You must be Ava?" he asked me.

I nodded.

Smiling, Dr. Farrah looked at his clipboard. "Headache aside, how exactly are you feeling, Mr. Bordellini?"

"Like I ran into a freight train," he muttered.

"I'll make sure they get you something for the pain," the doctor replied and then did a quick examination.

"When can I get out of here?" Dwayne asked when he was finished.

The doctor explained that he'd need to stay for a couple of days so they could monitor his head injury.

Dwayne groaned.

"It's better than dealing with the cops at the moment, right?" Dr. Farrah said with a grim smile.

He sighed. "I suppose I'm in deep shit, huh?"

"I'd advise you to contact your lawyer and to take an Uber the next time you decide to drive while under the influence," he replied. "Just so you know, a couple of officers will be checking in with you soon."

"What a fucking mess," Dwayne mumbled.

"Yes, but it could have been a lot worse. Next time, it might be," Dr. Farrah said. "Anyway, I'll stop back later and see how you are."

"Thanks, Doc. Don't forget the pain medicine," Dwayne reminded him.

"I'll get on that, too. It was nice meeting you," he said to me before walking out of the room.

"So, where were you going last night?" I asked him.

"I was heading to Minnesota, if you want to know the truth."

"Ah. From what it looks like, you're going to need to postpone the trip," I replied, sitting down next to him.

"Fuck that. Those guys are going to pay," he muttered and then winced.

"I agree that they should," I said. "In fact, I want to go with you."

"I told you last night it's not going to happen."

"Why? Because I'm a woman?"

"Because…" he lowered his voice, "you've never done anything like this before and I'm not putting you in danger."

"And you have?"

51

"I've come close to it for far less than this."

"But you've never actually killed anyone?" I whispered.

"No, but those bastards murdered my boy so now I have to," he said in a ragged voice.

"He was my brother," I reminded him again.

"Stop it right now. I won't allow it. Hell, chances are I won't walk away from this myself," he said, looking irritated. "Now, don't argue about this with me. I'm not putting your life in danger."

I sighed. "We'll talk about it when you're feeling better."

"Bullshit. My mind is made up. You stay out of this, Ava. I mean it."

I stood up as a nurse walked in carrying a small paper cup of pills.

"Those for me?" Dwayne asked with a look of relief.

She smiled. "Yep. I hear you're in a lot of pain."

He grunted. "You can say that again."

"I'm going to take off," I said, picking up my purse. "We'll talk later?"

He looked at me. "Yeah, but I'm not changing my mind."

From the look on his face, I knew he wouldn't, but that wasn't my problem nor did I care. I wasn't about to let him stop me.

I DROVE BACK to my mother's trailer and began searching for her financial records. Fortunately, I found a file cabinet in the back of her closet with old bank statements and the deed to her trailer. I learned that it was paid off, but the owner was listed as Andrew, so I wasn't sure what I needed to do with the place.

I smiled to myself. Although they'd had an estranged relationship, he'd made sure to keep a roof over her head, which made me love him that much more.

As I was going through some more of her records, my cell phone rang. Recognizing that it was the hospital again, I quickly picked it up.

"Ms. Rhodes? It's Dr. Farrah again," he said in a grim voice. "I'm so sorry to have to tell you this, but Mr. Bordellini suffered a massive stroke shortly after you left. He... he didn't make it."

I gasped. "What?! A stroke? I thought he was doing fine?"

"So did I, Ms. Rhodes. Unfortunately, this came on very suddenly and there wasn't anything more we could do. I'm so sorry for your loss."

The doctor went on, but I barely heard him. This was the third death I'd endured in the last week, all of them people I'd known or cared about as a child. It was true what they said — death happened in threes.

"Do you know if he has any surviving family members?" Dr. Farrah asked.

I cleared my throat. "I don't. I'm sorry. I have to go," I said, picturing Andrew. As far as I knew, he'd been the only living relative. But the Gold Vipers had taken care of that.

He started talking again, but I hung up, my mind on other things. In a sense, the Gold Vipers were also responsible for Dwayne's death now, too. It made me hate them that much more. They had to pay for this.

Murder.

Could I actually do it?

I reminded myself of what Dwayne had told me last night: these guys were animals who preyed on the innocent. They were involved with human trafficking, prostitution, and the kind of drugs that turned good people into addicts. Not to mention that the Gold Vipers were cold-blooded killers. I didn't know if I had it in me to actually pull the trigger, but I was hell-bent on finding out who was responsible for all of this. I wanted to confront them and make them pay. If it meant using a gun, I'd make sure that I was the last one standing.

NINE

AVA

I T TURNED OUT Dwayne did have an aunt still living, because I met her at his funeral a few days later. It was a small, private affair, and from what I gathered, paid for by a man he'd worked for. Someone definitely associated with the mob. At least, I assumed that was the case after meeting a few of the attendees, who literally reminded me of some of the characters from *The Sopranos*. From the way they spoke to the uneasy and shifty looks they were passing to each other. Almost like they were waiting for someone to waltz into the church and open fire. It was a little unnerving.

"You're Ava, right?" Dwayne's aunt asked me after the service. She was a short, squat woman who walked with a cane.

"Yes," I replied.

"My name is Beatrice. You can call me Bea."

"Nice to meet you."

"You, as well. Your brother, my nephew, used to speak so highly of you," she replied, smiling at me.

I smiled sadly and wondered if she knew that Andrew was dead. I didn't have the heart to tell her, considering how devastating the blow had been for me at my mother's funeral.

"It's such a shame. I always told him that he needed to quit drinking. Ever since Andrew left, he hit the bottle really badly though."

"That's too bad."

She sighed. "I don't know how to find Andrew and really don't know what I'm going to do with all of Dwayne's things." She put her hand on my arm. "You wouldn't be interested in helping me sell his house? I'll split whatever profit we make on it with you."

"I couldn't do that," I replied. "I'll help you, but you don't have to give me any money."

"At least let me pay you for your time," she replied firmly. "Please."

"Okay," I said. "If you want."

She smiled in relief. "Thank you."

I thought about the trip I was planning. "I'm going to be busy for the next few weeks, however. So, I won't be able to get to it for a while."

"No worries at all. Just call me when you're ready and we'll discuss what needs to be done at that time."

"Thank you."

"I know you were just at your mother's funeral a little while ago. I'm sorry for your loss."

"Thank you."

We exchanged phone numbers and then parted. Now I had two properties that needed my attention. I'd already decided to donate my mother's trailer and sell anything worth value, which was probably nothing. I had a feeling that Dwayne's house was a different story.

INSTEAD OF DEALING with either of the homes, I spent the next month preparing myself both mentally and physically for what was needed in Minnesota by visiting the gym every day, going to the shooting range, and researching everything I could about the Gold Vipers. From what I'd learned, there'd been a lot of scandals surrounding the club and they had a keen knack for staying out of jail.

As I dug deeper into their past, I learned that most of the drama related to the club had occurred with the Jensen, Iowa chapter. The current president, a man named Tank, was particularly interesting. An old girlfriend of his had apparently been murdered a few years back by a rival club and it was rumored that his father, a man dubbed "Slammer", had also been assassinated by the same group. Of course, nothing was ever proven and nobody went to jail. The writer of the article hinted that Slammer's murder might have been related to retaliation, but nothing was ever proven and violence continued on both sides. If that wasn't interesting enough, I also learned that Tank was now with a woman whose son had been caught in the crossfire of a war between the clubs, right after his father had been assassinated. The boy, who'd been two at the time, had recovered and the couple actually got married.

Married? Really?

I decided that the woman had to be a total nutcase. I couldn't understand why anyone would raise a child in such a dangerous environment, especially after he'd already been shot once. But then I thought of my own birth mother, who hadn't been a saint herself. I could still remember all of those times she'd gotten so high, leaving me unattended to fend for myself. It had been tough, especially during the week, when Andrew had been at his father's place. Most of my meals had consisted of Doritos or pretzels or whatever else I could get my hands on. I was forbidden to go outside when she was in her room "resting", so my life revolved around watching television and playing numerous video games.

Pushing the memories aside, I continued reading about the Gold Vipers until I eventually reached an article about Peyton Francis, the woman who'd claimed my brother had tried to assault her.

Seething, I continued reading. Apparently, she was involved with the vice president of the Gold Vipers in St. Paul, Minnesota. A man named Dominic Savage. Of course, he was nowhere to be found during the shooting. The man who killed my brother was the woman's neighbor, a retired cop. No charges were filed against him because it had supposedly been in self-defense and of course, Peyton had backed his story up. As far as I could tell, there were a lot of holes in the case, and to me, it was obvious there'd been more going on there than what it looked like. One thing I knew for certain was that Andrew wasn't a rapist or sexual predator.

Plus, the fact that she was dating the Gold Viper's V.P. was very suspicious. Reading the article made me even more determined to find out what in the hell had been going on. There was no way I could sit back and turn the other cheek. I was even more bound and determined bring justice.

BEFORE LEAVING FOR Minnesota, I purchased an old beater off Craigslist so I could leave my Lincoln Navigator at home. I didn't want to stand out or be remembered. I wanted to fit in with the type of crowd I assumed hung out with the Gold Vipers. The Chevy Malibu was a piece of crap, but that was fine. It just needed to get me to Minnesota. My plan was to do what I needed to, ditch the car, and rent a different one to get me back home. Another reason I wrote down a fake name and address when he sold it to me. I couldn't afford to have the car traced back to me.

After packing for the trip, I called Millie and reminded her that I was leaving town.

"Where are you going again?" she asked.

I told her that I'd been hired to do some stunt work in Minneapolis, but would be home soon.

"Another movie?"

"Yeah," I replied. "I'll tell you all about it when I get back."

"Okay, dear. Drive safely and call me when you get out there," she said.

"I will."

"Are you okay?" she asked.

"Yeah, why?"

"I don't know. You've just been so quiet lately." She sighed. "I can't even imagine how difficult it was, not just going to your mother's funeral, but finding out about Andrew and then of course, Dwayne. I know we've talked about it, but I just want to make sure you're doing okay."

"I'm fine," I replied. "Really."

She sighed. "Okay. I love you, Kiddo."

"I love you too, Mom."

After we hung up, I walked into my bedroom and pulled out the small gun safe from under my bed. I unlocked it and removed my .38 Special. As I held the revolver in my hand, I was suddenly hit with the reality of what I was considering and the gun felt like it weighed a ton.

Could I actually kill someone?

I had little doubt that if I confronted one of the Gold Vipers about murdering my brother, it would be the last thing coming from my lips, unless I was prepared. If anything, pulling the trigger would be an act of self-defense, which definitely helped to ease my conscience. I needed answers and someone had to pay for killing my brother.

I packed the gun, along with a box of bullets, and walked into the living room. I set the suitcase down on the carpeting and looked around my condo, wondering if I'd ever see it again. It was my first place and I'd spent a small fortune on the shabby-chic furnishings, trying to emulate something that wasn't just inviting, but cute. Oddly enough, I suddenly felt like a stranger in my own home. Maybe it was because I'd been visiting my past so much in the last few weeks, and this place was such a far cry from where I'd come from. Truthfully, I'd paid quite a bit for the condo, mainly because of the ocean view. I'd wanted to treat myself and hadn't thought twice about signing the paperwork. But now... I almost felt like I didn't belong here. That it was too luxurious for someone who'd come from nothing.

Angry with myself, I pushed the thought aside. There was no reason for a pity party. I'd worked hard for the money and I *deserved* it. Screw Hunter Calloway and anyone else who dared to try and make me feel inadequate.

Raising my head up high, I walked out of the condo, locked the door, and headed down to the parking lot, prepared to make sure others got exactly what they deserved, too.

TEN

AVA

THE DRIVE TO Minnesota wasn't bad, although I did stop in Tennessee to rest. I checked into a nice hotel, ordered room service, and tried to sleep, which was next to impossible, especially with everything on my mind. So, I tossed and turned for most of the night, dreading what was ahead of me. A couple times I caught myself wondering what in the hell I was even thinking, going out to Minnesota alone to take on the Gold Vipers. But then I pictured my brother getting shot and them grinning over his dead body. It kept me motivated.

When I did finally make it to St. Paul, I found myself stuck in rush-hour traffic, which was annoying as hell. Especially since I was new to the area, the car really *was* a piece of shit, and I was nervous as all hell. Eventually, I found my motel, a seedy one near a tattoo parlor the Gold Vipers were said to frequent. After thinking long and hard on the matter, I'd decided to bite the bullet and get a tattoo. It wasn't anything I'd ever imagined doing, but if it helped to get me closer to the club, then totally worth it in the end. Plus, whatever I got would be a tribute to Andrew.

My first night in town, I planned on taking it slow. I would visit the parlor, inquire about getting a tattoo, and see if it was true about it being a Gold Viper hangout.

After checking into the motel, I got to work. First, I changed into a pair of lacy white shorts and a black Harley Davidson tank. I then teased, fluffed, and spritzed my hair with hairspray until I looked like I belonged in an eighties rock video. From my research, it appeared that one-percenters, *especially*, preferred women with big hair, big boobs, and small brains. I'd been in show business long enough. The part wasn't hard to play.

Easier to control, I mused as I shakily applied dark eyeliner to my lids. As I concentrated on getting the line straight, I prayed that I wouldn't prove to have all three myself. Back home, I'd felt confident and courageous. Now I was trembling so badly, I could barely keep the liner straight.

After a few swear words, I finished my makeup and put on a pair of black Converse Chucks for an easier getaway because… one just never knew. Heels would have been sexy, but stupid as hell. I decided that if they weren't impressed with the package above the high tops, then it wouldn't matter anyway.

I kissed my lucky necklace for good luck and then stared into the mirror at the stranger looking back. In my line of work I was used to makeup and costumes, so it wasn't anything new. What I wasn't used to was being in charge of the transformation. Fortunately, I had to admit, I'd aced it.

I checked my ass in the mirror, grateful I'd been doing extra squats and leg lifts at the gym, and then finished my disguise with a spritz of perfume. It was new and smelled like candy, which is what I'd decided to call myself.

Candi.

I popped a piece of gum into my mouth and smiled at the mirror.

"Hi. I'm Candi. With an 'I'," I said, in my version of a bubble-headed bimbo. I popped my gum and smirked. *Maybe I should have gone into acting?*

On my way out, I slipped a small bottle of tequila into my purse, knowing I might need a little liquid courage.

DEVON'S TATTOO PARLOR was seven blocks away from the motel. I drove, mainly because I didn't want to be mistaken for a prostitute with what I was wearing.

Although it was just past eight, I noticed that the streets were already filled with shady-looking guys hanging out on street corners, and women strutting around in heels and eyeballing cars.

Hookers and drug dealers. Awesome.

Noticing that the women were dressed less provocatively than I was, I had to chuckle.

When I finally pulled into the studio's parking lot, which was located across the street from a strip club called *Danny V's*, I noticed a row of Hogs lined up, and that's when the panic set in. There was no doubt about it. I was in Gold Viper territory.

"Oh, my God... what in the hell are you thinking, Ava?" I whispered to myself, breaking out into a cold sweat. I stomped on the brake, feeling as if my heart was about to leap out of my chest. Trying not to hyperventilate, I reached into my purse, grabbed the bottle of tequila, and took a swig. The taste was horrible, especially without any lime or salt. Shuddering, I recapped the bottle, feeling the heat of the alcohol. It slowly began to do its job and calm me slightly. Blowing a curl away from my eyes, I cranked up the air conditioner and counted the motorcycles. There were ten.

Knowing I must look suspicious idling there, I took my foot of the brake and found a parking spot, away from the bikes. I cut the engine and took another swig of tequila.

"You're just getting a tattoo," I said breathlessly, talking myself off the ledge. "There's nothing suspicious or alarming about it."

Knowing it *would* look a little strange if I didn't do something soon, I grabbed my purse and got out of the car, leaving the tequila in the glovebox. Staring at the flashing neon sign, I mustered up some courage and walked to the entrance. When I stepped inside, music played in the background, a popular song from the *White Stripes*. Looking around, I thought the place looked edgy, but in a good way. It was also clean and smelled like disinfectant, which was a relief, considering I was getting a tattoo. There were no signs of bikers, however.

"Hey, sweetie," one of the gals called out to me, a busty woman with jet-black hair and tattoos sleeved over both arms. She was sitting down next to a burly-looking man and holding a tattoo gun. "If you're looking for the party, it doesn't start until ten and it's across the street at *Danny V's*."

My eyebrows shot up. "Party?" I repeated.

"Club party, you know?" Her mouth formed a circle. "Oh, shit. I'm sorry. Are you here for a tattoo?"

"Actually, yes," I replied and smiled. "I'm sorry, should I have made an appointment?"

"We usually prefer it if you do," she said. "But, we do accept walk-ins." She looked up at the clock on the wall. "I just don't know if we can fit you in for another couple of hours."

"I can wait," I replied quickly.

"That was *hours*, not minutes," she said, looking amused. "You sure about that? Maybe you should just come back?"

"No. I'll stick around. I've got nothing better to do," I said, glancing toward two other artists working on clients, one a bald guy with tattoos all over his head, the other, a heavy-set woman with red hair. They ignored me and continued what they were doing.

"You know what you want done?" the dark-haired woman asked.

"I have an idea," I told her.

"I'll be right back," she said to her client and stood up. She walked over to me and introduced herself as Devon.

"I'm… Candi," I said, the name still so foreign on my tongue.

"It's nice to meet you, Candi. Why don't you tell me a little bit about this idea of yours?"

Devon reminded me of an amazon, especially with the heels. Not only was she tall, but it was obvious she spent a lot of time at the gym. Although my arms were toned from lifting weights, she looked like she could bench-press me without breaking a sweat.

"I want the name 'Andrew' tattooed on my hip," I said, pointing to where I wanted it.

"Boyfriend?" she asked.

"No. He was my brother."

"Ah. I was going to say, I'm not a big fan of inking names on a person unless it's a family member or spouse. You said he 'was' your brother?" she replied, her eyes softening.

I nodded.

"I'm sorry for your loss, sweetie," she said, putting her hand on my shoulder. "And it think it's really cool that you want to honor his memory by getting a tat."

"Thanks."

"So, do you want just his name or an image with it?"

We discussed different ideas until I heard her mention something about a dragon.

"That's it. I want his name and maybe a small dragon." Dragons were supposed to be brave and fearless. That's how I wanted to remember Andrew.

She grinned. "I love it. You sure you want to go small with the dragon, though? I have a guy who I bet can come up with something that will look both sexy and cool on the side of your hip."

"I don't know. This is my first tattoo," I replied. I wasn't even totally sure I was all in with a small one.

"Let me show you my guy's portfolio of dragons. He's kick-ass at what he does. The last dragon he did was incredible."

"Okay."

She turned around and grabbed a white binder from the counter. "I'm sure if you want a small tat, he can probably do that, too. I just think with a hot body like yours, a larger one would look super sexy," she said, raking her eyes over my outfit.

"Uh, thanks," I replied, wondering if she was into girls.

As if reading my mind, Devon laughed and handed me the binder. "Relax, Candi-cane, I'm not hitting on you. I'm just telling it like it is."

"Thanks," I said, amused that she'd called me Candi-cane.

She looked up at the clock. "I'm going to ask Hollywood if he's free. I know he's in back."

My eyebrow raised. "Hollywood?"

She smiled. "Yeah, the artist. He's my fiancé's cousin. You'll love him. All the women do."

"Okay." I chuckled.

I watched as she headed toward a doorway in the back of the parlor.

"Today's your lucky day," the red-headed artist said, looking over at me.

"Oh yeah?"

She nodded. "Double yeah. He's a total hunk."

"Oh, really?"

"You'll see."

Assuming he was also a Gold Viper, I knew things were about to get interesting.

ELEVEN

HOLLYWOOD

I WAS IN the back of the clubhouse, enjoying my first beer of the night, when Devon walked in.

"Hey, Babe," said Brass, who was sitting across from me. "What's up?"

"I'm here for Hollywood," she replied and looked at me. "You free? I have a gal in front who'd like a dragon tat. Fresh canvas."

I held up my beer. "Shit… I just sat down."

I'd been working my ass off all day, helping Phoenix, the club prez, with some roof work. Between doing that part-time and prospecting, it didn't leave me a lot of energy to do what I really enjoyed, which was being an ink-slinger. But club business was top priority, whether I liked it or not.

"I hear ya, but she wants a custom job and has decided on a dragon. I could do it, but you're so much better. And… I think you'll enjoy the job a lot more than I will," she replied with a smirk.

"What do you mean?" I asked.

"Come up front and find out," she replied, turning around.

Devon had my attention.

"Hey, babe," Brass called out. "Who's watching Wyatt?"

Wyatt was their infant son.

"Lily volunteered again," she said over her shoulder before walking out.

Lily was Phoenix's Old Lady. He said she was getting 'baby fever' and kept talking about having one of their own. I think it made him nervous. Hell, the idea of having kids made most guys anxious.

"Devon still pissed at you?" Len asked, one of the older club vets. He was pretty cool and didn't demand much. Of course, he was always comfortably stoned.

"Probably," he replied.

I stood up. "Why?"

"She wants a big wedding and I want to elope," he replied. "Big weddings aren't my thing."

"Brother, you'd better marry her the way she wants to be married," said Phoenix, listening in. "Take it from me, you don't mess with a woman's wedding plans. This isn't like picking out a restaurant. This is something many of them have been planning on ever since they received their first *Wedding Day Barbie*. You don't take that away from them and live happily-ever-after to tell about it. Especially with a woman like Devon."

Dom, the V.P. also agreed. "He's right on the nuts. Make her happy, Brass. You'll regret trying to get out of it later."

Brass groaned. "Fine. I guess if Tarot's warning me, then I'm doing a big wedding."

We called Dom *Tarot* because he had some kind of freakish psychic ability. He didn't like to call himself a clairvoyant, but that's exactly what he was.

I downed the rest of my beer and then went into the shop. Devon, who was seated next to a male client, looked up at me and winked. "Over there."

A young woman was standing by the cash register, paging through my portfolio. At first, all I saw was a cute chick with big hair and a tank top that appeared to be filled out rather nicely.

I approached the counter. "Hey, how's it going?"

She looked up and smiled.

I felt like someone knocked the wind out of me. She went from being just a pretty, young thing to being absolutely gorgeous.

"I'm doing good," she said. "You must be Hollywood?"

I held out my hand. "That's me. Nice to meet you. What was your name?"

She shook it. "I'm Candi."

71

Fuck, she sure smelled sweet. If her big brown eyes and beautiful white smile wasn't enough to get my blood boiling, she was also blessed with one hell of a body. Tan with long legs, a curvy ass, and the kind of tits that caused boners and fistfights.

"I'm Hollywood," I repeated, without thinking.

Devon snorted loudly.

Candi looked amused. "Yeah. You mentioned that."

Trying to hold onto a little dignity, I picked up the binder and asked her to follow me to my station. As we passed by Devon, I ignored the mocking smile she gave me.

"So, let's start from the beginning," I said, when we were in the back of the parlor. "You're looking for a dragon tattoo?"

"I think so," she replied, looking unsure enough to warrant 'the speech', which I used to weed out what I called "Regretters." People who weren't as serious about getting inked as they should be. Those were usually the ones who complained the most about the needles, the time it took for the tat, and the price. Getting a tattoo shouldn't ever be done on a whim. The only people I wanted wearing my ink were the serious ones.

"A tat is permanent, for the most part. It's important to make sure you're absolutely definite on *why* you're doing it and determine if it's something you really want to do. " I said, sitting down on a stool. "So… why don't you tell me what it is that really brought you in here tonight, Candi?"

TWELVE

AVA

MY STOMACH DROPPED. Had he figured it out? He looked so serious, it made me wonder.

"What do you mean?" I asked, forcing a smile to my face.

"You look a skittish about getting inked. If I'm going to put my time in, I want to make sure you're doing it for the right reasons, so you won't regret it later."

I relaxed. "Oh."

"Now, tell me why you're considering this," he said, staring up at me.

I explained that I wanted to honor my brother and thought a tattoo sounded cool. "He died last year," I explained, noticing Hollywood was wearing a Gold Vipers vest with the word "Prospect" on it. I knew it meant that he wasn't an official club member and realized that he might not have been around when Andrew had been murdered. The thought made me a little bit more comfortable, although the other gal had been right. He was a hunk. In fact, Hollywood was a work of art himself. Tall and muscular, with blond hair buzzed on the sides and long on top, a five-o'clock shadow that was edging more into six p.m., and eyes the color of the sky on a clear day. To be perfectly honest, he was as hot-as-sin. And I say sin, because I found myself responding to his hotness, which I knew was wrong on so many levels.

"I'm sorry to hear that," he said, his eyebrows knitting together. "That couldn't have been easy. Were you close?"

"We were. A long time ago," I replied, shifting my gaze. The guy was watching me with an intensity that was unnerving.

"Okay. So... where do you want it?"

I turned sideways and touched the back of my right hip. "I was thinking I'd like it here. Something small with my brother's name near it."

"I thought she should get one that runs all down her side," called out Devon.

He tilted his head and stared at my hip. "But, you just want something small?"

"I guess it depends on the design," I replied, imagining him leaning over me while I was half-naked. I'd seen some of the tattoo shows on cable and knew it would take hours to complete. I also knew it wasn't going to be a walk in the park. But, it would give us time to talk about the club, and the more I knew, the better.

He opened up the portfolio and began sifting through the pages. "Was there anything in here that caught your eye?"

All of the artwork had been impressive, but there'd been one I'd particularly liked. I showed him. The dragon was red with blue spikes and claws. The details were incredible enough that I imagined it had taken him hours to complete.

"So, it's the colors you like?" he asked, still all businesslike.

"Yes, plus I love all of the details. I've never seen anything like it," I said and began pointing out the areas that really impressed me.

Nodding, he closed the book. "Okay. Just so you're aware, every design of mine is original, but it helps to get some ideas on your preferences. Like, the colors that attract you the most and what kind of a feel you're going for. From what I'm gathering, you want a fierce-looking dragon?"

"Yes. Exactly."

He grabbed a sketchbook from the counter and flipped it to a blank page. "What about colors?"

"I like purple and blues. Maybe some green, too."

He nodded. "Sounds good. I actually have some ideas on where to place your brother's name, too."

"Cool."

Hollywood looked up from the sketchbook. "We just need to figure out the size."

I looked down, imagining a sleek, colorful dragon on my hip and thigh. It wouldn't just signify the love I had for my brother, but what lengths I was willing to go for the people I cared about. It would be a sign of loyalty, justice, and retribution.

But did I really want someone associated with the gang who had been responsible for my brother's death doing the tattoo? Wouldn't I always be reminded of them when I looked at the tat?

I glanced up at Hollywood. He was staring at me, hopeful and handsome. I flicked my gaze down at the Gold Vipers patch on his chest, then back into his icy blue eyes. He just didn't seem like the type... but then again, what did I know? There was no turning back now, though. This was for Andrew anyway.

I nodded. "Let's do it."

"Yeah?" he said.

"Yes. I want it big and long."

Devon burst out in laughter.

"Don't we all," drawled Red from her station.

Hollywood's lip twitched.

"Did Mr. Serious smile?" Red asked.

"Almost," I replied, grinning.

This produced a grin and a head shake from him.

"Good," Red said. "You need to learn to smile more, Hollywood."

Before he could answer, the door leading to the clubhouse opened and an attractive guy with jet-black hair and an annoyed expression stepped into the parlor. He also wore a Gold Viper cut with a patch that read *Sergeant at Arms*.

He was one of the higher-ups, I thought, stiffening up.

"Uh oh," said Red. "Here comes trouble. What's shakin' Brass?"

"The roof as soon as you kick off the party later, Gigi," he replied with a wink.

She smiled. "You know I will, Brassy-boy."

Smiling, he walked over to Devon's station and said something to her quietly.

She squealed in delight and stood up. "Really? You're serious?"

"Anything for you, Mama," he replied.

She threw her arms around him. "I love you."

"I love you, too. Let's go make some more." Devon was a big woman, but he picked her and threw her over his shoulder like she weighed nothing. I suddenly realized that he meant to take her back for sex.

"Hey! Wait, I'm not done with Jimmy's tat!" she cried, laughing as he turned on his heel to head back to the clubhouse.

Brass stopped and turned around. "Jimmy, you don't mind if I borrow her for a few minutes, do you?"

"He means seconds," Devon said wryly.

The man she'd been inking said, "No, man. Whatever you want, Brass. Take all the time you need."

"You're a good man, Jimmy. Her hand will be a lot steadier after I'm done with her," he replied.

"Have a cigarette, Jimmy. I'll be back before you put it out," Devon said, looking up.

Gigi laughed. "You know, they do make pills for that."

Brass slapped Devon hard on the ass, making her gasp. "You think you're funny, talkin' smack about your old man, woman? You aren't going to be laughing when you walk back here sore from —"

"T.M.I., Brassy-boy," Gigi interrupted. "This woman isn't getting any, so I don't want to hear about something I'm missing."

"Len's available," he replied. "You know he likes you."

"Not as much as he likes the ganja. I'll pass," she replied.

"His loss. Hey, man. Looks like it was worth it," he said, winking at Hollywood as he carried Devon past us.

I didn't know what that was all about, but I had a feeling it had to do with me.

Not responding, Hollywood looked at me. "Make yourself at home." He nodded toward the reclining chair and then turned his back to work on the sketch.

I sat down.

"You want anything to drink? We have bottled water, coffee, or soda," he said, looking over his shoulder.

"I'm good. Thank you."

"Let me know if you change your mind."

"Okay."

I looked around the parlor, wondering again what I was thinking. Here I was about to get a tattoo from a guy who belonged to the hoodlums who'd killed my brother. Sure, he might not have been involved with it directly, but he was tied to the killers and that made him just as dangerous.

Reminding myself that I was doing it for Andrew, I looked down and found a magazine rack next to the chair. I leaned down and grabbed a mag about tattoos. As I started flipping through the pages, the back door opened up again, and this time a group of five menacing-looking Gold Vipers stepped into the parlor. As they walked toward the front of the parlor, a couple of them looked my way.

"Hey there, gorgeous," one of the men said, stopping by the station. He was thin and wiry with greasy brown hair and long sideburns. "You getting a tat?"

I cleared my throat. "I think so."

78

"Where?" he asked, his roving eyes moving up and down my body.

"She's not sure yet, Len," Hollywood said, turning around. "You guys heading to the party?"

"Yeah," he replied and then looked back at me. "I've never seen you around here before, sweet thing."

"It's my first tattoo," I said, forcing a smile to my face.

"Nice. Fresh canvas," he said, grinning. "Hollywood, you got yourself some virgin skin. Gotta love that."

"Yep," he replied, once again concentrating on the drawing.

"You know what they say about tattoos, once you get the first one, you're hooked. You want to keep coming back for more," Len said. "Kind of what the chicks say about me. What about you, beautiful? You seeing anyone?"

I wanted to tell him 'yes' so badly, but I knew it would be easier to get information from these guys if they thought they had a chance with me.

"I'm just getting over a relationship," I replied instead.

"On the rebound," he said. "Well, if you need someone to take your mind off of the idiot who let a beauty like you go, I'm your man."

Hollywood grunted.

"I'm doing fine, but thank you," I replied.

The door opened again and another Gold Viper stepped into the parlor by way of the clubhouse, which was attached to the parlor. I had to do a double-take as he walked by.

"Hey, happy birthday, "Gigi said, turning in her stool to look at him.

"Thanks, darlin'," the man said, smiling at her. "You stoppin' by the party later?"

"I wouldn't miss it, Tarot," she replied.

"Good. I'll save you a seat." The muscular, dark-haired guy looked at me curiously and I quickly turned my head. He reminded me so much of my brother, it was almost eerie.

"You comin', Len?" the man asked.

"Yeah." Len looked over at me. "Good luck with your tattoo. What was your name?"

I almost said Ava, but caught myself. "Ah, Candi."

"Mm…" he said, a wicked gleam in his eyes. "I bet you taste as sweet as your name."

The thought of him tasting me made my skin crawl.

"Goodbye, Len," Hollywood said sharply.

Chuckling, Len winked at me and headed toward the front door.

"Sorry about Len," Hollywood said. "He sees a pretty face and can't help himself."

"It's okay." *No, it wasn't. Shudder.*

I watched as the group of men left the parlor, still wondering about the man who looked like Andrew.

THIRTEEN

HOLLYWOOD

I WANTED HER dragon to be my best work of art to date, so I took my time with the details until I finally produced something I hoped would impress her. Unlike many other tattooists, I was usually pretty fast with my sketches. Some people took days. Some took hours. I normally finished the first draft in fifteen minutes and would then consult with the client to make any necessary changes. For Candi, I spent forty-five minutes, which was a lot more than usual, concentrating heavily on the details and shadowing. When I was finished, I held it up and her eyes widened.

"Wow," she said, moving closer. "It's incredible. I've never seen anything like it."

Flattered, I smiled. "Thanks. Obviously, I still need to color it. I just wanted to know if there was anything you'd like me to change?"

"No. Nothing. I really love what you did with my brother's name, too."

Instead of just a dragon, I had the beast wrapped around a medieval sword with Andrew's named etched down the front of the weapon. Even I had to admit, it looked pretty badass.

As we were discussing the sketch, Devon and Brass walked back into the parlor.

"Bye, babe," he said, patting her ass again. "Text me when you're ready to close the shop and I'll return."

"Okay," she said.

Brass winked at Jimmy as he passed him by. "Sorry, man." He said looking back. "She put me up to the challenge. I had to save face."

"Dude, you don't have to explain nothing to me. I understand," he replied.

"You're a good man, Jimmy," he said before leaving the parlor.

Devon sat down and apologized again for leaving him stranded.

"No problem, Devon," he said.

"Hollywood, did you finish the sketch?" Devon called out from her station.

"Yeah," I replied.

She stood back up. "Sweet. Let me see." She walked over and I showed her. Devon gasped. "Oh, my God, that's fucking gorgeous. You outdo yourself every time, Hollywood."

"Thanks."

"I can't wait to see the finished product. Are you going to leave it black and white or colored?" she asked Candi.

"Colored," Candi replied and then told her which colors she'd chosen.

"That's going to be breathtaking," she replied.

I looked at the clock. It was nine-thirty. "It's getting late and this thing is going to take hours. We'll have to start on it tomorrow."

Candi looked disappointed. "Darn. How long will it actually take?"

I shrugged. "Probably eight to ten hours. Plus, it depends on your pain threshold. Some people can only handle a couple hours at a time."

She sighed. "I understand. So, when can we start it?"

"I'm free tomorrow afternoon. Around three? I wish we could do it earlier, but I have some shit I've got to do tomorrow."

"It's fine."

"I'll work on the coloring during my lunch break and should have it ready for your final approval by three."

She nodded. "Okay. What kind of a price are we looking at?"

I told her and she whistled.

"It's a good price," Jimmy called out. "Considering the work he does. I paid two grand for my wife's tattoo, and to be honest, I wish I'd have come here. You get what you pay for."

"No, it's fine," she said. "I've just never gotten a tattoo and had no idea the cost."

"We charge by the hour, and obviously, this one will take a while. I know it's very detailed, but I want you to love it," I told her.

"I do already."

"Good. Tell you what," I said, lowering my voice. "How about you have a drink with me at the bash we're having and... I'll give you my 'friends-and-family' discount?"

FOURTEEN

AVA

R EALIZING THAT HE was inviting me to the birthday party, I tried not to panic. Things were happening so much faster than I'd planned, catching me off-guard. Not to mention, I'd heard about how rowdy and chaotic biker parties could get. Still, it was definitely a great opportunity.

"Sure. Why not…? Who's the party for?" I asked.

"It's Tarot's. Our V.P. I should probably warn you, we're having it across the street at *Danny V's.*"

My heart started to race. *Tarot!* The man who looked like my brother was the same one responsible for his death. It seemed to make it even more disturbing. "No problem."

"It should be a pretty tame party, considering. It's in the back room, and some of the Old Ladies are going to be there. Tarot was adamant that he didn't want any strippers around when he found out we were throwing it there."

"Why at a strip place then?" I asked.

"Because the owner offered. I'm sure he'll make a killing off of the booze and food. Plus, if any of the guys want a lap dance, they can always visit the club area," he replied.

"Makes sense."

"So, what do you say?"

I made a face. "Len's going to be there, right?"

He chuckled. "Don't worry. He's all talk anyway. If he makes a move, I'll kick his ass."

"Okay. As long as you promise to be my bodyguard." I batted my eyelashes at him.

Hollywood stood up. "Nobody will mess with you. Let me clean up my station and then we'll head over there."

I nodded.

FIFTEEN MINUTES LATER, we stepped into *Danny V's.* Unfortunately, we had to walk through the front of the strip joint, which was crowded with rowdy customers. Loud music blasted out of the speakers as two girls on stage wrestled in a plastic pool filled with what might have been whipped cream. I noticed Len and a couple other Gold Vipers cheering the strippers on as one of girls pulled the other's bikini top off. The naked girl jiggled her breasts, causing the guys to clap, hoot, and holler.

"Nice place," I mused.

Hollywood looked down at me. "First time in a strip club?"

"Yeah."

And definitely my last.

Although I had nothing against strippers, watching the men get turned on brought back disturbing memories of my past. Especially of the times I'd been *forced* to get undressed to please others.

"Hey, Hollywood," said a half-naked woman walking by with a tray of drinks. "Haven't seen you here in a while."

"I've been busy," he replied. "How've you been?"

"Pretty good, considering." The waitress nodded toward the back. "They're all in *that* party room."

"Thanks, Kiki," he said.

Kiki glanced at me and then back to Hollywood. She winked. "You two have fun now."

He smiled. "We're planning on it."

"Come here often?" I asked after Kiki disappeared, unable to help myself.

"Not too much. Let's go."

Hollywood led me back to the party where, thankfully, the atmosphere was better and much more mellow.

"See, this isn't so bad," he said.

"No. It's nice," I admitted.

I took in the scene in front of me. Most of the guests wore Gold Vipers vests and were playing cards. There were also quite a few women sitting at separate tables, drinking, talking, and laughing.

After scanning the room, my eyes rested on Tarot. He was seated at a card table, holding a woman on his lap. They were engaged in a deep kiss, ignoring everyone else around them.

"Looks like a big turnout. Let's grab a drink," Hollywood said.

"Okay."

I followed him to the bar and a male bartender named Phil greeted us.

"What can I get for you?" Phil asked.

Not wanting any more tequila, I ordered a whiskey-sour.

"Sounds good. I'll have one of those, too," Hollywood said, scratching his chin as he looked at the bottles lined up behind Phil.

"You got it," the bartender said, turning away to mix the drinks.

As we waited, I looked back over to where Tarot was.

"That's Peyton," Hollywood said next to my ear. "His Old Lady."

My heart skipped a beat. It was *her*. The woman who'd accused my brother, which meant that Tarot was Dominic Savage.

I stared at them, my blood boiling.

"You've been intrigued with him ever since he walked into the parlor," Hollywood said. "I should have told you he had an Old Lady."

"I'm not intrigued and couldn't care less if he's with someone. He just looks familiar," I admitted. "It kind of caught me off-guard."

Hollywood looked back over at Tarot. "You think you've met him before?"

"No. I know I haven't. He just looks like a guy I knew a long time ago. A… friend," I added, although Hollywood didn't sound like he was jealous. In fact, it was hard getting a read on him at all. Although he'd invited me for a drink, I still couldn't tell if he was into me or just being nice.

"So, do you have a girlfriend?" I asked, deciding to get right down to it. I wanted to know what he wanted or expected from me.

He turned around and faced me again. "Nope. What about you?"

I smirked. "No, I'm not into girls."

"Funny," he replied, biting back a smile.

"Didn't you hear me tell Len that I'd just recently broken up with someone?"

He shrugged. "Yeah, but I figured you were just letting him down easy."

"You're right. He's not my type."

"What type is that?" he asked piercing me with a serious expression.

Admittedly, in a different world, it would have been easy to flirt with such a good looking guy. He was sexy, quiet, and his artwork blew me away. The man was definitely fascinating. But, he was also the enemy and I didn't want him to think he was getting down my pants anytime soon.

"A nice guy. One who doesn't come on as strong as Len," I replied, internally patting myself on the back for the answer.

Hollywood nodded. "I can appreciate that."

"What's your real name?" I asked, staring at his profile. The five-o'clock shadow gave him more of a rugged, bad-ass kind of look, but I could tell that if he shaved, he could also look like the boy-next-door.

"Jayce."

"Would you be insulted if I called you that instead? I just really like it better."

89

"No. Go ahead," he said as the bartender set our cocktails down in front of us.

Jayce paid for the drinks and then asked if I wanted to play darts.

"Sure."

"Let's go over and say hi to Tarot and Peyton first."

My stomach knotted up. "Sure."

We walked to where they were sitting. Peyton was now seated next to Tarot and scrolling through her phone.

"Hey, Peyton. How's it going?" Jayce said, addressing her first.

"It's going great, Hollywood. Who's your friend?" she asked, smiling up at us.

"This is Candi," he said and then went around the table, introducing me to the club members. Most of the names went over my head. All except for Phoenix, who I knew was the club president, and of course Tarot's.

"So, are you two dating?" Peyton asked, putting her phone away.

"We just met tonight," I said tightly. Although my intention was to try and come off as friendly, it was damn hard. I wanted to grab her by the hair and slam her face into the table.

Noticing my cool tone, she gave me a funny look.

I swore inwardly. Being a bitch wasn't going to help me any.

My eyes met Tarot's who was watching me intently. I forced a smile to my face. "Happy Birthday. So, how old are you?"

"Too old to think about it. Thank you," he said, tilting his head. "Have we met somewhere before?"

"I don't think so," I replied.

He shook his finger at me. "There's something familiar about you. I just don't know what it is."

90

"You *did* see me in the tattoo parlor," I reminded him. *There was no way he could connect me to Andrew.*

He scratched his whiskers and nodded. "That must be it," he said as a waitress named Bambi approached the table with a tray full of shots.

"Here we go, boys. It's Jägermeister time," she said, setting the shot glasses down, one-by-one.

"Uh, oh. Who ordered all of these?" Peyton asked, laughing.

"Me," Phoenix said, reaching over. He began handing them out. "Go ahead, Peyton, Candi. Help yourselves."

"I'm driving us home," Peyton said. "I'll stick with my Diet Coke."

"Take an Uber," Phoenix said. "Or crash at the clubhouse. We have plenty of rooms in the back."

"Thank you, but we've got to get home to Ruby, who's with a sitter," she replied. "Plus, I have a showing tomorrow and need to help get the house ready. The client is a slob."

"Hey, who you calling a slob?" Len said, coming up behind us. "I just want you to sell the damn thing. You don't need to clean it."

She sighed. "If won't sell if it's a mess."

"I cleaned it. Earlier today," he replied, looking embarrassed. "Hell, it's not that bad."

"No offense, Len, but I've seen your place. It's a pigsty," Tarot said with a smirk.

Len flipped him off.

"I thought you'd moved in with Chachi?" Jayce asked.

"I did about three weeks ago. The place I'm selling was my mother's house," he said. "Remember, she passed away."

"That's right. Sorry," Jayce said somberly.

"No worries. She was a mean old bitch who's probably sitting at the right hand of the Devil. If Satan had any offspring, she'd have been the black sheep of the family," Len said with a disgusted look.

Tarot sighed. "She had mental problems. I'm sure now that she's passed on, she regrets the horrible way she treated you."

"Doesn't help me now much, does it?" he replied and then turned toward me, his scowl turning to a grin. "What you doing here, gorgeous? Tell me you're looking for me."

"Sorry, brother. I talked her into having a drink with me," Jayce said, putting his arm around me.

Not expecting that, I forced myself to not pull away. I still had issues with guys touching me without warning, no matter how good looking they were.

Len gave me a strange look. "Thought you weren't in the market for a man right now?"

"I'm not," I said. "We're just having a drink together."

"Maybe afterward, you might want to share one with me, too?" he said, wiggling his eyebrows.

"Len, give it up. Leave her alone and find yourself a woman who's actually interested," Phoenix said dryly. "Everyone else, grab a shot so we can toast Tarot. I'm thirsty."

"You want one?" Jayce asked, looking down at me.

"No, I'd better not," I replied, holding up the whiskey-sour. "I still have to finish this, and to tell you the truth, I'm not much of a drinker."

Actually, I probably could have used a shot to calm my nerves, but under no circumstance did I plan on getting drunk. Not when Jayce's hand was starting to feel a little too good around my waist.

"No problem." He picked up one of the shots and held it up as Phoenix began making a toast. I raised my drink and Peyton held up her Diet Coke.

"To Tarot. May this next year bring you all that you desire. You deserve it more than anyone, brother," he said.

He deserved something, and as my eyes shifted between him and Peyton, I vowed to make sure he, along with his "Old Lady", got it.

FIFTEEN

HOLLYWOOD

I COULD TELL Candi was nervous around the club, which was no surprise, considering she was an outsider. They were good guys, though; even Len.

After we took the shot, I brought her over to a more intimate part of the club, hoping she'd relax and open up a little.

"So, where are you from?" I asked after we found a table in the corner.

For a split second, a look of panic flashed across her face. It made me wonder if she really was there just to get a discount on the tattoo and wasn't interested in me.

"Las Vegas," she said, stirring her straw in the drink. "A couple of weeks ago."

"Really? You have family here?"

She lowered her eyes. "No. I don't have any family."

"So, what made you travel up here to Minnesota? You thinking about moving?"

"Honestly, I don't know. It's still in debate." Candi smiled and turned the conversation around to me. "Have you lived here all of your life?"

I nodded.

"How long have you been a prospect?"

"Over a year." I told her about Brass being my cousin and sponsor.

"When are they going to make you a member?"

"Soon, I hope."

She nodded toward Tarot's table. "What's it like, being with these guys?"

I shrugged. "Basically, it's like we're one big family. We look out for each other, and if something happens to one of us, it happens to all of us," I said, trying to explain the camaraderie, which was why a lot of guys joined clubs.

"What do you mean, 'if something happens'?"

"We have enemies all over. If they strike out at one of us, it affects us all, and we work together to take care of it. We have each other's backs."

Her eyes hardened for a brief second. "Does that happen a lot?"

"Strikes?"

She nodded.

"It hasn't for a while. We had some issues with a rival club awhile back, but things have mellowed out."

Candi took a drink of her cocktail and then asked if the rumors about the Gold Vipers were true.

"Which rumors are that?" I asked, hoping she wasn't talking about any criminal activity. At the moment, we were only involved with some minor weapons trafficking. The Gold Vipers had stopped their involvement with drug running a few years back. In regards to prostitution, some of the chapters had their hands in that bullshit, but not us.

"I heard that you guys are a force to be reckoned with. Nobody screws with your club or they pay the consequences," she said, chewing on her straw and staring up at me with doe eyes.

"Yeah. Those rumors are true, but you have nothing to worry about unless you're plotting against us," I replied with a smile.

"You don't have anything to worry about from me. I'm just here having a drink with my new favorite tattoo artist," she said, laughing. "Seriously, I have nothing against you guys."

I reached forward and put my hand on hers. I'd obviously made her nervous. "I know. I'm just giving you shit."

"I know."

Damn, she was beautiful. It had been awhile since I'd gotten laid, being as busy as I was with the club and work.

Just thinking about Candi underneath me was getting me hard. "So, why did you really agree to come over here? Was it just the tattoo?"

SIXTEEN

AVA

CRAP. HE'S MAKING *his move.*

"I don't know. You seem like a nice guy. You're obviously handsome, too. I thought maybe we could get to know each other a little more. Especially since we'll be spending a lot of time together in the next couple of days."

"True. Handsome, huh?" he said as another waitress stopped at our table.

I smirked. "A little."

"You two doing okay, or would you like another round?" she asked.

"How about one more?" he said, looking at me.

I nodded.

He ordered the drinks and then the waitress walked away.

My cell phone went off, startling me.

I reached into my purse to see who was calling. It was Millie.

"My mom," I offered without thinking.

He gave me a puzzled look. "I thought you said you had no family?"

"She's my foster mother," I explained, kicking myself mentally. "My blood relatives are dead. She's all I have."

"You grew up in foster care?"

I nodded.

"What was that like?"

I laughed dryly. "A nightmare." I took another sip of my cocktail and decided to tell him about my past, without giving anything else away. I explained that my birthmother had lost custody of me because of her drug addiction, and I'd hopped from foster home to foster home up until meeting Millie.

"You moved around a lot. Why?" he asked, studying my face.

99

"Let's just say that some of the foster parents were either assholes or just far too 'nice'... if you know what I mean," I replied, finishing my drink.

"They abused you?" he asked angrily.

I nodded and looked up from my empty glass. "I survived, though. It's true what say, 'what doesn't kill you makes you stronger'. I can certainly vouch for that," I said with a brittle smile.

"Fuck, I'm sorry you had to go through that," he replied, a look of disgust on his face. "Did anyone get in trouble for it?"

"No. Nobody believed me. Or, decided not to because it was easier," I replied, remembering the first time I told the wife of the first degenerate who'd touched me. I'd only been eleven. She'd accused me of lying and trying to get them kicked out of the foster program. I told Jayce about it and he looked like he wanted to murder someone.

"That's fucked up," he said, reaching over again to grab my hand. "Really, really fucked up. I wish I'd known you back then. I'd have done something about it. See, that's one reason why I'm with the Gold Vipers. If they found out something like that was going on, they'd stop it."

I smiled.

"Do you know if these people are still involved with foster care? The ones who did it to you?"

From the look on his face, he looked like he wanted to pay them a visit.

"I don't know."

"Do you remember the neighborhood the asshole who touched you lived in or anything like that?"

Of course I did. One never forgot the places they were abused. At least I couldn't.

"I appreciate you wanting to help, but I'd rather just forget about it," I said, moving my hand away from his as the waitress returned with our drinks.

"Here you go," she said, setting our cocktails down in front of us. She included two shot glasses filled with orange liquid.

"What's this?" Jayce asked.

"Fireball. Compliments of Len," she replied, nodding toward the table of Gold Vipers. "He said something about you two needing something to heat things up over here."

We both looked over and Len raised his beer.

Jayce smiled and shook his head.

WE DRANK THE shots and talked for the next hour about the club and how 'great' they were. It was hard to listen to, but I kept a smile on my face. He also told me about his stint as a model, which intrigued me.

"How did you go from modeling to being in a biker gang?"

"Biker *club*," he corrected. "And I'd wanted to belong to one long before I modeled, especially after attending some of the parties with Brass."

He explained that his chapter used to be called the Steel Bandits before getting patched over. I'd already read about it online, but pretended to be clueless.

"Now the club is stronger and part of a bigger unit," he said with a glint in his eyes. "People really take notice when you're wearing Gold Viper colors, even as a prospect."

"And that means a lot to you?" I mused.

"Respect means a lot to me. But, it's more than that. It's about the brotherhood and representing something we take pride in. You know, outsiders only know about what they see on the news, and everyone knows that the media will write anything that sells — bullshit or not. They don't ever talk about the good things our club is involved in, like volunteering and raising money for local charities. Last month, we raised twenty-thousand dollars and donated it to a homeless shelter up the road. Was that ever on the news?" He snorted. "Hell no. Because they're only interested in making us look like criminals."

The Gold Vipers didn't need any help there, I mused.

"Wow, that's amazing," I replied. "Do you do this all year- round, then? Raise money for those in need?"

"During the holidays is when we do the majority of our charity work. It's a hard time for people during that season and we're committed to helping families who need help. Last year some of the clubs had guys dress up as Santa Claus and visit nursing homes. Tarot volunteered for our chapter. We all got together and delivered cookies Lily and some of the other Old Ladies made. You know, some of those people never get visitors, let alone presents."

"I bet. It's sad. I'm sure it was very special for them," I replied. It still didn't excuse the fact that they were a bunch of criminals.

He smiled. "Anyway, enough about me. What about you?"

I hadn't really learned much about him other than he was affiliated with the club, had modeled once, and was now a tattoo artist. For all I knew, he was a cold-blooded killer with a bad temper, a drinking problem, and dog he kicked around when he got home.

"There's not much to tell," I said.

He asked me what I did for a living.

"I've waitressed here and there. Nothing like this place," I said with a smile.

Jayce chuckled. "Obviously. Tell me about your foster mom. Millie."

I gave him the basics, explaining that she'd saved me from the system, provided me a loving home, and helped me to move forward.

"You love her very much," he stated, studying my face.

I nodded. "I don't know what would have happened if she hadn't come into my life. Like I said, before living with her, I'd been transferred from home to home. Of course, not all of them had been horrible, but none had been terribly great, either." I stared off into space, smiling wistfully. "The thing about Millie was that she actually cared from the get-go, although it took me awhile to figure it out. Thank goodness she had the patience to deal with my anger and stubbornness."

"She sounds like a great lady."

"The best."

"So, what is it that you're running from then?"

Surprised, I looked at him. "Why do you think I'm running from something?"

"Because you don't know where you're going and you're leaving behind a woman who supports and loves you. Coming out this way isn't work-related and you haven't mentioned anything about a psychotic ex hunting stalking you."

"Maybe I'm just trying to find myself?" I replied, smiling.

He raised his glass. "I can appreciate that."

I laughed and raised my drink, clinking it against his.

"Little did you know that you'd find yourself here. At a strip-joint with a total stranger," he added.

"Little did I know," I repeated. A stranger who I had to keep remind myself was the enemy, no matter how pretty he was.

SEVENTEEN

HOLLYWOOD

S HE FASCINATED ME and it wasn't just her looks. There was a hidden strength inside her that would pop up every once in a while. I couldn't begin to imagine the kind of horrors she'd suffered growing up. Not to mention, she'd not only survived, but here she was, all alone in a big city, trying to get her shit together. It was very admirable, considering she couldn't have been more then twenty-three or twenty-four. As far as her relationships with the opposite sex, I began to wonder if she might be batting for the other team, or maybe both teams. Especially after being hurt in the past by shithead men.

Fuck it. I decided to ask her if she was gay.

"I have a personal question for you. You don't have to answer it if you don't want to."

Her eyebrow raised.

"I'm just curious," I said, trying to be subtle, "has it been hard? Trusting men?"

"Depends on the man and the situation."

That didn't help. "What about relationships? Have you gotten close to anyone?"

She shrugged. "Not really. I tried dating a few times, but not everyone is as patient as I'd like them to be."

"What about other women?"

Candi smiled. "I tried that, too. Once. It didn't work out. Besides, I told you earlier I wasn't really into chicks."

That's right. "So, you really haven't had a decent relationship with anyone?"

"Not romantically. No. What about you? We keep talking about me, but you've never actually talked about *your* love life. I imagine being a Gold Viper, and as handsome as you are, women are always hitting on you."

"I get my share of dates."

She laughed. "Dates? Nothing serious?'

"I haven't had a real relationship with anyone for a long time," I said. "Hell, I'm too busy."

Of course, I still got laid whenever I wanted to. I didn't much care for sharing women, though, and it was always the same chicks hanging around the clubhouse. They were basically open to having sex with any of us, any time, and any place. I wasn't into sloppy seconds, so I stayed clear of them. If I was in the mood for sex, I used *Tinder* for quick, anonymous hookups. It had been a few weeks since the last time I'd logged into the app. Obviously, I wouldn't be getting anything tonight. Trying to get Candi into bed, after everything she'd told me, would make me a monster. As much as I wanted her, I wasn't going to be a fucking asshole.

"You want another drink?" I asked, noticing she was on the last sip of her whiskey-sour.

"No, I really should get going," she replied.

"Are you okay to drive?" It had been two hours and she looked sober enough, but it was hard to tell with some women.

"I'm fine. I should probably use the bathroom, though."

"I'll follow you there and then walk you out to your car. Are you parked outside of the shop?"

She nodded.

I quickly finished the rest of my drink and then we both headed over to the restrooms. She stepped into the Ladies' and I waited in the hallway. After a few seconds, Tarot and Peyton appeared as well.

"Having fun?" Peyton asked.

I leaned against the wall. "Yeah. Definitely."

She winked. "We can tell."

Peyton disappeared into the restroom and Tarot waited with me.

"You and Candi seem to be hitting it off pretty well," he said, checking his phone for messages.

I smiled. "Yeah."

He looked up from the screen. "This your first date?"

"First and probably last. She's just passing through town."

"Oh yeah? Why is that?"

"She's trying to 'find' herself," I said in a low voice.

"Maybe she needs you to do that for her," he said with a devilish grin.

"I wouldn't mind, let me tell you," I replied. "Anyway, she's had a tough time of things and needs to be handled with kid-gloves."

Tarot's smile faltered and I could tell that he was suddenly a million miles away.

"What's up?" I asked, recognizing that he was having some kind of premonition.

"I don't know," he said. "For some reason, I just had a flashback from last year. I keep seeing Blade's smug-ass grin."

"What do you think it means?"

Tarot shrugged. "Honestly? I don't know. He's long gone, but I feel like I'm not done with him yet."

"What if it just has to do with the Blood Angels?" I asked.

"Could be. Maybe they're plotting more shit, although Cane and Jet are gone, too."

"His club brothers could be plotting some retaliation."

Tarot nodded. "Yeah. Retaliation," he said, looking troubled. "That's the vibe I'm picking up. We'd better keep our eyes open."

"Agreed."

EIGHTEEN

AVA

I WAS WASHING my hands when Peyton walked out of one of the other stalls. Seeing me, she smiled and turned on the faucet.

"You and Hollywood seem to be hitting it off really well," she said, trying to be friendly.

"Yeah." I forced a smile to my face. I couldn't let my true feelings for the woman get in the way. It wasn't going to help my cause. I needed her to like me so we could become chummy. "He seems really nice. All of them do."

"They all have their moments, let me tell you," she said wryly.

"I bet. So, you and Tarot are together, huh?"

She turned off the water and pulled at the paper towels. "Yeah, he's so sweet."

"Sweet?" I laughed.

Peyton chuckled. "I know he looks like a real badass. The first time we met, he scared the hell out of me, to be honest. But, he's seriously one of the nicest men I've ever met."

"No offense, but you seem like such complete opposites," I replied, staring at her. Peyton wasn't like the other women I'd seen hanging around the guys in the bar. She wore slacks and a classy top while most of the others were dressed like me.

"I know. I guess opposites really do attract," she replied, smiling at me through the mirror.

"How *did* you two meet, anyway?"

"I used to work for this real estate company and he was looking to buy a house," Peyton replied, tossing the paper towel into the garbage. She turned back toward the mirror and began fussing with her hair. "I ended up showing him a couple of homes and we just kind of hit it off from there."

"So, you're a realtor?"

"I am. Back then, though, I was just an administrative assistant. I received my realtor's license a couple months ago, however. So now I'm doing it part-time."

Peyton explained that she'd quit the company she'd been working for to become a fulltime writer, but it hadn't been paying the bills. "So, now I'm back in the real estate world, only this time I'm enjoying it so much more because I'm working for myself. My last boss was such an asshole."

"Good for you." I turned the conversation back to Tarot. "So, when's the wedding?"

Her eyes sparkled as she stared down at the ring on her finger. "We haven't set date yet, although we were talking about having a winter wedding. I thought it would be really romantic to drive up to the North Shore and get married."

"Where's that?"

"Just past Duluth. It's gorgeous there. You should take a trip sometime."

I nodded. "Maybe I will."

"Are you sticking around? They're going to be doing karaoke soon. The guys love doing it."

I snorted. "Really?"

She chuckled. "Yeah. Especially Len. He has a surprisingly good voice. Reminds me of Joe Cocker."

"It sounds fun, but I was about to head out," I replied. "Anyway, it was nice meeting you."

"Same here."

An idea came to me. "You know, I might be in the market for a new house. Can I call you?"

Her face lit up. "Yes, definitely. Let me get you my number." She reached into her purse and pulled out a business card. "Call me when you're ready. I'd love to help you find something."

"I like it here. I'll probably be getting in touch soon and take you up on that offer. Just don't tell Jayce. If I do move out here, I want it to be a surprise."

She winked. "Don't worry. I won't say a word."

I grinned.

NINETEEN

HOLLYWOOD

CANDI'S FACE WAS beaming when she walked out of the bathroom, with Peyton right behind her. In fact, both women looked pretty happy about something.

"Uh oh," said Tarot, noticing it too. "What happened in there? Don't tell me Len gave you some of his ganja?"

"No," Peyton said, chuckling. "We were just having ourselves a little chat."

He raised an eyebrow. "About what?"

"Don't worry about it, Dom," she said, putting her arms around his neck. "Just worry about having a good time before I have to drag you out of here. Remember, Ruby's sitter has to be home by one."

He sighed. "I know. I was thinking of leaving soon anyway. I miss the little munchkin. I'm going to wake her up and give her a big hug."

She smiled. "You've been out of town so much lately. She'll like that."

"I know. Club business isn't always fun business. I'll make it up to her," he replied. "Maybe we can go for ice cream tomorrow. Then we'll give her the good news."

I could tell Candi was getting anxious to leave. "Hey, we're taking off, you two. Happy Birthday again, Tarot," I said.

He released Peyton and turned to me. "Thanks for stopping by and chipping in on the gift." He held out his hand. "Amazing, by the way, brother."

"Oh, you opened it?" I asked, shaking his hand. We'd pooled enough money together to send Tarot, Peyton, and Ruby on a Disney cruise. He'd been talking about booking one for a while, so we'd rounded up enough money to buy the tickets as a gift.

"Yeah," he pulled me in for a hug. "I can't wait to tell Ruby. She's going to love it."

113

I patted him on the back. "Good, you guys deserve it."

"Yes, thank you, Jayce. It *was* very nice of you," Peyton said. "We're really looking forward to it."

"I'm glad," I replied.

"It was nice meeting you," Tarot said, turning to Candi. He held out his hand. "Hope you had fun."

There was a slight hesitation, which I chalked up to her past. But then she relaxed, shook his hand, and wished him a *Happy Birthday* again.

Tarot thanked her. As he let go of her hand, I noticed he was looking at her strangely.

Another premonition?

I couldn't imagine what it was like having visions all the time. I had to be nerve-wracking. I made a mental note to ask him about it later. I was curious, especially if it had to do with Candi. I hoped she wasn't in any kind of danger. She'd already been through a lot of shit in her past and didn't deserve any more of it in her life.

After we parted, I walked Candi outside and to her car.

"You sure you're okay to drive?" I asked, wishing she wasn't that I could give her a ride. I wasn't ready to say goodbye just yet.

"I'm fine." She opened up the driver's side door of a beat-up old Chevy Malibu and then turned to look at me. "Thanks for the drinks."

"Thanks for joining me," I said, noticing that she suddenly looked like a frightened rabbit. I wanted to tell her to relax, but also didn't want to embarrass her. "It was fun."

"Yeah. Well, I guess I'll see you tomorrow. Around three you said?"

"Why don't I text you when I get into the shop? That way I can let you know if I'm running late or early."

Her eyes widened.

"Or… you don't have to. That's fine, too," I said, getting a clear vibe that she didn't want to.

"No. It's fine," she said and smiled. "Of course you can text me."

I pulled out my phone, went to my *contacts* list, and typed her name. "Okay, what is it?"

She rattled off the number.

"Awesome. I'll call or text when I'm twenty minutes away from the shop. I should have a pretty short day tomorrow and am hoping to be finished by three. Do you want my number?"

"I'll have it when you text me," she replied, tossing her purse into the passenger seat. "Goodnight, Jayce."

I wanted to kiss her. At the very least, hug the woman, but she looked nervous enough as it was.

"Goodnight, Candi," I said, not getting any closer.

Smiling, she got into her car.

I waited until she was safely out of the parking lot before I walked over to my bike and headed home.

TWENTY

AVA

D AMN, TALK ABOUT a close one.
When Jayce asked for my telephone number, it had caught me off-guard. Trying not to panic, I reversed a couple of the numbers instead of giving him my real one. The last thing I needed was to have the Gold Vipers track me down later. I honestly still wasn't sure what I was going to do, but more than ever, I wanted to find out what happened with my brother and learn why he was killed. Now that I had Peyton's business card, I planned on spending some time with her in hopes that she might confide in me. In the morning, I would purchase a small device to record our conversations, along with a prepaid cell phone. If anyone else asked me for a phone number, I'd have something to give them. As far as what I'd given Jayce, I'd worry about an excuse later. I was too tired to think straight.

When I reached the motel, I dreaded getting out of my car. There was a group of thugs standing around a pimped-out Cadillac, listening to loud music, and stealing sips from small paper bags. Of course, there weren't any cops around, and motel management didn't seem to care, apparently.

Sighing in irritation, I parked the car and got out. Keeping my head down, I quickly headed toward my room, hoping to stay out of their radar.

"Hey, sexy mama!" one of them shouted. "You want some company tonight?"

"Come and party with us!" another one yelled.

Ignoring them, I quickly opened the door, turned the lights on, and locked myself in. Sighing, I kicked off my Chucks and pulled my phone out of my purse to call Millie back.

"I was so worried about you," she said after picking up. "You didn't call me back right away like you usually do."

"Sorry," I said, lying down on the bed. I stared up at the ceiling and scowled. There were water stains and a couple of

117

tiny spiders crawling around above me. "I had some meetings to go to. I should have called you."

"It's okay. I understand that you were busy. Maybe you can just send me a text next time? You know I'm a worry wart."

"I will."

We talked for a while longer and then I yawned.

"I'll let you go," Millie said. "I'm glad you made it out there safely."

"Me, too."

"I love you, Ava. Be careful out there."

"I will."

"Where are you staying? Do you have an address? You know, in case something happens?"

Crap. I closed my eyes. "Nothing is going to happen."

"Just give it to me anyway. You know how —"

"Much you worry," I finished her sentence. "Sorry, I forgot it and I'm too lazy to get out of bed." I yawned again, proving my point. "Can I give it to you in the morning?"

"That's fine. I'm sure you're absolutely beat. Goodnight, sweetie."

"Goodnight, Mom."

I hung up and then killed the spiders, hoping those had been the only things crawling around in the room.

TWENTY ONE

ONE

HOLLYWOOD

I WOKE UP early the next morning, packed a couple of turkey sandwiches for lunch, filled a big jug full of water, and then drove to the construction site to wait for Phoenix.

"Hey, brother," Phoenix said, arriving shortly after me. He had his long, blond hair pulled back into a ponytail and was carrying a small cooler.

"Hey." I grinned. "What you got there? Beer?"

"I wish. It's lunch. Hope you're hungry. Lily packed up a shitload of fried chicken and potato salad. More than I could ever eat."

"I actually brought a couple of sandwiches, but your lunch sounds much better."

"Good. You can help me eat it," he said, leading me toward the house.

"Is it just us today?"

"Yeah. Why?"

"Just wondering what time we'll be getting out of here?"

He looked at me over his shoulder and grinned. "Let me guess. You got another hot date with that chick from last night?"

"I'm inking her today," I replied.

"Oh, yeah?"

I told him about the tattoo.

"Damn, that sounds cool and sexy as hell. Speaking of which, you get a piece yet?"

"Nope."

"You must be losing your touch," he said with a wry smile.

I chuckled. "Hardly."

"That's what she's going to say later. Hard-ly."

I flipped him off.

He laughed.

WE SPENT THE next couple of hours sheathing the roof and adding metal flashing. By lunchtime, we had some of the shingles on, but I knew there was still a long way to go. Especially with just the two of us.

"When are you supposed to meet Candi?" he asked as we were eating chicken.

I shrugged. "I told her I'd see how the day was going."

"I was thinking we could head out around four. We can finish up tomorrow."

"Sounds good."

We bullshitted for a while as we ate and then went back to work. As three o'clock loomed closer, I sent Candi a text, telling her I wouldn't be at the shop until closer to five. I knew I'd be needing a shower and a bite to eat before starting on her.

After sending her the message, I was about to put my phone away when I received a quick reply. It wasn't one that I expected, either.

Who's this?

Me: *It's Jayce. This is Candi, right?*

Person: *Uh, no. You must have the wrong number.*

Me: *Sorry.*

Person: *NP*

Frowning, I put my phone away.
"What's wrong?" Phoenix asked, noticing my expression.
"Nothing."
"You sure about that? You look like someone just shit in your Wheaties."

I wiped the sweat from my brow. "I think I may have typed in the wrong phone number last night when Candi gave hers to me."

His smile widened. "You sure she didn't give you the wrong one on purpose? Maybe she's ghosting you?"

"Nah, she wouldn't do that. I mean, why would she?" I replied, not so sure myself now. I thought back, trying to remember if she'd seemed distant at the end of the night. Admittedly, she'd paused before giving me her number.

Fuck.

Maybe she *was* ghosting me.

"I guess you'll know if she doesn't show up at the shop later," he said.

I nodded and pulled my phone out again. I called Devon's and left a message with Gigi, who'd just made it in herself.

"If she shows up, tell her all be in around five," I said.

"Will do," Gigi replied.

I thanked her and hung up.

"You get ahold of Candi yet?" Phoenix called out.

I picked up the nail gun. "Nope."

"Did you happen tell her how much the tat was going to cost? She might have gotten sticker shock and decided not to do it. Or you," he added, cracking himself up.

Snorting, I shook my head.

"You know… you should have told her you'd take payment in trade."

I smirked. "No shit." The truth was, after getting to know her more, I'd have done the tattoo for free. She'd seemed like a cool chick and definitely one I wanted to get to know better. The way things were looking, however, I wasn't so sure I'd ever even see her again.

TWENTY TWO

AVA

I WOKE UP around six the next morning to the sound of a couple arguing in the next room. Groaning, I tried falling back asleep, which proved to be a joke. Especially since the couple decided to make up by having loud, headboard-banging sex a short time later. As I listened to their moans and grunts, which was actually kind of comical, I thought about my own nonexistent sex life. Of course, the idea of having it for enjoyment was almost foreign to me. Admittedly, I was attracted to men, and at times, imagined being held, which was about as intimate as I was comfortable with. But, letting my mind go beyond the cuddling to having flat-out intercourse, was hard. Oddly enough, being naked didn't freak me out. It was the act of sex itself that I had a problem with. I'd tried it a couple of times, but once I found myself underneath a man, it would get to be too much. Memories would come flooding back of the abuse and the moment would get ruined.

Tired of listening to the couple, I dragged myself out of bed and made a pot of coffee. Afterward, I took a shower and then put on a pair of black running shorts along with a lime-colored T-shirt. I pulled my hair into a ponytail, put on a baseball cap, and went out for a jog. Fortunately, the neighborhood was quiet.

Pushing my earbuds into my ears, I turned my music on low, and headed toward Devon's Tattoo Parlor, as I was curious as to what was happening on that side of town. When I reached the shop, the *CLOSED* sign was up and the parking lot was bare.

I jogged around the building and noticed, to my chagrin, that there weren't many escape-routes, especially in the back where the clubhouse was. Not that I'd allow myself to get trapped in the building, but I still hadn't narrowed down a plan of attack yet.

When I returned from the jog, I was completely covered

in sweat, so I took another shower. Afterward, I slipped into a black thong and matching push-up bra. Over that, I pulled on a pair of light-colored Daisy Duke shorts and a black tight-fitting *AC/DC* T-shirt. Satisfied that it was sexy enough, I worked on my hair and makeup, turning myself once again into a biker groupie. I finished it off with a little more perfume, and then left the motel to eat and run the errands I needed to before meeting up with Jayce.

A couple hours later, I walked out of Walmart with a cheap, prepaid cell phone and a small, voice-activated digital recorder. After activating the phone, I called Millie with my other one. She didn't answer, so I left a message.

"Hi, Mom. I am going to be super busy today, so I'm leaving you the address for the house I'm staying at." I rattled off one for a townhome I'd found on the Internet that was for sale. I hated having to lie to her, but I certainly couldn't tell her that I was staying at some seedy motel in St. Paul. She'd start asking too many questions.

"Anyway," I continued. "I love you and I'll call you again when I get a chance."

After hanging up, I took out Peyton's card and stared at it. The woman had seemed nice enough, but I couldn't let that influence me. She had been directly involved with Andrew's death and I needed to get her alone, so we could talk. Someplace without interruptions.

I called the number with my prepaid phone. When she didn't answer, I left her a message.

"Hi, it's Candi. From last night. I'm actually really considering a move to Minnesota and was wondering if you'd have time to show me a few homes in the area? Please call me when you get the chance."

I left her my new cell phone number, hung up, and then headed back toward the motel. As I was pulling into the parking lot, my phone rang.

125

"Hey, it's Peyton. Yeah, I'd love to show you some houses," she said with a smile in her voice. "Have you talked to a mortgage lender yet?"

"Not yet, but I know my credit is great, so there shouldn't be a problem getting a loan."

"I have a broker who can probably get you pre-approved right away. That way if we find something, you can make an offer. I can give you his number if you'd like?"

I paused. Obviously, I wasn't going to go through with that. An idea came to me. "Thanks, but I do have a friend in the mortgage industry. She'd kill me if I didn't go to her for my home loan."

"That's fine. I understand."

"Can we still look at some homes before I get my approval letter?"

"Sure. What price range are you thinking?"

Because I'd been going through the home sales earlier, I gave her a price-point that I thought sounded reasonable.

"Okay," she replied. "Which area are you thinking?"

We discussed location and what I was looking for. Afterward, she asked when I'd want to start looking.

"Tomorrow maybe? I'm getting a tattoo this afternoon and will probably be unavailable all evening."

"That's right. With Jayce?"

"Yeah."

"Tomorrow is fine. When's a good time for you? I can pick you up."

Crap.

"Why don't I meet you? I have some errands I'm going to be doing tomorrow," I lied. "I should be done around two, though."

"I have to be home when Ruby gets off the bus. How about five o'clock? Dom should be home by then."

"Sounds good."

126

"If he's not, I could always bring her with, I suppose," she said.

I groaned inwardly. Not that I was planning on torturing her for answers, I didn't need a kid around to distract me. "Yeah, of course."

"Let me give you our address," she said.

"Can you text it to me? I don't have a pen around."

"Of course."

We confirmed our plans again and then hung up. A few seconds later, she texted me her address. As I put my phone away, I began to wonder how hard it would be to break into their home.

My stomach felt queasy at the thought of what I was actually considering.

Murdering a couple in their sleep?

Not to mention, they had a child in the next room.

The very idea sounded horrific. Especially if I left the little girl without parents. As bad as they were, they couldn't be as terrible as the foster system.

Sighing, I decided that if someone would die, it would be Tarot. Hopefully, it wouldn't come down to it, but I was there for justice. I couldn't get soft now.

TWENTY THREE

HOLLYWOOD

Cassie Alexandra

AFTER LEAVING work, I grabbed some Taco Bell, scarfed it down quickly at home, and then took a shower. By the time I was on my Hog and heading toward Devon's, it was almost five. I had no idea if Candi was going to show up for our appointment, but had been thinking about her all day.

When I arrived in the parking lot, I noticed her car was parked there and sighed in relief.

She hadn't ghosted me.

"Here he is," Devon said as I walked into the shop. It was just her, Gigi, and Candi inside.

Candi, who was sitting in the waiting room and reading a magazine, looked up and smiled. Seeing her there, looking so gorgeous and sexy, made my stomach do a flip.

I grinned back at her like a kid walking into a candy store. "I hope you weren't waiting too long for me."

"No. I just arrived here myself about ten minutes ago," she said.

"That's cool. You know, I wasn't sure if you were going to show or not," I replied.

"Why not?"

"You gave me the wrong number. That's why I wasn't able to send you a message."

She looked puzzled. "Really?"

"Yeah." I pulled out my phone and read it off to her.

Her cheeks turned red. "Oh, crap. I must have been more buzzed than I thought. That's my old phone number. I just had it changed a little while ago. I'm *so* sorry."

I shrugged. "Honest mistake. I figured it was something like that," I lied. "So, you ready?"

"Yeah." She stood up and pulled at the lower hem of her short shorts. My eyes moved from her lean, tanned thighs to her crotch and my cock woke up.

"Ah, let's go," I said, looking away. Obviously, it had

129

been too far and few between since I'd gotten laid. Even worse, I was going to have to remain professional when she removed the shorts.

Devon looked up from the magazine she was reading and winked at me. "Have fun," she said with a smirk.

Ignoring her, I led Candi to my station and then draped a long curtain around us for privacy.

"So, you're still interested in my dragon?" I said, setting my phone down on the counter.

I heard a snicker from Devon.

"Does it shoot fire?" Gigi called out, laughing. "We might *all* be interested in seeing that."

Smiling, I rolled my eyes. "Sorry. Their minds are always in the gutter."

"Says the choir boy," Gigi said loudly.

Devon laughed. "No shit."

"I swear, they're worse than the guys in the clubhouse. Hell, I'd put in a complaint to HR, but Devon's in charge of that, too," I joked.

All three women laughed.

"Anyway," I sat down on my stool and opened up the notepad. "I finished it up. I hope you like it."

I'd added colors to the drawing, which really made it pop. I was excited to see how it looked on Candi after I was finished. It would take several hours to complete, but in the end, I thought we'd both be satisfied with it.

"Wow, it's stunning," she said, her eyes widening. "I was impressed yesterday, and now... I can't even describe how cool this is."

"Okay, I have to see it," Devon said from outside the curtain. "Can I take a peek?"

"Me, too," Gigi said.

"No. You're gonna have to wait and see the finished product," I replied, winking at Candi with a smile.

130

"But, you'll be here all night," pouted Gigi. "I have to leave at seven. I'm going to miss it."

"We might not finish tonight," I replied, knowing the tat was going to take, at the very *least* six hours, and that was if Candi could handle the pain. Most first-time clients couldn't go too much longer in the first sitting. Although, she was a woman and their threshold was usually pretty impressive.

"Really?" Candi said, frowning. "I was hoping to do this in one session."

As I explained the process and my concerns, I had to admit I was disheartened that she wanted to get it over with. I wanted to take my time and do it right. Plus, I didn't know if afterward, we'd see each other again. Especially if she was just passing through town.

"Okay. I guess we should get started and see what happens," she replied. "What should I do?"

"I'll need you to fill out some paperwork," I answered, opening up the file cabinet under the counter.

"Release forms so I don't sue you if I get an infection?" she asked with a smirk.

"That, and we need your medical history. I should probably take a look at your ID, too. Make sure you're over eighteen," I joked.

Her face turned pale. "I'm twenty-seven. I would hope you wouldn't need to card me."

Her response was a little odd, considering that I'd meant it more as a compliment. Not that she needed one. Candi was all woman and definitely didn't look like a teenager.

"Legally, I'm supposed to take a copy of it, but… we'll worry about that later," I replied, grabbing a pen. I handed her a clipboard with the form she needed to fill out. "For the record, you look younger than twenty-seven."

She relaxed. "How old?"

"Twenty-six," I joked.

131

Candi swatted me playfully and I laughed.

"How old are you?" she asked me.

"Twenty-eight. Going on forty," I replied.

She looked down at the form and began writing. "I hear you. I feel like I've already passed by my thirties," she said dryly.

"We should do something about it."

She looked up at me with a little smile. "Really? What do you suggest?"

"I don't know. Hit up an amusement park one of these days together? You like rollercoasters?"

She tilted her head. "You asking me out?"

"I'm just asking if you want to go and have some fun together."

"What if amusement parks aren't my idea of fun?" she asked, her eyes twinkling.

"What about zoos? Or taking a ride on the back of a motorcycle?"

"Devon, I don't know about you but his voice is dripping with desperation. Don't you think?" Gigi said loudly.

"No shit. I also haven't seen him smile so much. Hell, if I was Candi, I'd wait until after the tattoo to give him an answer. Guys are more attentive when they have to work for it," she replied. "The harder it is for them, the better it is for us."

"Quite literally," quipped Gigi.

Both women laughed.

"Speaking of work, don't the two of you have something better to do than listen in on our conversation?" I hollered.

"Actually, I was thinking about grabbing something from Panera. You want to join me, Gigi?" Devon asked.

"Yeah. Let's do it," she replied.

"Looks like you two will have the place to yourselves," Devon said loudly. "Behave, Hollywood."

"Only if she wants me to," I replied.

TWENTY FOUR

AVA

I'D MOSTLY BEEN ignoring the banter between Jayce and the others, but I definitely heard his response. I looked up and our eyes met as the two women left the shop.

He grinned. "Just seeing if you were paying attention."

"I was, and yes. You'd *better* behave. Especially holding a needle," I teased.

"Don't worry. The moment I start inking, I'm all business and no play," he said in a low voice. "Even if you begged me to be bad, I just couldn't do it."

"Work ethics?" I asked with a smirk.

"Of course," he replied with a glint in his eyes. "No compromises either. So, if you're even thinking about coming on to me, don't bother. My mind will be on one thing... and one thing only. Your body... art."

"Good. Maybe we'll get this tattoo done tonight then," I said in a serious voice.

His smile faltered.

"And then afterward, we'll talk about amusement parks and zoos," I added. "Because the truth is, I'm kind of an adrenaline junkie."

Jayce looked impressed. "Oh yeah?"

"I love fast cars and fast motorcycles. I especially love being behind the wheel."

His eyebrows shot up. "You ride?"

I nodded. "I used to, at least," I said, not wanting to give him too much information.

"What kind of bike?"

I told him that I once owned a Kawasaki Ninja, H2R. Which I still did.

"Those just came out a couple of years ago. You sold it already?"

I lied and said that I'd lost my job and had to sell it.

He started asking me more questions.

135

"Shouldn't we start the tattoo?" I cut in quickly.

"Yeah. Of course. Why don't you take off your shoes and shorts while I grab a clean razor?" He opened up a drawer and began rummaging around.

I kicked off my tennis shoes. "Wait a second? A razor? Why?"

He explained that he needed to make sure there wasn't any hair on the area he was going to ink.

"Uh, okay," I replied, unbuttoning my shorts. "I don't have much there, though."

"Even a little can get in the way," he said, pulling out a disposable razor.

"I understand," I said, letting my shorts drop to the ground. I bent down and picked them up. "So, should I pay you before we start?"

"No. We'll work it out later," he said in a weird voice.

I looked over at Jayce. "You sure?"

TWENTY FIVE

HOLLYWOOD

S EEING CANDI STANDING there in the lacy black G-string gave me an instant boner. Especially when she turned to the side and I saw the curve of her round, firm-looking ass. I imagined what it would feel like under my palms, and my cock practically lurched out of my jeans.

Fuck.

"No. We'll figure out payment later," I said, looking away.

"Okay. What now?"

I had her sit in the lounge chair and then began cleaning her skin with rubbing alcohol.

"Should I remove my panties?" she asked in a low voice.

Abso-fucking-lutely.

"We'll move it down when we need to. There's not much to it anyway," I replied casually. There was barely more than a couple of strings holding it over her hips. Normally, nudity wasn't a distraction for me. But with this girl, I knew I was in trouble.

"Okay," she replied.

"I'm going to turn on some music," I said. "It helps me concentrate."

"Go for it."

I turned on the radio; the Stone Temple Pilots were playing. "Too loud?"

"Not at all."

I began preparing the thermal fax, which would create a stencil from the drawing I'd made. Afterward, I applied the stencil to her hip and prepared the tattoo machine. After the ink caps were filled and the needles were prepared, I put some ointment over the transfer design, while she sat there quietly.

"You doing okay?" I asked, excited to get started.

She opened her eyes and smiled. "Yeah, this isn't so bad."

I bit back a smile. I hadn't even touched her with a needle yet.

"Would you like something to drink before I begin with the line-work?"

"I'm good."

"Good. Now, remember, one thing, okay?"

"What's that?"

"There's beauty in pain."

"Right," she said.

Smiling, I leaned forward and began.

TWENTY SIX

SIX

AVA

ALTHOUGH IT WAS uncomfortable, the needle didn't bother me as much as I thought it would. Or Jayce touching me. He did wear gloves, however, so it made it feel less intimate. Regardless, the pain was bearable and within a couple of minutes, I felt totally at ease with him touching me. I wasn't sure what was going through his mind, but I had to admit, there were a couple of times I found myself enjoying his touch more than I'd ever care to admit. Maybe it was because he *wasn't* doing it in a sexual manner.

As the minutes ticked by into hours, I began learning more about Jayce, and despite my reason for being there, I genuinely started liking the guy. Especially after he began telling me about his younger half-sister, Emily, who was slightly autistic. She'd just turned ten and I could tell from the way he talked about her, that Emily was very special to him.

"She loves to draw and paint," he told me with a smile in his voice. "She's damn talented, too."

"Like her older brother, obviously," I said, closing my eyes.

"Thanks. She actually drew one of my tattoos," he said. "Devon inked it."

I re-opened my eyes. "Really? Can I see it?"

"Sure." He got up and walked around to stand in front of me. He raised his T-shirt and showed me the tattoo, which was of a smiling frog wearing a crown of jewels. It was actually very cute. I noticed he had several other tattoos too, most of them depicting something from medieval times. He looked down at the frog, which was near his heart, and smiled fondly. "I just wish I could spend more time with Emily," he said. "My mother and Gus, her old man, moved to Iowa recently."

"So, it's just you out here?"

"I have an older sister, Jackie. She lives in Maplewood

141

with her boyfriend."

So, he had two sisters. "Why did your mom and Gus move to Iowa?"

"His father died, leaving him a pawn shop. So, they're out there running it now."

"So, you hardly ever see her?"

"Well, I usually take a road trip out there once a month. She cries whenever I leave, though." He sighed. "It breaks my heart every time."

"I bet. The frog is adorable. How long ago did you get it?" I was impressed with the canvas under the tattoo as well. He was slim and muscular, with an impressive six-pack. Tanned from the sun, I imagined he spent a lot of time shirtless, and that vision was something even I could appreciate.

"Last year. She's really into frogs and always loved fairytales. In fact, when Emily was really little, I used to read her The Frog Prince all the time, which was her favorite."

"That's so sweet."

He smiled sadly. "I try and bring her something related to frogs whenever I get out that way. Last time I brought her a pendant, and she refuses to take it off now."

I touched my own necklace from Millie. I hardly ever took mine off either. "She sounds like a sweetheart."

"She is."

My eyes went to his arms, where there were more tats. I asked him about them. "You're really into fantasy and medieval stuff, aren't you?"

He grinned. "Yeah. Pretty obvious, huh?"

"I bet you're a *Game of Thrones* fanatic?"

Jayce chuckled. "Yeah. I also loved *The Hobbit* and *Lord of the Rings*. Anything to do with middle-earth or the dark ages, too."

"So, King Henry, wizards, and knights are your thing?"

He nodded. "I admit it. I'm a nerd at heart."

I asked, "Do you read a lot?"

"I used to," he said, sitting down on the stool behind me. "What about you?"

"No, I'm not much of a reader," I admitted. "Although, I never really gave it much of a chance."

"I love it. It takes me away for a while. Growing up, I used to wish that I could travel back in time to the middle-ages, although it was the made-up shit that I was intrigued with."

"Yeah, you'd have been pretty disappointed to learn that there weren't any dragons or wizards around, huh?"

"Exactly."

"So, were you into D and D, too?"

"Dungeons and Dragons? Yeah. I *really* got hooked into online fantasy gaming though. I'd spend hours on my computer, going on quests with other gamers. My mother used to get so pissed off. I eventually stopped when I found something else I liked even more than that."

"Motorcycle clubs?"

"Girls," he replied, getting back to work on my hip. "That's what brought me back into the real world."

I winced a little, noting that I was beginning to get sore.

"You okay?" he asked.

"Yeah." I was determined to get the tattoo finished during that session. Especially since I was beginning to really like Jayce, which wasn't going to help my cause.

The rest of the evening flew by pretty quickly. We stopped only to eat when Jayce ordered a pizza from a place up the road, which turned out to be amazing. Afterward, he went back to work on the tattoo, a comfortable silence settling in around us.

At around eleven, Devon left, leaving us alone in the shop.

143

"How's it looking?" I asked him several minutes later.

He cleared his throat. "Great. But I'm not going to be able to finish it up tonight."

"Really?" I replied, disappointed. He'd warned me, though.

"Yeah, I really don't want to rush it. In fact, I was going to suggest that we stop soon."

"When do you think we should finish it?"

"That depends on you. We can try doing it tomorrow if you're in a hurry. Otherwise, I'd wait a couple days."

I sighed. Looked like I'd be in town longer than I'd been planning. "Tomorrow I'm busy. How about the day after?"

"Saturday? I might be going out of town. Club business," he said, not looking happy about it. "What about Monday?"

I seriously didn't want to wait until then, but it looked like I wouldn't have a choice. Unless, I didn't have him finish it.

"That's fine," I said. "So, just Monday and that's it?"

"I hope that will be enough time to complete it. I'm sorry to make you come back in."

"It's okay," I replied.

"Let's get you cleaned and bandaged," he said.

After cleaning the area, he put a warm towel on the tattoo, which felt soothing. After it cooled, he removed it and asked what I thought of the dragon.

Since I'd been lying down, I hadn't been able to get a good look at it. Once I was standing and able to see what he'd been up to, I was left speechless.

"You like it?" he asked, studying my face.

"I'm overwhelmed," I said, staring down at the design in awe. It was even better than the drawing, and as far as I could see, almost completely finished. The only thing missing was Andrew's name on the sword and some of the color. Other than that, it was incredible.

144

"We'll put some ointment on it and bandage it up."

"Okay."

He dressed the tattoo and then put on a bandage. As he was finishing up, he explained how to take care of it.

"You'll want to leave the bandage on for a few hours. You should be able to remove it in the morning, before you take a shower. I recommend taking a quick, cool shower, because your skin will be extra sensitive to the heat. Also, your pores could open up and some of the ink may leak out if the water is too warm. Just be really careful with it."

"What about soap?"

"Use something that is unscented and hypoallergenic. To dry it, pat your skin gently with a paper towel. I'm going to give you a small tube of moisturizer to apply after it's completely dry. It's also unscented and hypoallergenic and one that I like using myself."

"Okay."

"I'll give you an instruction sheet," he said. "So, you won't forget any of this."

"Thank you."

"You can get dressed now," he said, handing me my shorts.

"Thanks. So," I leaned over to put them on, "I imagine you're used to seeing half-naked women and men coming through here."

"Pretty much."

"Perks of the job?"

"I get a lot more guys than women, so it's not usually a perk," he replied, scratching his chin with a smile. "Today was definitely an anomaly."

I smiled. My cell phone went off and I groaned inwardly. It had to be Millie.

It was late and I hadn't called her. I loved the woman, but she was far too overprotective.

I picked up my purse and reached inside, muting the ringer. "So, we'll finish this up on Monday?" I asked, looking back at Jayce.

"Yeah. I should be here around six."

"Okay, I'll be here. Let me give you my number, in case something changes. My *new* number."

"Sounds good."

I gave it to him and then pulled out my wallet. "So, how much do I owe you again?"

"Let's not worry about it until Monday."

I had to admit, I was surprised he wasn't collecting on it now. He'd put a lot of hours into it and if I really wanted to, I could walk away and be totally satisfied with the way it was now. But, I wanted Andrew's name on it. I also wanted to find out more about the club.

"You sure?"

"Yeah."

"Okay." I put my wallet away. "I suppose I'd better get going then."

He yawned. "It's late. Let me walk you to your car."

"Okay. Thanks."

We walked out of the shop and he accompanied me to my vehicle. The parking lot was completely empty.

"No club gatherings tonight?"

He shook his head. "Nah. Thursdays are usually pretty quiet here. At least lately."

"I've never been in a biker clubhouse before," I said, looking back at the building. "Or a party."

He smiled. "That's probably a good thing."

"Why?"

"Because you'd probably be claimed by now."

"Claimed?"

"Someone would want you as their woman. You're pretty... special."

146

TWENTY SEVEN

SEVEN

HOLLYWOOD

I'D WANTED TO say "hot", but it would have made me sound like a punk. From the smile on her face, I guessed I'd made the right choice.

"Thank you. That's sweet," she replied, her cheeks flushing.

"It's the truth. Anyway," I leaned back against the counter. "My club is having a party tomorrow night. You want to come?"

"Aren't you going out of town?"

"If I do, it'll be Saturday morning. We don't have to stay very late. I just figured since you've never been to one before, this would be the perfect opportunity."

She nodded. "Okay."

"I should warn you, though, this one could get a little crazy. You'll be with me, though. You won't have to worry about anything."

"Okay. Are they having it here?"

"No. This one is going to be at a farmhouse in Chisago. We needed more room because some of the other chapters will be showing up. It should be a pretty big bash."

"Sounds like fun."

I nodded. "Why don't you give me the address to where you're staying and I'll pick you up?"

"Why don't I just meet you here, instead?"

I smirked. "You don't want me to know where you're staying, do you?"

She snorted. "That's not it. I'm actually just up the road at a motel. I'd rather not leave my car parked there unattended for too long—not that it's worth stealing. Last night there were some shifty characters in the parking lot, drinking and partying. I could see one of them deciding to take it for a joy-ride, because I'd ignored them when they tried talking to me."

"This definitely isn't the best area." I didn't like the idea of her staying at some shitty motel, but knew if I offered her

148

my sofa, she wouldn't take it. "Maybe I should follow you back there tonight, so you don't get hassled by anyone?"

It took her a few seconds to answer; I thought she was going to refuse, or make up some other excuse, but then she nodded. "That would be nice. Thank you."

"I'll lock up the shop and then we can go."

"Okay."

THE MOTEL WAS definitely a dump. I followed her to the parking lot, and sure enough, there were two cars parked near her room, surrounded by punks. I recognized one of them, a guy named Sharpy. He was a knucklehead drug-dealer who wasn't even supposed to be in the area. Phoenix had warned him before about selling on our streets and Sharpy had promised to stay away. Apparently, he'd forgotten all about it.

Normally, I didn't deal with guys like him unless I was armed. Although I kept a pistol in my truck, I didn't carry one on me. But the hell if I was gonna drive away without checking on him.

I parked my Hog next to Candi's car and shut it off. As I got off of my bike, I could see Sharpy and his five friends watching me warily. They were listening to loud music, and from what I could tell, passing around a small pipe.

I nodded to Sharpy and he nodded back.

"See what I mean?" whispered Candi after she got out of her car. "I mean, who parties in a motel parking lot?"

"Losers. They hassled you last night?"

"Just some catcalls. Nothing serious."

I looked over at the group again; they were still watching us silently. "I'll walk you to your room."

"Okay."

I followed Candi to the door and she unlocked it. She flipped on the lights and then turned around to face me.

149

"So, what time should I meet you at the shop tomorrow night?" she asked.

"I'm picking you up here."

Her eyebrows knitted together. "But, what about them? What if they mess with my car?"

I knew her car wasn't of any interest to the likes of them. If she owned a Mercedes or something worth selling, then I'd have been worried.

"It will be fine. How about I pick you up at eight?"

"How do you know it will be fine?" she replied, frowning.

"Because I'm going to talk to them."

Her eyes widened. "Are you sure that's a good idea?"

"Relax. They know who I'm associated with and wouldn't dare make a move."

She bit her lower lip, not looking very convinced.

"You worry too much," I tapped her bottom lip with my finger with a smile, letting it linger there. "Now" — I moved my finger from her lip and traced it along her smooth jawline — "go and get some sleep. I'll see you tomorrow night."

Her eyes widened. "O... okay."

"Would you mind if I kissed you?" I whispered. "I want them to think you're my girl. That way, they'll for sure leave you alone."

"Um, sure," she said, running her tongue along her bottom lip.

My pants immediately felt like they'd shrunk two sizes as I pulled her into my arms and kissed her softly. At first, Candi was rigid, but she slowly relaxed and slid her arms around my neck.

Hungry for more, I deepened the kiss, and after a few seconds, she seemed to be into it as much as I was. Unfortunately, the punks in the parking lot began whistling and howling, ruining the moment.

I let her go reluctantly.

"I guess that worked," she said, her cheeks flushed.

"Apparently. Thanks for playing along."

She smiled.

"I'd better go. Goodnight, Candi."

"Goodnight, Jayce."

She shut the door and I waited to hear the lock engage before I walked over to Sharpy.

"Hey, what's up?" he asked, looking nervous.

"Not much. Aren't you a little far from home?"

His eyes hardened. "I'm just visiting my buddy, John," he said, nodding toward the guy standing across from him.

I looked at John. "You staying at this motel?"

John, who was tall, skinny, and looked a little nervous himself, nodded.

"When are you leaving?"

"Tomorrow night," he replied.

"Do me a favor and keep an eye on my girl's car. You see anybody fucking with it, or her, you get ahold of me," I said firmly.

The guys all nodded.

"How do we get in touch with you?" asked John.

"He's a prospect for the Gold Vipers, dumbass," Sharpy said, spitting out a wad of chewing tobacco. "I told you that. See his cut?"

"You just have to get a message to my clubhouse," I said to him. "Sharpy knows where it is."

"Okay," John said.

"Thanks." I looked at Sharpy. "I'll let Phoenix and Tarot know you said hi."

Sharpy gave me a dirty look. "Why? I'm not doing anything wrong here. Just visiting. I'm not dealing."

"So, you *don't* want me to tell them that you said, hello?

151

That's kind of rude, isn't it?" I replied with a smirk.

"You know what I mean," he mumbled.

"I know exactly what you mean, but you're in Gold Viper territory and if memory serves me right, you're banned from this area. Now, I'll tell them you said hi and if they ask if you were dealing, I'll tell them the truth, which is, I didn't see anything. Maybe they'll leave it at that. Maybe they won't. But, if I were you, I'd make myself scarce."

He glared at me.

I looked back at John. "Around here, it's important to know who your friends are and who they aren't. Stay out of trouble and you might even make some new ones."

He nodded.

I looked at the other three guys, who were silent. I didn't recognize any of them. "You all have a good night."

"You, too," they each replied.

I turned to head back to my bike when I noticed Candi peeking through the curtains. As I swung my leg over my Hog, I smiled at her. She smiled back and closed the curtain.

TWENTY EIGHT

AVA

I DON'T KNOW what Jayce said to the guys in the parking lot, but soon after he pulled away, they took off.

Relieved, I called Millie and apologized for not answering and for calling her back so late again.

"It's okay. You're a busy girl. I understand."

"You have no idea."

"You work too hard. How long are you going to be away?"

"A week or two. It might be longer. It's hard to say."

"I hope you find time to relax so you don't overwork yourself."

"I do."

"Good."

"By the way, I'm going to a production party tomorrow night," I said to her. "So, I probably won't call you until Saturday."

"Oh, that sounds like fun. I'm glad you're able to enjoy yourself a little out there."

I thought of Jayce's kiss, which admittedly, I'd enjoyed the hell out of. "Yeah, me, too."

We talked a little longer and then hung up.

Yawning, I headed to the bathroom, removed my makeup and changed into an oversized T-shirt. As I got into bed, my mind lingered on the kiss we'd shared. It had been unexpected and had taken my breath away. The man certainly knew his way around a woman's mouth and I started to wonder if he was just as talented with the female body, too.

Reminding myself that he was associated with the enemy, I closed my eyes and went to sleep. I dreamed that I was Jayce's girl, riding on the back of his bike and happy to be there. At first, it was all good, but then his club surrounded and then tore us apart. At one point, they were threatening to kill Jayce for being with me, and that's when I awoke.

Relieved that it was just a dream, I turned to look at the clock and saw that it was almost nine a.m. I crawled out of bed, used the bathroom, and then prepared for my shower. I took the bandage off carefully and saw that the skin under my tattoo was still very pink. After taking a cool shower, I followed Jayce's instructions by drying the tattoo carefully and then putting the moisturizer on. I then put on a two-piece bikini with a pair of loose-fitting black cotton capris and a midriff T-shirt, featuring *Tweety Bird* on my boobs. I wound my hair up into a messy bun, grabbed the car keys, and left my room.

The weather was perfect. The sun was shining and almost eighty degrees. Humming to myself, I got into the car and drove to a bagel shop a couple miles away. I bought myself something to eat, a along with a cold-pressed coffee. Not knowing what else to do with my time before meeting up with Peyton, I stopped at a bookstore. Remembering that Jayce liked fantasy books, I headed over in that direction, and after a few minutes of searching, found *The Hobbit*. Although I'd never read it or had seen any of the movies, I decided to give it a try. It would give us something to talk about later.

After buying the book, I went to a nearby park and began to read. Admittedly, it wasn't the easiest book to get into. Especially for one who wasn't into reading to being with. But, I forced myself not to give up.

About an hour later, when I was actually starting to enjoy the book, I received a text on my new cell phone.

It was Jayce.

He asked me about my tattoo and then after I answered him, apologized for forcing me kiss him.

You didn't make me, I typed back, thinking it was kind of sweet. *Besides, it was for a good cause.*

Jayce: *I agree. It was also a good kiss.*

Me: *I thought so.*

Jayce: *I might have to do it again at the party tonight. Just to make sure you're left alone by other guys.*

I grinned.

Me: *If you think it will help.*

Jayce: *Definitely.*

He sent me a devil emoji, which made me smile again. I was about to flirt back, when I caught myself. As much as I was enjoying the banter between us, and the kiss, it was dangerous. I couldn't let myself get too comfortable or I'd fall for him. And, from the butterflies in my stomach, I was already heading in that direction.

Me: *Have a good day at work.*

Jayce: *Thanks. What are you up to on this beautiful day?*

I told him that I was in a park, reading *The Hobbit*.

Jayce: *Cool? How's it going?*

I admitted that it was hard to read, but I was still enjoying it. He then asked if I'd seen the movies and I told him I hadn't.

Jayce: *I have the entire series. We should watch it together.*

Me: *Sure.*

156

He sent a happy face and then told me he had to get back to work.

Me: *See you at eight.*

Jayce: *Looking forward to it.*

I put my phone away, frustrated that I was giddy about seeing him later. Almost like a love-struck teenager. He was definitely getting under my skin and I couldn't have that. I picked up the book and started reading again, determined to take my mind off of Jayce.

A COUPLE OF hours later, I was stiff from sitting on the bench, my side was aching where the tattoo was, and the park was getting crowded. Kids were racing around and laughing and screaming. Not that I disliked children, but it was hard to concentrate.

I closed the book, headed to my car, and ended up at a nearby mall. As I was walking by one of the shops, enjoying an ice-cream cone, a summery, wrap-style dress caught my eye. It was white with yellow flowers and spaghetti straps. Flowy and cute and maybe even a little sexy. I finished my cone, tried on the dress, and purchased it for the party.

TWENTY NINE

HOLLYWOOD

I FINISHED WORK early again and headed to the clubhouse for a meeting.

"You all know that Tank, Raptor, and some of the others are coming down here for the party tonight, so it should be a kickass time. Even better, *Doug's Smokehouse* is catering it for free, which is pretty fucking generous. Especially knowing how much you fuckers eat," Phoenix said after calling the meeting to order.

Doug's Smokehouse was some of the best barbecue in the state, so it put smiles on all of our faces.

"As far as booze goes, you want some, you bring your own bottle. There will be beer supplied, of course. I've ordered four kegs, which should be enough." He looked at me. "I need someone to bring 'em out to the farm before the party starts. You up for it?"

I groaned inwardly, but couldn't refuse. "Yeah," I said. "Can I deliver them around seven?"

He nodded. "That's fine. Bring one of the other prospects, too."

I sighed in relief. I wanted enough time to pick up Candi and already couldn't wait to see her again. All day long she'd been on my mind. I thought it was cute how she'd started reading *The Hobbit*.

Knowing that she wasn't sure about staying in Minnesota or traveling on, I pulled Tarot aside after the meeting about getting Candi a job. He owned *Wild River Saloon* and was always in need of good waitresses.

"I'll hire her if you think she'd do well," he said and then lowered his voice. "By the way, Peyton mentioned that Candi called her yesterday. She wants to look at some houses. She's meeting her at five."

That surprised me, especially since she hadn't mentioned it. I was stoked, though. I definitely wanted to see more of her.

"Sweet. I hope she finds something. She's staying at this shitty motel. Oh, by the way, I ran into Sharpy in the parking lot there." I told him about our conversation.

Tarot's face darkened. "He'd better not be dealing his shit over here."

"He said he wasn't, but you never know."

He leaned back and got that faraway look in his eyes. "I think he might be up to no good, regardless. I'm going to have a little talk with him next week. In the meantime, if you see him again, let me know."

"Will do."

"And, don't tell Peyton or Candi that I mentioned anything about house-hunting. It's supposed to be a surprise."

"Don't worry. I won't say anything."

"You like this chick a lot, don't you?"

I nodded.

His face grew serious again. "Be careful with her."

"What do you mean?"

He sighed and ran a hand over his face. "I don't know. I feel like she might be hiding something. Something big."

"Like she might be married?"

He shook his head. "No, but I feel like it has to do with another man. Just... be careful."

Knowing that she'd been sexually abused as a child, I wondered if was picking up on that, somehow.

"She had a bad childhood. With bad men, if you know what I mean," I said in a low voice. "You think that might have something to do with it?"

He nodded slowly. "Yeah. It's possible. Regardless, you need to be careful."

Fuck. That's not what I wanted to hear.

I smiled grimly. "You think she's dangerous?"

160

Thinking that he was going to tell me "no", I was shocked when he nodded.

"How so?"

"That part is gray," he replied. "But, my gut tells me that things aren't exactly how they appear with her."

I trusted Tarot. Especially after the incident the year before. Peyton had been attacked by a psychopath, who'd called himself Blade. He'd been hired by the Blood Angels to impersonate Tarot and cause a shitload of problems. The resemblance between the two had been pretty significant, at least from a distance. Fortunately, Blade didn't have Tarot's psychic skills, which in the end had been his downfall. If he thought there was something up with Candi, I had to take it seriously. Even if I didn't want to.

"I'd better call Peyton and warn her, too," he replied, reaching for his phone. "I might be wrong. Hell, I *hope* I'm wrong. But if I'm not, we all need to be wary of her."

THIRTY

AVA

NOT KNOWING HOW long we'd be looking at houses, I put on the new dress and fixed my hair and makeup. This time, I didn't go as crazy with the hairspray and opted for more of a natural look. After one last glance in the mirror, I went into the bedroom, grabbed the gun, and loaded the clip with bullets. My hand was shaky as I shoved it into my purse, along with the box of bullets. I still didn't know what the hell I was planning on doing, but it felt right to bring it.

I arrived a couple minutes early to Peyton and Tarot's place. It was a split-level home with a huge yard and a three-car garage. It was a few years old, but looked like it had been freshly painted, and I could see that there was a fenced-in backyard.

As I was getting out of my car, I heard the rumble of a motorcycle in the distance. Noticing that it was getting louder, I looked down the road and saw Tarot approaching. He pulled into the driveway and shut off the engine.

"Hi," I said, trying not to feel so intimidated by the cold-blooded killer.

"Hi." He smiled at me as he got off his bike. "Excited about looking at houses?" he asked, removing his sunglasses.

Still a little weirded out by his resemblance to Andrew, I nodded. "Yes. Very."

"Good. I know Peyton mentioned that she had a couple for you in mind earlier. Come on in," he said, walking toward the house.

I followed him inside, where we were met with a Siberian Husky he called Chilly, and a little girl with dark hair and light blue eyes. After calming the excited dog, he picked up Ruby.

"How's my big girl?" he asked, carrying her into the living room.

"Good. Who's that?" she asked, looking at me over his shoulder as I followed them.

"That's Candi. Candi, this is Ruby," Tarot said.

"Hi," I replied, feeling a little sick to my stomach as I leaned forward to pet the hyper, young Husky. Not having been around many dogs in my life, I wasn't sure how to handle her, and she kept jumping on my dress. Luckily, Tarot noticed and ordered her to get down. Chilly whined a little, but obeyed.

"Chilly does that to everyone," Ruby said. "She's still a puppy, even though she's as big as a moose."

I smiled. "It's fine."

"Speaking of growing, you need to slow down. You're going to be taller than me pretty soon," Tarot asked, tickling Ruby.

Ruby squealed and laughed. From the way she was staring at Tarot, I could see how much the child adored him. It was a pity that he was a piece of shit when he wasn't teasing his daughter or playing fetch with Fido.

"So, is your name is really Candi?" Ruby asked, her eyes wide. "That's cool!"

Hating that I was lying to a little girl, I could only nod.

Peyton suddenly appeared in the living room, looking very professional in a black pin-striped suit and pointy heels. Her reddish-brown hair was pulled into a soft chignon and she wore dangly, tanzanite earrings and a matching necklace.

"Hey, Babe," Tarot said, setting Ruby down. He gave her an appraising look. "You look like you just stepped off of Wall Street, sexy mama."

She laughed and shook her head. Then she turned to me and her smile faded. "Hi, Candi. You look really pretty this evening."

I glanced down at my dress and brushed away some of the white dog hair. "Thanks. I don't usually dress like this. I have a date with Jayce tonight. I just didn't know how long we'd be and wanted to make sure I was ready to go when he picked me up later."

"Hollywood?" she said and then turned to look at Tarot.

"Yeah." I thought Peyton was acting a little strange, although I didn't know the woman very well. She seemed a little uptight compared to the other night.

"He mentioned something about it to me, too," Tarot said. "He's bringing you to the bash later, huh?"

I nodded. "Are you two going?"

"I am," he replied. "Peyton is staying home with Ruby."

"Yeah. Those parties get pretty crazy," Peyton said.

"We're going to watch a movie, right?" Ruby asked.

Peyton smiled at her. "Yes. Your dad is going to help you pick one out later. You can surprise me."

Ruby's face brightened. "Yay! I know just the one, too."

"Remember, no scary ones. I don't like them," Peyton said and looked at me. "Last time she wanted to rent *Annabelle*, not that she could have watched it anyway. She's way too young."

"That *was* scary," I replied, looking at Ruby. "I saw it. You didn't miss much. Maybe a few nightmares."

"What about *IT*?" Ruby asked.

"Pumpkin, you know you're too young for that one," Tarot said. "When you're old enough, I'll watch it with you, though. I want to see it myself."

She let out a dramatic sigh. "Fine."

"I'm sure you'll find a good one. We should get going," Peyton said, looking at her watch. "I'll be right back."

"I wish I could come," Ruby said, as Peyton disappeared down the hallway. "I love looking at houses. I'm going to be a realtor just like Peyton when I grow up."

"I thought you wanted to be a doctor?" Tarot replied.

"I'm going to be a house doctor," she explained. "Like on

165

those shows where they fix houses up and sell them."

Smart kid, I thought.

"She loves watching home remodeling shows," Tarot said to me.

"I like those shows too," I replied, smiling at Ruby.

He crossed his arms over his chest. "Speaking of, what do you do for a living?"

"Mostly waitressing."

Studying my face, he frowned. "You've done some acting too, haven't you?"

Acting?

My heart skipped a beat.

"No. I've been told I look like this one actress, though."

"Jessica Alba," he said, nodding. "Yeah, you do. But, are you sure you've never been behind a camera before?"

"Well, yeah. I've been behind a camera, but have never acted," I said, chuckling. "Although there was that one time on spring break…"

He just stared at me, either not amused or still trying to figure me out.

Thankfully, Peyton walked back in the living room with her purse and a manila folder. She kissed Tarot and Ruby goodbye.

"Keep in touch," he said.

Peyton nodded. "I will."

We walked out of the house and got into her car, which was a gray Cadillac CTS.

"Wow, this is nice," I said, putting my seatbelt on. It was so refreshing to be getting into a luxury car again and not the rusted-out Malibu.

"Thanks. Dom bought it for me last winter. So," she said, opening up the folder. "After talking to you yesterday, I found a couple homes I think might have what you're looking for. I hope you don't mind, but I took the liberty of making appointments to actually view them inside."

"Sounds good," I replied, looking at the information she'd printed out.

"This one right there is in Gem Lake," she said. "It's small, but very private. A good distance from the neighbors, which is what you were looking for, right?"

"That's exactly what I was looking for," I replied.

"Good." She gave me a strained smile and then started the engine.

"Is everything okay?"

She glanced at me. "Yes. Of course. I... I just have a little headache. That's all."

"Oh, I'm sorry. Did you want to do this another time?"

Peyton waved her hand. "No, no, no. I took some aspirin. I'm sure it will kick in very soon."

Her excuse sounded logical, and yet, I still felt as if something was off.

As we backed out of the driveway, I took one last look at the house and noticed Tarot staring at us through the window. His expression was grim and I had to wonder if he'd figured out who I was. Realizing there wasn't much to connect me with Andrew, I brushed it off to paranoia.

Peyton's headache must have been getting better, because she talked a mile-a-minute on our way to look at the first house. When we arrived in Gem Lake, I was only half-listening to what she was saying, my mind on other things. Like... how was I going to get a confession out of her without giving myself away?

"Here we are," Peyton said a few minutes later as we pulled up to a small cottage-style house.

"Nice," I said. It was cute, but obviously I wasn't really there to shop for homes.

We got out of the car and headed inside. She started giving me a tour of the place and that's when an idea hit me.

167

"I wish this had a security system," I said, walking over to the sliding glass door in the kitchen. I reached into my purse, making sure I had the recorder. "I had some crazy guy stalking me last year, and one night, I caught him staring at me through one of these. It freaked the hell out of me."

"Wow, that's creepy," she replied. "Did you know him?"

"Not really. I mean, I saw him around town. He was always staring at me. Anyway, he moved from just being a weirdo to a total stalker."

"Did you call the police?"

"I did, but I couldn't really prove anything. Anyway, he did it a few more times, and that's when I had some friends take care of it. Or, I should say *him*."

Her eyebrows raised. "Oh?"

"Yeah. I probably shouldn't be telling you this, but I feel like I can trust you." I gave her my most honest smile. "Anyway, I don't know exactly what they did, but he never came around again. Thank goodness." I looked down, feigning shyness. "They belonged to a biker club, too. My friends."

"Which one?"

I made up a name. "Silver Daggers. They're not well known," I said. "But, they kind of remind me of your man's club. You know?"

"How so?"

"Just that they're so close to each other and know how to 'fix' things when they need to be fixed," I replied.

"To be honest, I don't really know what goes on in Tarot's club," she said. "Where did you say you came from?"

Remembering what I'd told Jayce, I told her the same thing. "Vegas."

"Do you have family out there?"

"I was in foster care most of my childhood," I replied. "So, I didn't really have anyone."

"Oh, that's too bad," she said, her eyes softening.

I shrugged. "Anyway, is this a good neighborhood?" I asked, looking out the window. "Not a lot of break-ins or crime?"

"It is," she replied.

I was getting frustrated, although I didn't exactly expect her to tell me about Andrew. I knew it was probably time to start pressing her.

"I was talking to Jayce and he mentioned that last year, you had an issue with some guy stalking you," I said, walking over to the kitchen's island separating us.

Her eyes widened. "He mentioned that?"

"Yeah. We were talking about my crazy admirer and that's when he told me."

She turned away to look out the kitchen window and that's when I reached into my purse and turned the recorder on.

"What exactly did Hollywood say about it?" she asked quietly.

"That the man broke in and tried hurting you."

"More like rape and kill me," she said in a bitter voice. "I managed to escape... but then he came back again when I had Ruby. It was... terrifying."

"But, you obviously escaped," I said. "What happened to him?"

"The neighbor shot him," she answered, still looking away.

"Who was the guy?"

She shrugged and turned around to face me. "Some asshole who called himself Blade." She grimaced. "He told me that he liked cutting people. Can you believe it? God, he was... a horrible, horrible man."

The person she described didn't sound like my brother Andrew.

169

He liked cutting people?

That was fucked up.

Either, she was lying her ass off, or he'd changed into someone else over the years. A monster who got off using a knife.

No. I refused to accept that.

I began to wonder whether there was more going on here than I knew about. Was it possible the guy who'd tried attacking her was someone else and that my brother had taken the fall? I had to dig further.

"I'm surprised Tarot didn't want to kill him, considering what Blade had done to you. You mentioned getting away from him once?"

"Believe me, he wanted to destroy the guy. I'm glad he didn't, though, because with his luck, he'd have ended up in jail. Fortunately, the neighbor was a cop and took care of the guy."

How convenient.

"I heard Blade was affiliated with another biker club. Was he going after you in some kind of retaliation thing? Because of your relationship with Tarot?"

"Probably. Look," she sighed. I'm sorry. I'd really rather not talk about this anymore. It was a horrible experience, as you can imagine."

"No, *I'm* sorry. I shouldn't be badgering you," I replied, seeing that she wasn't giving me anything else. Things had changed, however. I truly did believe that someone had terrorized her. I just didn't know who, and I still refused to believe that it was Andrew.

THIRTY ONE

HOLLYWOOD

I COULDN'T STOP thinking about Tarot's warning. Although I didn't want to believe Candi was hiding anything, I had to take him seriously.

After running my errands, I took off with Syd, another prospect, to deliver the kegs to the farm. After unloading them into a section of the barn surrounded by ice, we headed back toward St. Paul in one of the vans the club owned.

"This party should be kick ass," Syd said. "I heard someone say that *Crow Magnum* is playing there tonight, too."

Crow Magnum was a cover band from Minneapolis. Their specialty was playing *Metallica*, *Megadeth*, and *Slayer* songs.

"Cool," I replied.

"Phoenix mentioned that some of the other chapters might be showing up. Not just Jensen. This party is going to be huge."

Syd went on and on about the bash. He'd just turned twenty-one and was all about getting wasted every weekend. Of course, now that he was new, it wasn't happening as much as he thought it would. Prospects had to be ready and alert for whatever task was asked, and that could happen anytime.

"You bringing that chick from the other night?" he asked me. "She was smokin'."

"Yeah."

"Normally I'd say, *why bring sand to the beach*? But I don't blame you for taking her. You tap that ass yet?"

"No."

He looked shocked. "You're fucking kidding me. Why not?"

I shrugged. "Haven't had time."

Syd grunted. "If I were you, I'd make time. I can't believe you haven't banged her yet, man," he said, pulling out a cigarette. He shoved it into his mouth. "You're slackin', Hollywood."

We went back and forth on the ride back to the clubhouse, giving each other shit about who was and wasn't getting laid. I found out that Syd had just broken up with his girlfriend, who didn't like the company he was now keeping. Meaning, the club.

"She doesn't understand why I want to join and gave me an ultimatum. Either her or the Gold Vipers. Hell, I don't need that. No chick is going to tell me what to do."

My cell phone began to buzz and I pulled it out of my pocket. It was Tarot.

I answered it. "Hey, brother. What's up?"

"Just thought you should know that Peyton just arrived back home after taking Candi house-hunting."

"Yeah. How did it go?"

"Fine. They only visited a couple of homes and she didn't seem to find anything. She did ask a lot of questions, though."

"About what?"

"That thing with Blade last year," he replied. "She mentioned that you told her about it."

My eyes widened in shock. "*What?*"

"I wouldn't have thought much about it, but Peyton said that Candi was pretty inquisitive about the entire thing. It has me wondering if she's actually a cop or a Fed."

"I fucking hope not," I said angrily. "I spent all that time inking her, and… shit." The very idea that Candi could be a cop made me sick to my stomach." What does your sixth sense tell you? That she's undercover?"

It took him several seconds to answer. "Honestly, I'm having a hard time figure her out. I feel like she's digging for something, but I'm not really sure if it's because she's a cop. It's not out of the question, obviously."

"You sure you're not just being paranoid?"

He let out a ragged sigh. "I'm usually not feeling like this unless something is really off. You're bringing her tonight,

173

right?"

"Yeah."

"See if you can get her drunk and maybe she'll slip up and tell you something. At the very least, you might be able to search her purse. You know… if she loses it. You know what I'm saying?"

"Totally."

"I hope I'm wrong," he said solemnly. "I can tell you're pretty bummed about this."

"I'll be fine," I replied, although he was right. The woman was getting under my skin already. "Anyway, if she's up to no good, I'll find out."

"I know you will, brother. Good luck."

"Thanks."

We hung up and Syd, who'd been eavesdropping, started hounding me about the conversation. I didn't tell him shit, because he had a big mouth. That last thing I needed was for everyone at the party to start jumping to conclusions. It could turn ugly. Especially when there was going to be drinking involved.

Sid and I made it back to the clubhouse around seven-forty-five. I dropped off the keys to the van, jumped on my bike, and headed to Candi's motel.

THIRTY TWO

AVA

I HEARD JAYCE'S Hog approach as I was applying more lipstick in the mirror. I'd just gotten back from Peyton and Tarot's place a few minutes before, and wasn't really in the mood to party. But, I needed answers. I was hoping that, at some point, I might even be able to chum up to some of the bikers and get them talking. If I did find out anything and manage to get it recorded, I would bring it to the police and demand that they re-open the case.

Jayce knocked on the door.

I grabbed my purse from the bed, making sure it was zipped up, and answered it.

"Hi," I said, beaming a smile up at him. It was such a shame that he was part of the Gold Vipers. The man was so damn handsome. Tonight he had on a light-blue cotton shirt under his cut, which brought out his tan and made his blue eyes really pop.

"You ready?" he asked, looking distracted and impatient.

My smile fell. Not that I was one to fish for compliments, but I hoped he'd at least notice how different I looked compared to the last couple of days. The style was a reflection of the real me.

"Yes. Is everything okay?"

He nodded and then looked down at my dress. "Not sure if that's the best choice for the back of my bike."

I really wanted to keep the dress on. Especially since I didn't have anything else appropriate for a biker party. I told him that we should take my car instead if I had to change.

"Sorry, but I'm not showing up in a cage. I'd have brought my Mustang if I was going to use one. We're taking my bike."

My eye twitched. His testosterone was shining bright tonight. "I know. Why don't I follow you out there?"

"Nah." He scratched his chin and sighed. "I guess you'll

be fine wearing that. You have everything?"

"Yeah."

He stepped inside. "You have a jacket? It could get cold tonight on the way back."

"Okay." I walked over to the closet and pulled out a short, white denim jacket. I put it on and turned around. "Will this work?"

He nodded.

"You look nice, by the way," I said, pulling my hair out from under the collar.

"Thanks. You too," he said. "Too nice to have road rash. You sure you want to go in that short dress?"

"Okay, now you're making me nervous. Maybe I should drive your bike if you're so worried about crashing?" I teased.

"I'm not worried about my driving. There's going to be a lot of drunks out later. I'm just being cautious and thinking of your safety."

"Would it make you happier if I slipped on a pair of jeans under my dress? Or maybe a snowmobile suit?"

He grunted. "Let's go."

"Next time, I'll make sure to rent some chainmail. I bet they have some across the street at that costume shop."

Jayce smirked. "Smartass," he said dryly as we headed out.

I turned around and locked the door. "So, where is this party?"

"Chisago. It's about a forty-five minute drive."

We walked over to his motorcycle and he handed me a helmet. "Here."

"You're really into safety, aren't you?" I mused.

"I'm into keeping you alive."

"What about you?" I replied, seeing that he was giving me his helmet and didn't have another.

"If anyone's brains are going to be splattered on the

177

concrete, I'd rather have them be mine," he replied.

"You're so sweet," I said, putting the helmet on. As I tried adjusting the straps, he reached over and did it for me.

"How's your tat doing?" he asked softly.

"Okay. Tender."

"Have you been putting the moisturizer on it?"

"Yes."

Jayce gently pushed some hair away from my eyes. "Sorry in advance about the helmet hair. I like it much better this way," he said, tugging at one of the strands playfully. "I bet it's a lot softer, too, without all the hairspray."

I smiled. "True."

Jayce stared into my eyes and I could see a question in his. Just when I thought he was going to ask me something, he looked away. "You ready?"

"Yeah."

"Why don't you let me put your purse in my saddlebag?"

I thought about the gun and it made me nervous to let it go. But, what choice did I have?

"Sure," I said, handing the purse to him.

"Damn, it's heavy. What do you have in here?" he asked with a chuckle. "A bomb?"

"Just an arsenal of makeup," I said, feeling the hair stand up on the back of my neck. "A girl has to be prepared for anything, you know?"

"I guess," he said, putting the purse in the saddlebag and buttoning it back up. "You don't need any makeup, though. I have a feeling the less you have on, the better." Jayce's eyes dipped down and he grinned. "Actually, I can already vouch for that in more ways than one."

I just laughed.

He swung his leg over the bike and then I got on behind him.

"Ready?" he asked, after starting the engine.

I slid my hands around his waist.

Was I ready to surround myself with a bunch of hell-raising, dangerous bikers who were going to get drunk and rowdy? "Yep."

THIRTY THREE

HOLLYWOOD

CANDI WAS LOOKING hot, especially in that dress. Although she had more covering than usual, it was still very sexy and very distracting. Especially for someone who needed to keep a clear head. My other one apparently had a mind of its own. The moment she put her hands around my waist, I wanted them under my zipper.

Fuck, I need to get laid.

Fortunately, I calmed down during the ride and kept my mind on the conversation I'd had with Tarot earlier. I still couldn't believe Candi had insinuated that I'd told her about Blade.

Where in the fuck had that come from, and how did she even know that shit about Blade to begin with?

I hoped she wasn't FBI. They'd been trying to pin his murder on the Gold Vipers for a long time, although when it came to Blade's death, there'd been a fairly tight alibi. Yeah, Tarot had killed him, but Peyton's neighbor had shot the bastard afterward, because even he knew the guy had deserved to die. Even better, he'd been willing to take the blame so Tarot wouldn't end up in jail. The psychopath had gotten what he'd deserved.

When we arrived at the party, there were already a lot of people there.

I parked my bike at the end of a long row of motorcycles and shut off the engine. Old time rock-n-roll music drifted through the air, along with the smell of barbecue.

"I feel like I'm at some roughneck, bad boy biker festival. Is this what Sturgis is like?" Candi asked.

I chuckled. "No, this is *nothing* compared to Sturgis. This is much tamer, although it will get pretty rowdy after dark, I'm sure."

We got off the bike and started walking down the gravel driveway.

"Hey," I said, holding my hand out. "You'd better take it. I want people to know we're together so they don't mess with you."

Her eyebrow raised. "Mess with me?"

"Whenever you mix alcohol, testosterone, and pretty women, it's asking for trouble. Especially in this setting."

"Point taken." She took my hand.

We began walking again and then suddenly, she stopped abruptly. "Damn, I forgot my purse."

"I'll get it." I turned around and jogged back to my motorcycle. I unbuttoned the saddlebag and pulled it out, thinking again that her purse felt damn heavy. Unfortunately, she was watching me like a hawk, so I didn't have a chance to peek inside. I wrapped the strap around it and jogged back to Candi. "Here you go."

"Thanks." She took it from me and hung it over her shoulder.

"No problem. Ready to have some fun?"

She nodded.

I took her hand again and we walked around the farmhouse to the backyard, where two large canopies were set up. Underneath were long picnic tables where people were eating and drinking. On the other side of the canopies was a stage where guys from the band were setting up the equipment.

"Live music, huh?" Candi said. "Cool."

"Yeah. Have you heard of *Crow Magnum*?"

"No. Can't say I have."

I explained that they were a cover band. "They're good. Hopefully you'll like them. They play a lot of heavy metal and rock."

"Cool. I like rock. I can't wait to hear them."

"You want a beer?"

"Sure."

182

We headed toward the barn, exchanging greetings as we walked by the others. I noticed some of the guys were already eyeballing Candi, which I'd expected. She stood out in the sundress, especially since most of the other chicks wore the usual Harley tanks, leather halter tops, and ripped denim. It was just... different, and that was always sexier in my book.

"Hey, long time no talk," said Tarot, who was filling up a red Solo cup with beer as we approached. He poured out some of the foam on top and added more to top it off. "You two just get here?"

"Yeah," I said, grabbing two cups from a plastic bag sitting next to the keg. "It's busy already."

He handed me the beer faucet. "I know. Tank and his group are already here. Bastard is also with them."

"No shit?" I replied, surprised. Bastard founded the Gold Vipers. He didn't make many appearances, so this was a big deal. I met him once, after the thing with Blade. He'd paid us a visit and had complimented me about putting my life on the line for Tarot's fiancé, Peyton. I'd confronted Blade when he'd been trying to break into her place. Unfortunately, he got away that time, but it all worked out in the end.

"Yeah. He's playing horseshoes on the other side of the stage," Tarot replied.

"Cool. I'll go say hi." I began filling Candi's cup with beer. "I didn't know Bastard was coming. That's pretty cool."

"Neither did I. Anyway, you two have fun now," he said before winking and walking away.

"You, too," I replied.

I handed Candi a cup and then filled the other one. "You hungry?"

She nodded. "Yeah, a little."

"I'm starving. Let's go and say hi to the others and then grab some food."

"Sounds good. Who are Bastard and Tank, by the way?"

"Tank is the president of the Jensen chapter. He's the one who patched our club over when they were Steel Bandits. Bastard is the president of our mother chapter. He founded the Gold Vipers. "

"Cool."

I took her hand again and we headed over to the area where the guys were playing horseshoes. I recognized Bastard, Tank, and Raptor right away. There were a couple other guys who looked familiar, but I couldn't quite remember their names. Noticing us approach, Bastard smiled.

"Hey, Hollywood." He looked down at my cut. "They haven't patched you yet?" he asked, shaking my hand.

"Not yet," I replied.

"I'm sure it won't be long. Who's this pretty lady?" he asked, smiling at Candi.

I introduced him to her.

"Where's April?" I asked. She was his Old Lady, a real looker about half his age. He told everyone she kept him young, which I didn't doubt. The old geezer still had a spring in his step.

"Back in Sacramento. She's pregnant," he replied.

Shocked that he was having a kid when he had to be well past fifty, I congratulated him.

"Thanks." He looked beyond us toward another group of people. "Oh. A friend of mine just showed up. You two have fun now. It was nice seeing you, Hollywood, and meeting you, Candi."

"You, too," I said, fist-bumping him.

"Same here," Candi answered.

When he was out of earshot, Candi turned to me asked about April.

"That's his Old Lady."

"And she's pregnant?" Candi replied, looking surprised. "He looks so old to be fathering a baby. No offense."

184

I chuckled. "April is young enough for him to be *her* father. Anyway, they love each other, so what the hell. I'm sure she'll be the one chasing after the kids anyway. Or he'll have prospects doing it."

"You guys babysit, too?" Candi said, looking surprised.

"I've never had to do it, thank God."

She smirked. "Lucky you."

"No, more like lucky *them*. I wouldn't know what to do with a kid."

"Me neither," she said with a wry smile.

We watched Tank and Raptor play horseshoes for a while, and when they took a beer break, I brought Candi over to meet them.

"Hey, Hollywood," Tank said, shaking my hand. He was a powerhouse of a guy, towering over us at six-foot-five, with bulging muscles that rippled down from his shoulders and chest. As intimidating as he was, Tank was warm-hearted and would give you the shirt off his back if he though you needed it. "It's been a while. They haven't patched you yet?"

"Nope. I guess they're having too much fun ordering me around."

"You behaving?" he asked with a grin.

"Behaving?" I chuckled. "Hell yeah. Maybe that's the problem?"

"Could be. I was always a hell-raiser, even as a prospect. My old man used to get so pissed off. I was young, though, and cocky. I didn't care if I was fully patched or not. I just wanted to be part of the club."

Tank's old man, Slammer, had been the previous president of the Jensen chapter. Just like our club's prior president, he'd been murdered by a rival club. At least that's the presumption. There was a lot of speculation and rumors going around. The fact was, nobody knew for sure because the other clubs never took credit or boasted about being

185

responsible for Slammer's death. Which was odd, considering many of our enemies loved to brag.

"I'm sure." I put my arm around Candi's shoulders and introduced her.

"Nice to meet you," she said, looking nervous.

"You, too." He looked at me and then back to her. "Anyone ever tell you that you look like that actress who's was in that movie, the *Fantastic Four*? And *Spy Kids*?"

She smiled. "Jessica Alba? Yeah, I've heard that before."

"You watch *Spy Kids*?" Raptor asked, chuckling as he approached us with two full beers. "I guess that makes sense."

Raptor was Tank's V.P and best friend.

"Billy loves it," he replied as Raptor handed him a beer. "I bet Sammy has watched it."

From what I understood, Billy was Tank's stepson, and he also had a toddler named Grace. Raptor had a son name Sammy and a set of twin girls.

"I've heard him mention it before. Hey, Hollywood, how's it going?" Raptor asked, holding out his hand. He was somewhere in his early thirties, with blond hair and a goatee. We were the same height, which was a little over six feet.

I shook it. "Not bad. What about yourself?"

We shot the shit for a minute, and then of course, I introduced him to Candi, who seemed like she was finally relaxing under my arm. When I'd first pulled her close, she'd been as stiff as a board. Unfortunately, it had slipped my mind that she was squeamish about guys touching her. I felt like an idiot afterward and reminded myself to apologize later.

"We'd better finish up this game," Tank said after taking another sip of beer. "Catch you later?"

"Of course," I replied.

After a few more words, they went back to playing

horseshoes and Candi and I headed toward the barn again, where the food was. As we walked, I released my arm and apologized.

"It's okay," she replied. "I know why you did it."

We were just about to enter the barn when I grabbed her hand and pulled around the corner, where there was some privacy.

"What are we doing?" she asked, looking up at me in surprise.

THIRTY FOUR

AVA

"THAT'S JUST IT. I don't know," he murmured, his eyes searching mine.

Having had a few sips of beer, I was slightly buzzed. I was also feeling more attracted to him than ever, which was stupid and very, very dangerous. Not so much for my safety, but my sanity.

"I thought we were just enjoying a nice evening together," I replied, my heart hammering in my chest from the way he was staring at me. It was almost like he was inside of my head, trying to dissect my thoughts.

"We are," he replied, touching my arm lightly with his fingertips and making me shiver. "I guess what I'd like to know is if we're enjoying it as friends or... something more."

Nervous, I brushed a lock of hair away from my eye. "What... what would you like it to be?"

He smiled slowly. "You can't tell?"

Of course I could, but the words wouldn't come out. I just stared at him, breathless.

Jayce slid his hand along my cheek and leaned in to me. I closed my eyes as his lips touched mine and he began kissing me. Enjoying the moment, I opened my mouth to his. My body felt like it was humming when his tongue moved in and began exploring my mouth. Although we'd done it before, this time it seemed different. It was a slow, leisurely kiss, both of us taking our time and enjoying the moment. I involuntarily pushed myself into him, and his hand immediately dropped from my cheek, slid lightly down my neck, brushed over my shoulder, and after trailing down my arm, landed on my waist, pulling me against him. He smelled so good, and his kisses were so intoxicating that I could feel myself begin to respond to him.

My body was igniting with desire. Everywhere.

It may have been the alcohol, or maybe it was just that I was so completely and utterly attracted to Jayce, but I was

189

suddenly on fire. I dropped my cup onto the grass and slid both my hands around him, feeling hungry and desperate for more. My legs felt like jelly as I kissed him back with a passion I didn't know lived inside of me.

Jayce groaned in the back of his throat, and soon both his hands were on me, one in my hair, the other holding me up. I could feel his hardness pressing against me, and unlike all the other times I'd considered a man's erection, I was suddenly aching to feel it inside of me. Knowing that it wasn't the time or the place, I managed to find the strength to pull away from him. When our lips separated, we were both out of breath and practically panting. We stared at each other. Jayce finally opened up his mouth to say something when a stranger walked around the corner, unzipping his fly with the intention of relieving himself.

"Oh, shit," he said, looking embarrassed. "Sorry, my bad."

"No problem," Jayce replied. He put his arm over my shoulders and guided me around to the front of the barn.

"We forgot our cups," I said, picturing them still lying on the grass.

"Forget about 'em. I'll throw them away later. Let's get some fresh ones," he said softly. "You still hungry?"

"Yeah," I replied.

His eyes met mine and they were lit with a blue flame of desire. "I'm hungry, too. Just not for what's being served in there," he murmured, kissing me on the temple before we walked into the barn.

I know the feeling.

We grabbed some food and more beer and then walked out of the barn to a picnic table, where a bunch of his club brothers were already seated. I recognized some of them from the birthday party the other night. This time, however, there were less wives, but plenty of club groupies. One of them, a tall, pretty brunette, looked at Jayce and then at me. Her eyes widened for a second and she opened her mouth. I thought she was going to say something, but apparently she changed her mind because she remained silent.

Jayce and I sat down across from Phoenix and Brass. They both greeted us and then began talking about motorcycles and trips they were planning to take. I listened as I ate, my mind still on what had just happened. It had felt too right and that was wrong. Very wrong. I couldn't afford to lose myself like that again. I decided to ease back on the beer to try and stay focused. Soon there would be a lot of drunk bikers and loose lips. At least, I hoped.

"Where are you from, Candi?" Phoenix asked.

I cleared my throat and looked up from my plate. "Vegas," I said with a smile.

"What are you doing in Minnesota? Do you have family here?" asked Phoenix.

"No. I was just tired of Vegas and decided to move on," I replied.

"I can appreciate that," Len said from the other end of the table. "Although, I'd be more inclined to leave Minnesota and go to Vegas."

Some of the others agreed.

"Sin City, man," Len said. "Gotta love it."

"Why did you pick Minnesota?" Tarot asked, staring at me intently.

"I haven't exactly picked it yet," I replied. I don't know if it was the way he was looking at me, or my own paranoia, but I suddenly felt like I was being cross-examined. "I was on my way to Canada and that's how I ended up here."

"You thinking of staying?" Brass asked.

"I'm not sure yet," I replied.

"I think it's cool how you decided to just leave everything behind to start over somewhere," said a girl named Eve, one

191

of the club groupies. "I'd love to be able to do that. I just couldn't afford it."

"It's definitely an expensive and risky move," said Tarot. "You looking for a job at all? Phoenix mentioned you'd done some waitressing. We're always in need of a good server at my establishment."

I relaxed. Maybe my paranoia was just acting up again. "I might just be. Thank you."

"No problem." He looked at Jayce. "Bring her by the *Wild River Saloon* next week sometime. If she decides to stay in town."

"Yeah. Definitely," he replied and looked at me. "I *hope* you stick around."

I smiled at him. "I'm definitely thinking about it."

He grabbed my hand under the table and squeezed it. "Good."

The tender gesture warmed my heart, but it also made me feel guilty as hell. Jayce was turning out to be a really nice guy and didn't deserve the lies I was feeding him. When he found out later, he'd hate me. The idea made me sick to my stomach.

THIRTY FIVE

FIVE

HOLLYWOOD

D AY TURNED INTO night and more people showed up from other chapters. Several Tiki torches were lit and then the band took the stage. This kicked the party up a few notches, and soon, everyone was dancing, drinking, and having one hell of a good time.

"Can I get you another beer?" I asked Candi as one of the songs ended. We were standing close to the stage and she seemed to be enjoying herself, dancing and singing to some of the songs.

"Sure," she replied, turning her cup over to show it was empty. "I could use a refill."

"Let's go."

She bit her lower lip. "Maybe I should meet you back here? I have to go to the bathroom."

I looked around. Some of the guys were getting pretty hammered and there was no way in hell I was letting her out of my sight.

"We'll do that first," I said, touching her elbow. I began guiding her toward the porta-potties. Unfortunately, there were only two and the lines were long.

"I'll be fine here by myself," she said as we waited. "Go grab us a couple of beers."

Needing to relieve myself too, I glanced toward the barn and then back.

"Seriously. Just go," she prodded.

"Okay. Watch out for the wolves," I said, smiling. "They're everywhere tonight."

She laughed. "So, what does that make you?"

"A lucky dog who has what everyone else wants," I murmured near her ear, making her shiver.

Candi smiled and I leaned over and kissed her before heading over to the barn. At the last minute, I took a detour around the side to take a much needed piss. As I was zipping up, I heard someone gasp behind me.

194

"Sorry. I didn't know anyone was back here."

I turned around and saw Magpie, a chick I almost banged after the club's Christmas party last year. We'd both been drunk and things had started getting hot and heavy, but then something had come over me at the last minute. Maybe it was the fact that she'd been with several of my club brothers, which wasn't exactly an aphrodisiac. Whatever the case, I'd made up some excuse about not feeling well and we'd gone our separate ways.

"No problem," I replied. "How've you been?"

"Okay." Magpie took a step closer to me and lowered her voice. "So, how long have you been seeing Candi?"

"Just a few days," I replied. "Why?"

"I've seen her before and... her name isn't Candi."

I frowned. "What are you talking about?"

"When you first walked up with her, I thought she'd looked familiar. Then Eve mentioned that Candi was from Vegas. I was out there last month and pretty sure that I saw her on the set of a movie being filmed," she replied.

Magpie's sister was a set designer and sometimes she'd pay for her to fly out to watch some of the movies being filmed.

"I think you have her confused with someone else," I said, smiling. "Candi is definitely not an actress."

"No, you're right. She's a stuntwoman."

I laughed.

"I'm serious," Magpie said. "I saw her, or someone who looked exactly like Candi, on the set of a movie last month. I mean *exactly*."

I could tell by the look on her face that she truly believed that Candi was someone else and wouldn't rest until I was convinced.

"Who's this stuntwoman? You have a name?"

"I'll ask my sister if she can find out her last name," she

195

said, pulling out her phone. "I know her first name is Ava."

"I'm telling you, it's not her," I said, shaking my head. "Why would a stuntwoman drive all the way out here, in a shitty car, and lie about her identity?"

It wasn't to get a tattoo... that was for certain.

Magpie shrugged and then began typing out a message on her phone. "I don't know. But, I'm telling you... Candi *is* Ava. They even have the same mannerisms." She looked up from her cell. "Plus, they both have really toned arms, like they work out a lot. Obviously, stunt people need to be super fit."

Candi obviously spent time at the gym. Even I could see that. But it didn't mean anything.

"Hold on, my sister is typing back," Magpie said, staring down at her phone. After a few seconds, her face lit up. She looked at me. "She remembers who I'm talking about. The stuntwoman's name is Ava Rhodes. I bet if you Google her, you'll find out more information."

Sighing, I pulled out my phone and did what she suggested. Images and information pulled up about Ava Rhodes, who was a stuntwoman from Florida. She'd been in numerous commercials and a couple of independent movies.

As I looked at one of the close-up shots, my heart skipped a beat. The resemblance was definitely a little unnerving. They even had the same left-side dimple.

Fuck.

That definitely seemed like too much of a coincidence.

"See," said Magpie, who was also looking at my phone. "It's her."

Tarot's warning rang in my ears. If Candi really was Ava Rhodes, why was she lying? I could see if she wanted to protect her identity, especially since she was somewhat of a celebrity. But, we'd spent hours talking about her life, including the shitty abuse she'd received in the foster homes.

It made me wonder if she'd lied about that as well.

"What are you going to do?" Magpie asked.

"Figure this shit out," I growled, putting my phone away. "Have you mentioned it to anyone else here?"

"No."

"Keep it that way for now. Okay?"

She flinched. "Yes."

"I'm serious," I said, knowing how much she liked to gossip. I pinned her eyes with mine. "Not a fucking word."

Magpie nodded. "I promise, Hollywood. You can trust me."

THIRTY SIX

AVA

I DON'T KNOW what happened to Jayce, but he was gone longer than I had to wait in line for the porta-potty. Not seeing him, I walked toward the barn where the beer was, and that was when I ran into Len. He was *trashed*.

"Hey, pretty girl. Where's Hollywood?" he asked, swaying back and forth.

I looked past him toward the barn door. "I don't know. He's supposed to be getting me a beer."

"I just walked out of there. I didn't see him," he said, holding up his own beer. "I'll help you look for Jayce, though. You shouldn't be wandering around out here unchaperoned."

"Why?" I asked, amused.

"'Cause if you're not someone's Ol' Lady, you're free for the pickin'," he said.

"Don't I have some say in that?" I replied dryly.

"Not enough. Mind you, most brothers would leave you alone, but there's some guys here I've never met before," he said, lowering his voice. "They might mistake you for a club whore or something."

My eye twitched. "Wow. Thanks for that."

"Sorry," he said and laughed. "Not that you look like a tramp or anything. But, around here we get a lot of chicks willing to do anything for one of us Gold Vipers."

Len wasn't exactly a handsome or suave guy. He was tall and lanky with a lot of miles on his face already. I'd have guessed him to be in his forties, although I'd heard someone say he was in his thirties. He partied hard and smoked a lot of hash, at least that's what Jayce told me. I imagined that without the club whores, Len would have had a pretty dull sex life.

"It's okay. I understand," I replied, realizing that the opportunity had finally presented itself to start digging. "Let's go find Jayce. Maybe he's over by his bike?"

He shrugged. "I suppose we could look there."

199

I didn't think Jayce was by the motorcycles. I just thought it was a great opportunity to talk to Len.

We started walking toward the long gravel driveway, and I reached into my purse, and turned on the recorder.

"So, how long have you been in the club?" I asked.

"Since I was nineteen," he replied and began to talk about how he'd joined up after going to a biker party.

I cut in to his story. "So, you were around when poor Peyton was attacked by creep last year."

"Yep," he said. "That motherfucker. He was trying to frame Tarot for some shit. The Blood Angels… they recruited him."

He started going on about how they'd been dealing with the Blood Angels for the last few years.

"They're disbanded now, though. At least the ones bothering us," he said, taking out a cigarette and a lighter.

"What happened to Blade?" I asked, not really expecting him to answer me truthfully. But, he kept talking, which was a pleasant surprise.

"He got what he deserved. Tarot killed the asshole. I would have, too, if he'd been going after my woman and my child." Realizing that he probably said too much, Len stopped abruptly and swore. "Me and my big fuckin' mouth. Don't you go repeating what I said."

"Don't worry. Jayce already told me about it," I lied.

He relaxed. "Good."

We started walking again.

"Hollywood was lucky he didn't get killed that night," Len said after a few seconds.

My heart started pounding. "What do you mean?"

"He was there, too. He surprised Blade and had him at gunpoint."

"Jayce was there that night?" I said, the blood rushing to my ears.

He'd been involved in my brother's death?
The very idea made me want to vomit.
"Oh yeah. In fact—"
Someone shouted my name. We turned to look and saw the the devil himself.

THIRTY SEVEN

HOLLYWOOD

I DIDN'T KNOW why the hell Len was with Candi, or whatever the hell her name was, but it pissed the fuck out of me. I called her name and then jogged over to them.

"Where were you two going?" I asked.

"We were looking for you," Len said. "Where'd you disappear off to?"

"I was talking to Phoenix," I replied, noticing that he was drunk.

Tarot had left the party already, but I'd told Phoenix and Brass about what Magpie had told me. They didn't have much to say other than I needed to figure out what was going on and make sure that it didn't have anything to do with the club.

"You can't leave a sweet thing like this unattended around this kind of party, brother," Len said before taking a drag of his smoke.

"I didn't think I'd be gone that long. Sorry," I said to Candi, who looked like she wanted to ring my neck herself.

"It's fine," she said, her expression clearly telling me that it must not have been fine at all.

"You sure about that?" I said, trying to keep cool. I had so many questions and wanted answers right then and there. But, I'd been advised to take the drama somewhere else.

"I'm tired. Could you take me back to my motel?"

"Yeah," I replied, relieved. I'd been about to suggest that myself. I pulled out my bike key. "You can make it back by yourself, right Len?"

"Of course," he said, stumbling and spilling most of his beer.

I rolled my eyes. "Maybe you should go and find some place to lie down."

"I need to find me a woman first," he said and then laughed at himself.

"There are plenty to choose from," I said. "See ya, Len."

"Goodnight." He looked at Candi. "Nice seeing you again, Candi."

"You, too," she replied.

"Nice girl you got here," Len said and then hiccupped. "Damn it. Where the hell did all my beer go?" Mumbling under his breath, he walked back toward the party.

"Don't you have to say goodbye to your friends?" Candi asked coolly.

"Already did," I said.

She raised her eyebrow.

"Let's get you home."

THIRTY
EIGHT

AVA

THE RIDE BACK to my motel was chilly, in more ways than one. I was livid about what I'd learned, and for some reason, Jayce seemed to have an attitude as well. It was even more evident when he walked me to my room.

"Well… goodnight," I said, reaching into my purse for the motel key. I couldn't wait to be alone so I could process what I'd learned and listen to the recording.

"We need to talk."

I swallowed. "About what?"

"Things."

"If you don't mind, I'd rather not tonight. I'm really tired."

"It won't take long."

Sighing, I gave in and opened the door. We both walked in and I switched on the lights.

"Sorry, my maid took the day off," I said dryly, realizing that I'd forgotten to make the bed and my clothes were still strewn everywhere. I started picking them up.

"Don't worry about it," he said, grabbing my wrist. "*Ava.*"

My heart stopped.

How in the hell?

Trying to remain calm, I forced a smile to my face. "Excuse me?"

"Let me try again — Ava Rhodes. Does that name ring a bell?"

I thought about denying who I was, but knew he wasn't stupid. I also knew that even if he had figured out my name, it didn't mean he knew anything else. Especially that I was related to Andrew.

"Yes. That's my real name. How did you find out?"

"It doesn't matter. Why did you lie to me?" he asked angrily.

206

"I don't know. I guess I panicked," I said, my mind whirling with excuses to give him.

He frowned. "Why? Did you think I was some kind of a threat to you?"

"No. Not you. Look, I wasn't lying when I said I wanted to leave my past behind," I replied hoping he'd believe me. "I... I had some problems come up and decided to drop everything and just... leave."

"Leave where? Florida?"

I laughed harshly. "Wow, you really did your homework. Yes, Florida."

"What kind of problems?"

I rubbed my temple. "Personal things. I'd prefer not to get into them with you."

His face turned red with anger. "You'd prefer..." Jayce ran a hand through his hair in frustration. "You've been lying to me about who you really are, while I've been honest with you about everything. I *trusted* you. The least you can do is tell me what the fuck is going on."

"There's nothing to really tell. I had some problems with this guy and didn't want him to find me," I said, spinning another story.

"What guy?"

"An actor," I said, picturing how Hunter Calloway had pissed me off in Vegas. "This guy tried raping me and I—"

"He *what?*" snarled Jayce. "Who? Did you call the police?"

"No, because he didn't get away with it. I stopped him before anything happened."

"Who is the asshole?"

Jayce looked like a raging bull, ready to kill someone. I would have been flattered and amused if I wasn't so furious about what I'd learned from Len.

"His name was Hunter. Anyway, I needed to get away

207

for a while and that's why I came out here. To clear my head and figure out what I wanted to do. I'm sorry I lied. I shouldn't have."

His eyes searched mine. "What else is there?"

"Nothing."

"Bullshit. Tell me who you really are. I deserve to know."

"I already told you about the real me," I said, wishing he'd leave. "I just gave you the wrong name and occupation. Everything else we discussed is true."

"The stories about your foster parents?"

"Real. You can't make that shit up," I said quietly.

He sighed.

"Can we talk more about this tomorrow?" I asked. "I'm exhausted, Jayce."

He just stared at me.

"Listen, I promise you I didn't lie about my childhood. It was a nightmare from hell and… I don't just tell everyone about my past. I told you, though."

He sighed.

"Can we talk more about this tomorrow? Please?"

He nodded reluctantly.

"Look, I'm sorry I lied. I wasn't expecting us to start dating and I didn't know how to tell you the truth without looking like a nutcase," I said. "I wasn't trying to hurt you."

Jayce sighed.

"Let's have dinner tomorrow night."

"How about breakfast?" he asked.

"Don't you have to go out of town?"

"No. Not anymore."

I was planning on going to the cops in the morning. At least I had Len on tape confirming that Tarot had killed my brother. Hopefully, he'd be behind bars before the sun went down.

"I'm getting my hair and nails done tomorrow," I lied.

208

He looked at my nails, which were nothing special. "Okay. Dinner works. Unless you're planning on skipping town, Ava?"

I smiled. "No. I'm not going anywhere."

"I have to admit, I prefer your real name."

I smiled.

Jayce walked over to me. He slid his hands around my waist, drew me closer, and started kissing me.

Furious, I had to keep from shoving him away.

This man, who was as handsome as sin, with his boyish smile and passionate kisses, was disarming me by the second. I was more pissed off at myself than anyone for enjoying his touch. He was an amazing artist and probably a very talented lover. More than anything, however, he was an accomplice to murder. My brother's. For that... I would never forgive the jerk. But, I would make sure that along with Tarot, Jayce would also pay.

THIRTY NINE

HOLLYWOOD

AFTER I LEFT Ava's motel room, I still felt like things were unsettled and didn't know whether or not to trust her fully. As I walked by her car, I had to wonder why she was driving such a pile of shit, too. The vehicle couldn't have been worth more than a grand and something told me that a female stuntwoman could afford better. Of course, if she was running away from someone and trying to keep a low cover, it was definitely a good idea.

As I got on my bike and then headed home, I thought about the story with Hunter and decided to ask Magpie if she could find out anything about him. If the guy was real, and had tried raping Ava, he should be dealt with. The very idea that someone might have tried forcing her into sex made my blood boil.

When I reached my apartment complex, I checked my phone and found a text from Tarot. He wanted me to get in touch with him. I dialed his number and he answered right away.

"Phoenix called me about your girl. Her name really is Ava Rhodes, isn't it?" he asked in a low voice.

"Yeah," I replied. "She admitted it to me back at her motel."

I told him the story she gave me and he listened quietly.

"So, what do you think?" I asked, pacing back and forth in my apartment.

"Honestly, it feels pretty legit to me," he replied. "My gut is telling me it happened. Some douchebag tried throwing his weight and power around, to try and take advantage of her."

"Son-of-a-bitch," I growled. "I'd like to find the guy and beat the living shit out of the motherfucker."

"I don't blame you. There's something else I should tell you."

"What's that?"

"I think Ava is somehow connected to Blade. You know

how she was asking about him and everything?"

That was damn troubling. "Yeah."

"At first, I thought maybe she was FBI, poking around for answers. She's obviously not. But there is some correlation between the two of them. I'm just not seeing it yet."

"You don't think they were together, do you?" I asked, feeling sick to my stomach at the thought. As angry as I'd been about Ava's lies, I still wanted to be with her. And it wasn't just for the sex, which probably wouldn't happen anytime soon anyway. I was drawn to her unlike any other woman I'd met before.

"I don't know, brother. I don't know."

I sighed. "What do you think I should do?"

"You're really hung up on her, aren't you?"

"Yeah," I admitted.

He let out a ragged sigh. "If I were in your shoes, this is what I'd do..."

FORTY

AVA

I HAD A hard time sleeping. I kept expecting someone to come pounding at my door, especially now that Jayce had my full name.

And where in the hell had he gotten it anyway?

If they found out my identity, they could trace it back to my birthmother, and eventually learn that Andrew and I were related.

This was definitely bad.

After tossing and turning for the better part of the night, I got up early, made a pot of coffee, and then proceeded to call the St. Paul Police Department.

"Hello, I was wondering who I could speak to regarding a murder?" I asked the person who answered the phone.

"Ma'am, did you see someone get killed?" the man replied.

"No, but I know someone *was*. I also know who did it." I began telling the guy about the Gold Vipers and he immediately transferred me to a unit that apparently handled street gangs.

"Detective Olson," a man answered briskly.

I cleared my throat and asked to speak to someone about the Gold Vipers.

"You can talk to me," he replied, sounding a little more enthusiastic. "What did you say your name was?"

I was about to tell him, but suddenly my paranoia kicked in.

What if the Gold Vipers were paying off some of the police?

I wouldn't know until it was too late.

"I'd prefer not to tell you. I do have some information on a murder that occurred last year."

"Which one is that?" he asked.

I told him about the one involving a guy named Blade.

"Andrew Bordellini…. Oh, yeah. That case was closed," he replied. "We know who shot the assailant. It was done in

214

self-defense."

"Andrew was actually the *victim*," I said, trying to remain calm. "He was framed and then murdered by Dominic Savage, otherwise known as Tarot. In fact, I have it on tape that he *killed* Andrew Bordellini."

"Wait a second, he admitted it?"

"No. But, one of his club mates told me he killed him."

"So, you have *him* on tape?"

"Yes."

The man sighed. "First of all, the tape would probably be inadmissible in court, especially since it's not a confession. Second of all, the woman's neighbor, who admitted to the shooting, is a retired cop. He confessed to killing Bordellini."

"He lied."

"I'm sorry, ma'am, but unless you get Tarot to admit that he killed Andrew Bordellini on tape or video, we can't help you."

"So, Tarot is going to get away with murder?" I replied angrily.

"Let's be frank here. Andrew Bordellini was by no means a choir boy. He had a rap sheet a mile long."

"For what kind of charges?" I asked, feeling a lump in my throat.

"I don't rightly remember. Let's just say that he wasn't a stand-up guy."

"Maybe not, but he didn't deserve what he got."

"I don't know. Some would say he did," he said, a smile in his voice. "The world is always a better place when a criminal gets his wings. Or in this case, his horns."

Clenching my teeth, I growled, hung up on the asshole, and threw my phone onto the bed. No wonder the Gold Vipers got away with murder. The police treated them like vigilantes.

Knowing that I wasn't going to get any help legally, I

thought about going to the press with my information. It might force the police into taking action. But, I knew that doing something like that would not only put me in danger, but also Millie. I couldn't risk it.

Sighing, I knew that there was no other choice. I'd have to do what I came out there to do—avenge Andrew's death by myself.

I took a shower and put on a pair of black shorts and a gray long-sleeved T-shirt. I pulled my hair back into a ponytail and grabbed a baseball cap. After finishing up in the bathroom, I packed up my belongings and was about to check out of the motel, when there was a knock on the door. I checked the peephole and saw that it was a delivery man holding flowers. I opened the door.

"Ava Rhodes?"

I nodded.

He smiled and handed me a stunning arrangement of multicolored flowers. "These are for you."

"Thank you," I said, staring at them in confusion.

After the delivery guy left, I looked at the card.

Ava,

Like these flowers, your beauty is radiant and stems from within, regardless of anything else. I'm looking forward to seeing you tonight and I hope you feel the same.

Jayce

They were beautiful and I would have melted had I not known what I now did. If anything, the flowers depressed me and made me feel empty inside. It figured that the one guy I'd started to have real feelings for was an accomplice to murder.

Instead of putting them in water, I threw them in the garbage and checked out of the motel.

As I started the engine of my car, I still wasn't exactly sure what I was going to do. After blindly driving around for twenty minutes, I pointed the Malibu toward Tarot and Peyton's place. I needed to get this over with. There was no point in wasting any more time or money.

I drove down their street, and it appeared they were both home. I parked farther up the block and shut off my car. After sitting quietly for several minutes, I managed to find the nerve to call Peyton and get things rolling. She answered on the second ring.

"Hi, it's… me. I just wanted to say thank you for taking the time to show me those houses yesterday," I said, biting my nail nervously.

"No problem. Did you want to look at any more?" she asked, a smile in her voice.

"Actually, I really liked the last one and was wondering if we could check it out again?" I replied, an idea forming in my head.

"Sure. I could call the realtor and ask if we could do it today?"

"That would be great."

I would wait for her to leave and then shoot her bastard of a fiancé. Afterward, I would meet her at the other house as quickly as possible, my alibi set. Besides, I was quite certain Tarot had plenty of enemies. His murder would look like some kind of retribution. Which, it really was.

"I was just about to take Ruby to her dance lesson. It will have to be later in the afternoon, though."

"No problem. I'll be free."

Shit.

I closed my eyes. How could I have forgotten about Ruby? She was just an innocent child, about to lose her father.

217

By my hand.

Didn't that make me just as bad as the Gold Vipers?

But again, if he raised her, what kind of person would she grow up to be?

"Okay. I'll call you back and let you know what I find out."

"Sounds good. Thanks."

My plan was changing. If there was one thing I knew, I couldn't kill Tarot in front of Ruby. It would have to be now, while he was home alone.

"No problem," I said, eyeing my purse.

We hung up and I waited for Peyton to leave with the little girl. When I saw their car pull out of the driveway, I moved mine over to the next block. Then, I shut off the engine, grabbed my purse, and quickly walked back to their house with my baseball cap pulled down. Trembling, I unzipped my purse, put my hand on the gun, and knocked on the door.

FORTY
ONE

TAROT

WHEN I OPENED the door, I was surprised to see Ava Rhodes standing on my doorstep. The moment our eyes met, I saw turmoil in hers and felt a rush of apprehension.

"Hey," I said, eyeballing her purse. She held it close, like she was afraid to let it go, with her hand inside. "What's up?"

"We need to talk. Can I come in?" she asked in a shaky voice.

I stood back, letting her in. As she stepped into the foyer, I felt an incredible urge to grab her handbag. One so strong that I couldn't ignore it.

"Hey!" she hollered, as I yanked it from her and slammed the door shut. "Give me that back!"

I blocked her from leaving and opened up the purse. Inside, I found a revolver. I pulled it out and looked at her.

"What in the hell were you planning on doing with this?" I snapped.

"It's for protection," she said, looking guilty as hell.

I checked the gun and noticed that it was loaded. "Why do you think you need protection from me?"

"I didn't think anything like that," she said, not looking in my eyes directly.

She lied.

"Sit down," I ordered, nodding to the sofa.

Ava didn't move.

"Sit *down!*" I snapped.

She flinched and then quickly did what I asked.

I pulled out her wallet and looked at her license. Her name was definitely Ava Rhodes and she lived in Miami, Florida. What I didn't understand was why she was in my house with a loaded gun. I'd never met the woman before Hollywood had introduced us.

"You just called Peyton about looking at a house. I

overheard her tell you that she was leaving to take Ruby to her dance class. So, you are obviously here to see me," I deduced out loud, trying to figure out what the hell was going on.

She didn't say anything.

I sighed. "This has something to do with Blade, doesn't it?"

Her eyes gave away that it did. "Blade?" she repeated, as if it was the first time she'd heard the name.

I began pacing back and forth in front of the sofa. "Yes. You're here because of him." I stopped. "Why?"

She bit her lower lip but remained quiet.

"Who is he to you?"

Her eyes filled with tears and she looked away.

"Ava, believe it or not, I *want* to help you," I said, not seeing a killer, but a broken woman on my sofa. "Tell me, why are you here?"

Ava looked up at me again. "You killed him," she said hoarsely. Tears began to stream down her cheeks as she screamed at me, "He was my brother! The only blood relative who meant something to me... and you fucking killed him!"

I was stunned. I certainly hadn't seen that coming. I'd thought that maybe the two had been dating or married, and that she was a grieving widow.

"He didn't have a sister," I replied.

"Yes, he did. Andrew Bordellini was my brother, you asshole. My half-brother."

Still, my gut told me I was right. The man named Blade had no family. Nobody alive, at least.

"That man wasn't your brother," I said firmly.

Ava stood up. "He was. We had the same mother," she said, tears continuing to stream down her cheeks. "A bad one at that. But we were blood-related."

More information started coming at me out of nowhere.

221

"Your mother just died," I said, staring off ahead as visions flashed before my eyes. I could almost picture the woman. "She… had an addiction. But, she's free of it now."

Ava stared at me, her mouth open.

I looked at her again and smiled grimly. "I don't know if Hollywood told you, but I'm psychic. I get these… visions. Recently, it's been more than that. It's like the dead are trying to send me messages."

She looked at me like I was crazy.

"Your mother… she's with us right now," I said, sensing her presence in the room. Images began flipping through my brain, like an album of memories. I could see her mother doing drugs and drinking to the point of passing out. This was followed by a deep sadness that washed over me. "She's sorry for what she put you through."

"What?"

"She was weak. She felt so ashamed," I said, as more images were shown to me. I saw Ava as a child, frightened and scared. Someone… a man… put his hands on her and forced her to…

Angry at what I knew had taken place, I shook my head to clear my mind of the sick images. It was horrible, but it also gave me an insight on the woman who'd come to shoot me.

"Ava," I said softly. "You weren't ever going to shoot me."

She swiped at her tears but didn't say anything.

"Andrew is dead," I said as another spirit called my attention. "But, I didn't kill him. In fact, the man named Blade wasn't your brother. He was actually… his murderer."

FORTY TWO

AVA

I DIDN'T WANT to believe him, but there was something about the look in his eyes that made me wonder if there was any truth to what he was saying.

"What do you mean? Are you saying that Blade wasn't Andrew?" I asked, my heart pounding wildly.

He nodded.

"But, they identified him. I read the newspaper article. Plus, they looked alike." At least, as far as I could remember. It had been many years since I'd seen Andrew.

"Blade stole Andrew's identity after he killed him," Tarot said.

"Wouldn't they know by his fingerprints who he was?"

"If your brother was never arrested, then they wouldn't have any to match them with. Blade must have known this."

I slumped down to the couch, feeling almost defeated. I just didn't know what to believe. "But, then Blade must have never been arrested, either."

"Or, he could have filed away his fingerprints somehow," Tarot replied. "I've known guys to do that."

"Why should I believe you?"

"Because I'm the one with the gun right now. Why would I spin all of these lies and then let you go if I was the evil guy you thought I was?"

I swallowed the lump in my throat. "You're going to let me go?"

"Yeah. You need to find out what happened to your brother, because Blade wasn't him."

"How am I supposed to do that?"

Tarot was silent for a several seconds and then his eyes lit up. "I have a friend who might be able to help."

"Why do you want to help me after I came here to destroy you?"

"Because, you're confused and hurting, Ava," he replied with a sad smile. "And, it's gone on long enough."

FORTY
THREE

HOLLYWOOD

TAROT CALLED ME when I was in the middle of an ink job. He left me a message but, unfortunately, I didn't get it until a couple of hours later.

"Your girl, Ava, paid me a visit today. We're getting things sorted out, but she needs you, brother. Call me as soon as you can."

I quickly dialed his number and apologized for not getting back to him sooner.

"It's fine. She's already taken off, though."

"Where'd she go and why in the hell did she pay *you* a visit?" So much for the nail and hair appointment. Obviously, another fucking lie.

He explained what had taken place, shocking the hell out of me.

"So, she came all this way to kill you?" I growled angrily.

"Yeah, you too, and anyone else associated with Blade's death, I recon."

I swore. I still couldn't believe she'd played me like that. I felt betrayed and hurt.

"Why did you let her go?" I asked. "How do you know she's not going to try killing you or one of us again? Hell, she might even go after Peyton."

He told me how he'd explained to her that her brother wasn't Blade, and that he'd somehow taken Andrew's identity.

"Did she believe you?"

"I think so. She was pretty shaken up when she left here."

I grunted. "I bet. So, what now?"

"I called Tank and he's going to see if the Judge can help us figure out who this Blade guy really was. Or, what may have happened to the real Andrew Bordellini. I promised her I'd help with that."

This news stunned me more than anything else he'd told me. "Why are you doing this for her?" I replied. "She tried killing you today."

"She even didn't get the chance to try. Besides, her brother was murdered. The only guy she ever trusted and... it tore her apart," he said in a grim voice. "Someone needs to help put her back together again, if it's at all possible." He sighed. "I know you have feelings for her."

"I did." I laughed coldly. "Not anymore." I was too angry at the moment to feel sorry for Ava. She'd lied to me the entire time. Even last night. Obviously, she'd been using me all along and probably would have shot me dead if Tarot wouldn't have set her straight.

Feelings?

Yeah, mine consisted of boiling rage at the moment.

"She came out here to find justice for her brother," Tarot said. "You have to almost admire the courage it took to try and pull it off. A little thing like that, trying to avenge her brother, who she obviously loved. I'd have done same damn thing. We all would."

"Sorry, but I don't admire the way she played me," I ground out bitterly. "And if it's all the same to you, I'd like to stay out of what you're trying to do for her. I know I'm just a prospect and expected to follow orders, but this is not something I want to be a part of."

He sighed. "I understand."

We said a few more words to each other and then hung up. As far as I was concerned, I was completely done with Ava, or whatever the hell her name was. If Tarot wanted to help her out, that was on him. I wanted only to forget her and move on with my life.

FORTY
FOUR

AVA

I WAS STILL there when Peyton and Ruby returned. Peyton had been surprised, but not Ruby. Apparently, she had the same psychic gift as her father. Not only did she know why I was there, but she wanted me to know about the bad man who'd tried hurting them.

"Honey, you don't have to talk about it," Tarot said gently.

"It's okay. She's sad and thinks it's because of you." Ruby looked at me. "That man was bad. He wasn't who you thought he was either." She looked at Tarot. "Right, Daddy?"

He nodded.

She turned back to me with her big, innocent blue eyes. "Your brother liked little kids, but Blade hated them. He hated everyone." As she went on as we all stared at her in astonishment. "Your brother used to take you to the park and play hide-and-seek with you," she said with a smile. "Just like my daddy."

She then went on to tell me how she'd been living with her mean aunt and how her father had rescued her the year before. The love in her eyes had almost brought me to tears again while I listened to the story. Thankfully, I'd pulled myself together and had found the courage to leave when they invited me to have lunch. I knew there was no way I could share a meal with them, knowing why I'd come in the first place.

Before I left, Tarot told me that he was going to talk to a friend of his, to see if they could find out what really happened to my brother.

"I don't know what to say," I said when he walked me to the door and handed me back my gun. "You've been so nice. I doubt very many people would forgive me the way you have."

"I'm not like others," he replied. "I *see* things differently. *People,* differently. You're someone who wants justice. Not a

229

cold-blooded killer. That's why I don't think you would have even pulled the trigger. It could have been your downfall."

"I'd like to think I could if my life is in danger."

He nodded. "You would. You might not be a murderer, but you're brave."

We walked outside.

"Where did you park?" he asked, looking around.

I told him.

"Need a ride?"

"No, I'm fine." I sighed. "Does Jayce know yet?"

"No. I left him a message to call me."

"He's going to hate me when he finds out," I replied, imagining how angry he was going to be. He had every right, too.

"He'll get over it," Tarot replied. "Something tells me it will take a little while, though. He's a stubborn guy at times."

My heart felt heavy. Now that I knew he was innocent and not involved in Andrew's death, I longed to be near him. But something told me Jayce wasn't going to be as forgiving as Tarot.

I held out my hand. "Let me know what you find out and… thanks again."

He shook my hand. "I will. Hopefully we can put this thing to rest for you."

I couldn't have agreed more.

I WALKED BACK to my car and got in. Curiously, I felt as if a big weight had been lifted from my shoulders. Apparently not committing murder will do that to you.

I started the engine and was driving away when I received a call from Millie's sister, Clara. We didn't talk much, so I knew something was wrong.

"What's going on?" I asked after answering.

"Ava, Millie's had a heart attack," she whimpered, tears

in her voice. "Please, come home."

FORTY FIVE

HOLLYWOOD

I DIDN'T HEAR from Ava. Not even about the flowers. I tried to pretend that it didn't bother me, but it did.

I hooked up with Tarot that night, meeting him at *Wild River Saloon* to discuss what had happened. He was already on his second beer when I showed up.

"I ordered you one already," he said, when I sat down next to him at the bar. "*Dos Equis.* Your favorite."

"Thanks." I took a swig, and it went down damn good. Too good. The truth was, I felt like getting wasted, but knew it would lead to some drunken calls or texts, and my pride was insisting that I calm the fuck down. Ava wasn't worth it.

"Have you talked to her?" he asked me.

I looked up at the television where the Twins were playing baseball. "I told you I was done with her."

He ignored the comment. "Did she try calling you?"

I grunted. "No."

"Did you try calling her?"

I looked at him. "Fuck no. If she wants to talk, she can take the initiative. I'm not chasing after her. Especially after the shit she pulled."

"You're being too hard on the woman," he said.

"You might forgive her, but... I just can't. Not right now at least." I looked at him for a reaction.

He didn't say anything.

"You have no idea how many times she lied to me. She played me like a fool," I said, looking back up at the television. "I don't think she told me anything that was true."

"Did she tell you about her foster home?"

I sighed. "Yeah."

"The abuse?"

I shrugged. "So, you're saying that part is true?"

"I think so. That kind of stuff can really mess you up," he replied.

"Maybe, but it doesn't justify all of the lies. Not to

233

mention that when I had my tongue down her throat, she was giving as much as she was taking," I said, feeling disgusted. "Obviously, it was all part of the act. All lies from the very beginning."

"Maybe, but I think something changed along the way for her. I know she was worried about you being mad at her."

I raised my beer to my lips and took another drink. "Not worried enough to call me, though. She probably just said that to make herself look less heartless."

He sighed.

"Did you talk to Tank yet?" I asked, changing the subject.

"Yeah. He's got the Judge looking into Andrew Bordellini."

From what I'd learned, the Judge was an ex-hitman who could find intel on almost anyone or anything. Very few knew about him, and those of us who did, had never actually met the guy in person. Except for Tank.

Tarot told me that Ava's brother had contacted him from the other side. Listening to him describe what had happened gave me the chills.

"Her mother made contact, too," he said, after taking another sip of beer.

"So you're seeing dead people now?" I asked with a wry smile.

"Not so much seeing them in front of me, but in my head."

"That's creepy."

He shrugged. "Not to me. I imagine that these spirits are looking out for her, though. I could have killed her had I not known what was going on."

"She's lucky."

"*I'm* lucky I grabbed her purse before she had a chance to pull the gun on me." He emptied his beer and pushed it toward the edge of the bar. The bartender, a blonde named

Alice, spotted the move and hurried over.

"You want another one?" she asked with a flirty smile.

"Yeah. Can you put in an order of nachos for me, too?" he asked.

She popped open a beer and slid it over. "Of course. What about you, handsome?" Alice asked, looking at me.

"I'll take an order of those Jamaican wings," I said. "Extra spicy."

"You sure? Those things make grown men cry the way they are," she replied with an amused grin.

Tarot shook his head. "He's looking to torture himself tonight." He smiled at me. "Pain is good, right?"

"In this case, yeah," I replied.

"You're going to need some milk," Alice said.

"Just keep the beers coming," I replied, raising the bottle to my lips. The more Dom talked about Ava, the more I wanted to drink.

She looked at Dom. "I think someone is going to need a ride later."

Tarot nodded toward a couple of chicks sitting across the bar. They were staring over at us and smiling. "Something tells me he won't have any problems finding one either."

"Not interested," I murmured. They were both attractive, but I wasn't in the mood to flirt after what had happened over the last few days. I wasn't in the mood to talk to any fucking woman unless she was serving me beer or food.

"Let's see how you feel in a couple of hours. You want to play some darts?" Tarot asked, standing up.

"Sure. I'll take another beer, too, please," I said.

"Yeah." Alice walked over to the cooler and grabbed a new one for me. "I'll put the orders in for your apps," she said, opening it. "And don't worry, Hollywood. If you need a ride later, I get off at eleven. I'll take you home."

She'd given me a ride before, but in the back of her car.

Something told me that if I kept drinking, we might end up there again. Especially after my dry spell and the fact that I was still angrier than hell at Ava. A few more beers and I'd be doing her just to get rid of my frustrations. I knew that would be a real fucking dick move, though. Literally.

"I'll be fine. I'm not staying too late," I said before following Tarot to the dart machines.

"You change your mind, let me know," she called out.

I turned around and smiled. "Of course. You'd be the first to know."

Alice grinned.

"You'd better stop flirting with her," Tarot said when I reached him. "She likes you too much."

"I wasn't flirting."

"Oh, right. *'You'd be the first to know'*," Tarot repeated in a high voice. "If I recall, you two left together another night."

"Yeah."

"I'd advise against hooking up with her again. You'll only hurt her in the long run."

"Alice?"

"Yeah. Like I said, she is into you."

"Don't worry. I'm not going home with her... or anyone," I mumbled.

Tarot dropped some coins into the dart machine and it came to life. "Just do me a favor, will you?"

"What?"

"Don't let your pride and stubbornness interfere with the heart."

"The heart?" I snorted. "I don't love Ava."

"You feel something. Don't lie."

"Tarot, right now I'd rather not talk about her or my 'feelings'," I said bitterly. "So, don't go all *Dr. Phil* on me."

"Just trying to help, brother."

"I know. I don't need it, though. I'm fine."

236

"Whatever you say."

Love.

Been there. Done that. Was bitten in the ass by it.

Kind of like now…

Was this love?

I refused to think about it. I needed to get my mind on something else. I needed a shot.

I pulled out my wallet and told Tarot that I was getting one. "You want one, too? It's on me."

"I'll take whatever you're having and it's on me, brother. After all, I own the place."

I grinned. "I won't argue with that. How about we order a few then?"

"You get what you want. Just get me one. I told Peyton I'd be home and sober by midnight."

"I guess that's another reason to be grateful that I'm single. I'm not pussy-whipped."

He smirked. "Man, when the pussy is worth showing up for sober, you won't mind at all. I guarantee it."

TWO HOURS LATER, I was still at the bar with him, drunk and doing exactly what I said I didn't want to do — ramble on about Ava.

"I thought you didn't want to talk about her," he said with a smirk.

Ignoring his comment, I kept talking. "Do you know how much time and effort I spent creating the perfect dragon? And let me tell you, it was fucking perfect. You should have seen it. I never even collected the money on it either. I should call her up right now and tell her she owes me for the damn dragon tattoo."

"You mentioned that earlier," he said, smiling in amusement. "I suppose you're going to tell me again how perfect her ass is, too, huh?"

237

"Yesss! Hottest fucking assss," I slurred. "Just like those babes in the James Bond movies, where the hot chicks are always the devious ones."

"So, you're like James Bond and Ava's your evil nemesis."

"Exactly," I replied. "Dammit, I should have at least gotten laid. James always nailed the enemy. What did I get? Lies and a couple of kisses…"

He laughed. "I think we need to get you home. Alice? You still interested in driving Hollywood to his place?"

"Of course," she called out from the other end of the bar. "I'm off in fifteen minutes!"

"Nooo…" I whispered loudly. "She can't drive me home. I'm in a bad place right now. I'll probably… I'll probably fuck her. I… I can't do that to Ava."

"Brother, you're not *with* Ava. You're through with her, right?" he reminded me, looking amused.

"I'm going to take an Uber," I said proudly, grabbing my cell phone. "It's safer. Could we roll my bike into the back room so nobody fucks with it?"

"Of course. Why don't I just drive you home," he said. "I've been nursing this beer for the last hour. I'm about as sober as you are drunk."

"I'm not drunk. Just feeling good. And, thanks." I put my phone away. "I'm ready whenever you are."

He stood up. "We're out of here. Alice, I'm taking Hollywood home."

She gave us a pouty look.

"Sorry, darlin'," I said, getting up off the stool and stumbling slightly. "I need some fresh air and a bike ride should do the trick."

"Just don't fall off the back," she said, looking amused. "And wreck that handsome face of yours."

"Thanks, Alice. Don't worry about me. I'm not even

drunk," I replied with a lopsided grin.

She laughed. "No. Not at all."

FIFTEEN MINUTES LATER, we were heading toward my apartment. When we stopped for a red light, I asked Tarot if he could make a pit-stop.

"Where?"

"Ava's motel. I want to talk to her."

He groaned. "No way, you are too fucking hammered. And don't start texting her and shit when you get home. Wait until you're sober and your head is clear."

"I'm not drunk!" I protested.

"Listen to me, I forbid you to contact her in this condition. It won't help the situation. It never does."

I sighed. "Fine. Can we at least stop at Taco Bell then?"

Tarot nodded. "Now that, I can do."

We went through the drive-through and we both ordered a shitload of food.

"You want to eat at my place?" I asked, after we paid.

"No. I've gotta get home. Besides, some of that food is for Peyton."

"Okay. Thanks for the ride, by the way."

"No problem, brother."

After Tarot dropped me off at home, I sat down at my kitchen table and began eating. After the second burrito, I pulled out my phone and almost texted Ava, but stopped myself.

Tarot was right. I shouldn't even be texting her. I would talk to her tomorrow, however. I needed Ava to look me in the eye and tell me the truth for once. I deserved that, at least.

FORTY SIX

AVA

I NSTEAD OF DRIVING, I took a plane home to be with Millie. When I finally arrived at the hospital to see her, I felt like a total wreck.

"Look who's here," Clara said when I walked into her hospital room. "It's Ava, Mill."

"Oh, honey," Millie said as I approached her bed. "You didn't have to rush back home. I'm fine."

Thankfully, she just looked tired and pale. I'd imagined her to be in much worse condition, with tubes and wires attached everywhere.

"What happened?" I asked, taking her hand.

She explained that she'd had a mild heart attack and that they'd injected a clot-dissolving agent to restore blood flow in one of her arteries.

"So, you're going to be okay?" I asked, furrowing my brow.

Millie smiled. "Yes. I'll need to make a few lifestyle changes I'm sure, but I should be just fine."

I sighed in relief.

"I wish you wouldn't have raced back home so quickly. I hope you aren't going to get into trouble with director or the movie producers," Millie said.

"Don't worry about me," I said, sitting down next to her. "You're more important to me than what was happening out there in Minnesota."

I felt that more than ever. I'd been so busy trying to find out what the hell had happened to Andrew that I'd taken for granted the most important person in my life. Not that I could have known she was going to end up in the hospital, but I'd neglected her in the last couple of days, just by not checking up on her. I felt guilty just thinking about it.

"What were you doing out in Minnesota?" Clara asked, looking intrigued.

Wasting time, I thought.

241

"You know… same-old-same-old. Working," I lied.

"Do you ever get to do any acting? Or is it all just stunts?" Clara asked.

I pulled some stunts and acted my ass off, I wanted to say. "Not very often."

"You live such and exciting life," Clara said. "It must be so thrilling, being around celebrities and doing those action scenes."

"She's quite the daredevil," Millie said, smiling at me proudly.

"I imagine. Did you do a lot of dangerous things out in Minnesota?" Clara asked, intrigued.

If they only knew…

FORTY SEVEN

SEVEN

HOLLYWOOD

I WOKE UP with one hell of a headache. After cursing myself out for drinking too much, I took some aspirin, heated up some of the leftover Taco Bell, and then found a ride back to the *Wild River Saloon*.

After retrieving my bike, I headed to the motel where Ava had been staying, unable to stay away any longer. When I arrived, I noticed her car was missing from the parking lot. Sharpy was back, however. He was by himself and sitting in an old, souped-up Chevelle. Noticing me, his face fell.

"Hey, Hollywood," he said, after I parked next to his car and shut off my motor.

"Hey. What's going on?"

"Just waiting for John," he said, nodding toward the motel. "What are you doing here?"

"I was just driving by and figured I'd see what you were doing."

He looked over toward the motel. "I figured since your girl was gone, it was probably something like that."

"Gone?"

"Yeah." He turned back to look at me, a surprised look on his face. "She checked out yesterday, from what I heard. She dog you, man?"

"No. I knew she left," I lied, not wanting to look ignorant or weak. I changed the subject. "Anyway, aren't you supposed to be staying out of this neighborhood?"

"Just waiting for John," he muttered.

"I thought John was supposed to leave the other night," I replied.

"It changed. He's leaving now, though. Seriously," Sharpy replied and then pointed. "See? He's got his shit."

I looked over at the building and saw his buddy carrying a suitcase. My eyes moved to Ava's empty motel room, anger burning a hole in my stomach.

So, that's how it was going to be...

No goodbyes.

No apologies.

Just a "Fuck you I'm out of here," apparently.

Feeling once again like a damn fool, I started my bike and drove to the clubhouse. Devon was there, as usual. When she noticed my dark mood, she asked me about it in that thoughtful, gentle way of hers.

"What's crawled up your ass today?"

"Nothing," I replied.

"It doesn't have anything to do with *Dragon Lady*, does it?"

"Why do you ask?"

"Brass told me what was going on." She gave me a sympathetic look. I'm sorry she played you like that. What a bitch."

I shrugged. "Shit happens. I'm over it already."

She gave me a knowing smile. "You ever need someone to talk to, a woman, I'm always here."

"Thanks," I replied. "Like I said, though, I'm good."

She nodded. "You working today?"

Devon pretty much let me work whenever I wanted, which I appreciated.

"Yeah, I was thinking of taking some customers," I replied, wanting to keep my mind on something else.

"Sounds good."

Fortunately, we were busier than usual with walk-ins, and I ended up doing four tattoos, all relatively small, but enjoyable to work on. Especially, since they brought me what I needed—a distraction.

As I was finishing the last one, Brass and Tarot walked into the parlor.

"Come and find me when you have a minute," Tarot said, as they walked by.

"Okay," I replied.

"SO, WHAT'S UP?" I asked him after my client left.

"Tank got back to me," he replied. We were in his office, sitting across from each other. "He had some news about Andrew Bordellini. Apparently, he was affiliated with a club in Florida."

He went on to tell me that Andrew had gone missing from the club a couple years back. The president swore that Andrew, who they called Pac Man, wouldn't have *ever* deserted the club, so they knew something had been up."

"Did they know about Blade being IDed as Andrew Bordellini?" I asked.

"They hadn't even heard about Blade's death," he replied.

"Maybe because the real Andrew went by Pac Man?" I said.

"That's probably part of it. Anyway, they thought it had been odd as fuck that Pac Man had disappeared in the first place. From what it sounds like, he'd been a faithful member up until that point."

"Huh," I said, scratching my chin.

He went on. "The good news is that Andrew's old man is supposed to be living in Florida. I was thinking of taking a road trip down there next week to try and see if he'll show me any pictures of the real Andrew Bordellini. You know, for curiosity's sake. "

"Good idea."

He made a steeple with his fingers. "You want to join me?"

A road trip sounded good, especially to warm, sunny Florida. Plus, I had to admit, this entire mystery was intriguing. "Sure."

"Good. Let's plan on leaving a week from tomorrow.

Hopefully, we'll be able to clear some of this shit up for Ava. Speaking of which, you didn't drunk-text her last night did you? Or call?"

"No," I said. "I'm sure she wouldn't have responded anyway. She left town."

He looked surprised. "You drove by her motel?"

"Yeah."

Tarot leaned back in his chair. "Don't feel too badly about it. I'm sure it has nothing to do with you."

I didn't doubt that. As far as I was concerned, Ava didn't give two shits about me. It was obvious after the way she'd been treating me.

"I'll call her and see if she can give me Andrew's old man's address or phone number. I imagine she might have it."

"Sure," I said without much feeling. As much as I wanted to know who Blade really was, I was beginning to get really tired of hearing about Andrew and Ava.

He reached for his phone and put his feet up on the desk. "Are you sure you don't want to be the one to call Ava for the information?"

"I'd rather not," I said, staring at him.

He nodded and made the call.

"Ava? Hey… this is Tarot. I have some news for you."

He paused and then told her the same thing he'd explained to me.

"I was wondering if you could put me in touch with your brother's old man? I'd like to see if he has some recent pictures of Andrew. Even if we can't find out who this Blade character is, I'd like to see what your brother actually looked like."

She answered him and Tarot frowned. "You're kidding? When did he die?" He paused. "That's too bad. Does he have any other family?"

He waited as she spoke and nodded. "Okay. I'd appreciate it. We're leaving next Monday. No, we're taking our bikes," he answered.

They said a few more words to each other and then both hung up.

"She said she's going to get a key for his old man's place. She doesn't think Dwayne had any up-to-date photos, but it's worth a shot."

"Okay."

"I'm going to try and set up a meeting with Andrew's old club president, too. They might be able to help us out, too. You never know."

"Okay."

Tarot studied my face. "Do you want to know if she asked about you?"

"Do you want to know if I care?" I snapped. From where I'd been sitting, there hadn't been any mention of me.

He threw his head back and laughed. "Your response alone gives away how much you fucking care. No, she didn't ask about you. But, I think she was too scared to. That's what I got out of it."

I shrugged. "Whatever."

He looked at the clock in his office. "I'm supposed to meet Peyton and Ruby at her recital soon, so I've got to haul ass. I'll let you know if I find out any more information. In the meantime, plan on meeting me at my house next Monday at nine a.m."

I stood up. "Sounds good."

FORTY EIGHT

AVA

I'D WANTED TO ask Tarot about Jayce, but the words wouldn't leave my lips. I figured if he'd wanted to stay in touch, he would have called me by now anyway. Obviously, he had nothing more to say.

With Jayce still on my mind, I called Dwayne's Aunt Bea, who was happy to hear from me. I made arrangements to get the key for his place and promised to get started on getting it ready to sell.

"Thank you again," she said, before we hung up. "It's just too much work for me. If you'd like to hire cleaners, feel free. I'll pay for it, of course."

"I might take you up on the offer, depending on what needs to be done," I replied.

"I would still prefer to split the proceeds on the sale with you," she said.

"We can talk about it later." I didn't need the money and felt weird about taking it. If she wanted to pay me for my time, however, I was open to that.

"Okay."

After our conversation, I took a drive to my mother's trailer and began the task of cleaning and preparing it for donation. Fortunately, she didn't have any liens on the place and the mortgage had been paid off in full years ago.

As I was boxing things up, I found another letter from Andrew in the nightstand next to her bed. Unlike the others, this one from him had a lot to say. It was dated back three years ago.

Dear Mother,

I'm enclosing more cash to help you with bills and things. Please don't use it for drugs. I worked hard for the money and would be pissed as hell if I found out you did.

By the way, I hope you were able to locate Ava. I feel like an asshole about what happened to her. I keep thinking that maybe I could have rescued her from the system and tried taking care of her myself. Too bad I'd been such an immature punk at the time. If you talk to her, let her know I want to get together. Tell her I love her and feel like shit about what happened. She was a great kid. I hope she can learn to forgive us both one day.

I'm enclosing my address and phone number, in case you want to get ahold of me. I have some good news, in fact. I think you'll want to hear what it is.

Anyway, I'm renting from this guy, Blade. I met him at a bike rally after a couple of chicks got us mixed up. Apparently, they thought we looked alike and introduced us. We hit it off right away and now I'm staying at his townhome for dirt-cheap. Talk about luck. Anyway, call me. I worry about you.

Love always,

Andy

I re-read the letter and then called Tarot back. When he answered, I told him about it.

"What's the address?" he asked.

I told him. My heart was pounding a mile a minute and my hands were shaking.

What if he was still alive?"

"It's been a year since the incident with Blade. I wonder if the place is empty, or if someone else is living there?" he replied.

"I'm going out there," I replied, excited. "I'll let you know. Who knows, maybe Andrew is still alive?"

"For your sake, I hope he is," Tarot said sadly.

I touched the necklace around my neck. The lucky one. "I'm not giving up hope."

"I don't blame you. In your position, I wouldn't either." He paused. "I wish I could meet you there. Dammit, I'm curious as all hell now. When are you leaving?"

"Tomorrow morning."

"Okay. What's your address? In case I fly out there. We can drive together."

I hesitated.

"You still don't trust me," he stated.

"No offense, but it's hard for me to trust anyone, if you want to know the truth."

"I get it."

After thinking about it some more, I gave in and told him my address. Tarot had every reason to be angry with me and was instead treating me like a friend. I'd been wrong about him. The more I thought about it, the more respect I had for his club, too. I could see why Jayce had been proud to be a part of the Gold Vipers, even if some of their ways weren't on the up-and-up.

"At least you know for certain that your brother was a good guy," Tarot said to me.

"I always knew he was," I said sadly. "I'm just glad you set me straight about everything else. I'm so sorry for what I did to you, your family, and everyone else."

"I forgive you, Ava," he replied. "And I want you to know that you can trust me with anything. I mean it."

"I know. The same goes here. I don't feel as if I deserve your trust, but I swear that I'll never lie to you again. Or… to Jayce."

"You need to tell him that yourself."

"I know," I replied, softly. "I just need to find the courage to do it."

"*You*? You're one of the most courageous young women I've ever met. Seriously."

I smiled. "That means a lot coming from a hard-assed

biker like yourself."

"Well, I appreciate that. Oh, I've gotta go. Peyton is calling me. I'll keep in touch."

"Sounds good."

I hung up, did some more packing, and then headed back to my place. As soon as I arrived home, I called Millie, who was staying a couple more days in the hospital, and we spoke for a few minutes.

"I'll give you a ride home when they're ready to release you," I promised her. "Just let me know when you can check out."

"Thank you, honey. I'll keep in touch."

I hung up and took out Andrew's letter again. I searched the Tampa Bay address on Google Maps and zoomed in on it. It was a newer-looking townhome and in a decent neighborhood, from what I could tell.

I logged out of the Internet and was about to put my phone away, when I thought about calling Jayce. The thought of him rejecting my apology terrified me, though.

"You already lost him," I told myself, staring at my phone. "Let it rest."

Sighing, I plugged it into the charger instead. I'd lied to him too many times and probably didn't deserve his forgiveness anyway.

FORTY NINE

HOLLYWOOD

TAROT CALLED AND told me about the conversation he'd had with Ava.

"So, her brother was actually living with Blade?" I replied, stunned. "Wow."

"Looks that way. I called Tank and we did some more digging, or rather the Judge did. Anyway, the townhouse belongs to a man name Felix Doberly."

"Blade?"

"I'm thinking so."

"So now what?"

"I want you to jump on a plane and accompany Ava to the townhouse."

I clenched my jaw.

"You still there?"

"Why me?" I said, trying to keep the anger out of my voice. "Can't you ask another prospect?"

"She trusts you," he replied. "And I want someone with her just in case."

"In case of what? Blade's dead."

"I know, but she might need help getting into the house. Besides, what if her brother's there? Dead?"

"Why doesn't she just call the police and find out?"

"Because we're doing it *my* way," Tarot said in a stern voice. "Now, I know you're pissed off at the girl, but you have to put that aside right now and get your ass out to Miami."

"Okay." I didn't want to piss him off any further. I'd worked too hard to not get patched. Disobeying a direct order would definitely get me booted from the club.

"I'm buying you the ticket," Tarot said. "And renting you a car."

"How about a bike?"

"Fine. I'll rent you a bike. Ten or twelve-speed?"

"Very funny," I replied.

255

He chuckled. "I'm going to check around for flights. I'll call you back."

"Okay."

TAROT GOT BACK to me twenty minutes later.

"I booked a flight for you on Delta. It leaves in two hours. You'd better pack a bag and get your ass to the airport."

I sighed. "Okay. Does she know I'm coming out there?"

"I thought it might be better to surprise her. A little friendly payback, you know?" he said, a smile in his voice. "Since she's the queen of surprises."

I smirked. "You have her address?"

"Yep. Grab a pen and paper."

He gave it to me.

"You sure this isn't all bullshit?"

"No way. She's the one who called me about this to begin with."

"Okay. You rent me a motorcycle?"

"Good try. I rented you a cage. I figure that way the two of you can talk while you're driving out to Tampa."

"Thanks," I groaned.

"My pleasure," Tarot said with a smile in his voice.

FIFTY

AVA

I SPENT THE next few hours obsessing over what I might find in Tampa Bay. I was even tempted to call the police, just in case my brother was buried in Blade's backyard. Considering my last conversation with law enforcement, however, I decided that they wouldn't be much help, which was frustrating.

In the end, I got tired of waiting around. I needed answers and sleep was eluding me. I took a shower, packed an overnight bag, and jumped into my Navigator. Almost forgetting to call Tarot, I sent him a text telling him that I couldn't wait any longer. He called me back immediately.

"Hold up, you're going out there now?"

"Yeah. I'm sorry. I just can't wait. I need to know if he's there," I replied.

"So, you're going by yourself?" he said.

"Yes."

"Have you left your place yet?"

"I'm about to, why?"

He swore. "I was hoping that this would be a surprise, but obviously that's not going to happen."

"What are you talking about?"

A loud knock on my side window startled the hell out of me. When I saw who was trying to get my attention, I almost peed my pants.

Jayce.

"Jayce is here," I said, rolling down my window.

"I know. Talk to him," Tarot replied.

I hung up with Tarot, my heart beating wildly in my chest. So many emotions rushed through me at once. I felt like jumping out of the SUV and throwing my arms around him, but the ornery look on his face held me back.

"Hi," I said, feeling a little self-conscious. All of the times he'd seen me, I'd been wearing makeup and had done something with my hair. At the moment, I wore a ponytail, a

258

baggy T-shirt, and running shorts.

"Where you off to?" he asked in a pissed off tone.

"Tampa Bay. What are you doing here?"

"Tarot wanted me to drive out there with you. He said you weren't leaving until tomorrow though."

"That had been the original plan, but I changed my mind. I need to know what happened to my brother, you know?"

"Why don't you move over? I'll drive."

"It's my SUV. Why don't *you* get in on the passenger side?" I replied, narrowing my eyes at him. This was definitely not going to be a friendly visit. Jayce had obviously been forced to help me, and it was very evident that it was the last thing he wanted.

"Fine," he mumbled and turned on his heel. I watched as he walked around my truck and got in next to me.

I frowned. "You don't have to come with me, you know. I can tell Tarot that you did and he won't be any wiser."

"Lying doesn't solve anything. Apparently, you haven't figured that out yet," he said coldly.

I growled between my teeth in frustration. "Look, I'm sorry I lied to you, okay? I thought I was going after the men who'd killed my brother. I had no idea that Blade wasn't Andrew."

"You used me to get information. We spent hours together and I was honest with you the entire time, but everything that came out of your lips was a lie," he said angrily. "And then after the party… when you *had* the chance to come clean, you still didn't."

"I still thought you were the enemy at that point!" I replied loudly. "And if your club had done what I thought they'd done, admitting the truth would have gotten me into some serious trouble. Hell, it probably would have gotten me killed."

"We don't go around killing innocent women," he

259

snapped.

"But I didn't know that. I thought you all were murdering assholes. And don't go acting like you guys are angels, anyway. Your club's history is surrounded by death."

"Oh, yeah? Where in the hell are you getting all of this information?"

"From the Internet." I folded my arms over my chest defiantly.

He laughed coldly. "Well, then it *must* be true."

Screw this. I didn't need him. I certainly didn't have to put up with his bullshit. "Look, this is obviously not going to work. Get out."

"I've got a job to do and I'm going to finish it."

"I'm *not* a job!"

He grunted. "Ironically, lady, you really are a definite piece of work. Now, I'm going out to Tampa Bay whether you like it or not. If you don't want me to drive with you, then I'll meet you at the address you gave Tarot."

I put both hands on the wheel and gripped it tightly, refusing to look at him. "Fine."

"Fine what?"

"I'll meet you there," I said coldly.

He let out an exasperated sigh and got out.

FIFTY ONE

HOLLYWOOD

I WAS SO pissed off at Ava that I could barely see straight. I went back to the rental car and got in. As I started the engine, I watched as Ava tore out of the parking lot with attitude. Admittedly, it was a little amusing seeing a chick burn rubber like that.

I shifted the car into drive, turned on some music, and soon caught up to her. I half expected her to try losing me, but she didn't.

The ride to Tampa took just over two hours. Eventually, my temper cooled, so by the time we faced each other again, both of us were calmer.

"So, that must be it," I said after we parked our vehicles across the street from the townhouse and I stood outside of her window again.

"Yeah. I wonder if anyone is staying there?"

Although the place was dark, the yard looked like it had been kept up.

"Someone's obviously been cutting the grass," I noted.

"Yeah."

I rubbed my eye wearily. After driving for the last two hours, and flying earlier, I was beat. "Obviously, it's too late to go knocking on the front door."

It was just after midnight. If someone *was* living there, we'd scare the hell out of them.

"Right."

I scanned the area. There were several townhomes on the street, and at the moment, they all appeared to be quiet. "I'm going to sneak into the backyard and see if I can look into any windows," I replied, already plotting my course.

"Didn't you get hurt the last time you tried something that?" she whispered. "Tarot told me about your meeting with Blade and how you got hurt."

"That was different. He caught me by surprise."

"Someone else might catch you by surprise." She

unbuckled her seatbelt. "I'm coming with you."

"No."

"I brought my gun," she said, ignoring me. "Did you bring anything?"

"My fists."

She snorted.

"Never underestimate the power of a hard right hook," I added.

"You're bringing fists to a potential gun fight."

I sighed. "Let me have yours. I'll go and check things out myself."

"You sure love to give orders, don't you?" she said dryly.

"One of us has to stay here and be the lookout." I held up my hand. "Give me the gun. Please."

Ava frowned and then reached into her purse. She pulled out a pistol and quickly handed it to me.

"It's loaded?" I asked, glancing around as I shoved it inside of my jacket pocket.

"Yes, and the safety is on."

"Okay."

"Text me if you see something unusual. I'm going to go around the block and come up through the alley."

"Good idea."

I sprinted down the street and around the block, eventually entering the backyard from the alley. There was a small metal fence. I hopped it and crept up to the patio door, which was covered in blinds. Unable to see anything below, I looked up at the deck and made a decision to climb it. It was a pain in the ass, but once I made it up there, I was awarded with a clear view inside the kitchen from the sliding glass door. Inside was a distressed ebony dining table with matching buffet on the wall behind it.

I was about to try the slider door when a large, orange cat leaped onto the dining table, startling the hell out of me. We stared at each other for a few seconds and then it hissed at me.

Fuck.

From the looks of the cat, it wasn't missing any meals. Someone was definitely living there.

A light went on in one of the bedrooms above us. Not wanting to risk an arrest, I quickly climbed down and made my way back to the vehicles.

"What did you find?" Ava asked.

I told her.

"At least it wasn't a dog you saw. It would have barked and woke up everyone in the house."

"Yeah, well someone *did* get up, though. I saw a light turn on inside," I said, glancing back at the house. Fortunately, nobody seemed to be looking out of the windows or turning on any front porch lights.

"We'd better get out of here before someone notices us and calls the police," she replied.

"I agree. Let's meet at the gas station up the road. From there, we can decide what to do tonight."

She held out her hand. "My gun?"

"I'll give it back to you later. Let's worry about getting out of here quietly, first," I replied.

"Okay."

FIFTY TWO

AVA

J AYCE SEEMED TO be in a much better mood, which was a relief. I had a feeling that he was still angry with me, though, but at least we were on speaking terms.

When we reached the gas station, we talked about getting a room for the night and both agreed it was the best solution. We looked online and found a hotel room not too far away, with two queen beds available, and booked a reservation. It wasn't anything fancy, but both of us were too tired to care.

Thirty minutes later, we walked into the room and both of us collapsed on separate beds.

"Not bad. Better than that shithole you were staying at in Jensen, huh?" he asked, stretching his legs out and looking over at me.

"Very much so." I kicked off my tennis shoes. "This place is actually... clean."

"Speaking of clean, I could definitely use a shower," Jayce said, rolling out of bed and then removing his leather jacket and cut.

"I'm taking one right after you," I replied, watching him pull his T-shirt out from the waistband of his jeans. He raised it above his shoulders and took it off, leaving me a little breathless as I stared at his hard muscles and medieval tattoos.

"Would you like to go first?" he asked, not noticing the effect he was having on me.

I swallowed. "No. It's fine," I said, staring again at some of the artwork on his body. Although I'd caught a quick glimpse at the studio, it was nothing like seeing him without a shirt. "Sorry, I'm just in awe of your tats. They're incredible."

He looked down and ran a hand over his six-pack "Thanks. It's become an addiction. The more you have, the more you want."

"I bet."

"How's yours healing? If you want, I can take a look."

"Great. In fact, I'd still really like you to finish it for me sometime."

"Sure. If you ever make it out to St. Paul, look me up."

"I'll be around," I replied. "I can pay you for what you've already done, too. Anytime."

"We can talk about payment later."

"Sure," I replied, noticing glint in his eyes.

He turned around and began walking toward the bathroom. "I'll be out soon. Unless," he looked back at me with a grin tugging at his lips, "you're in a hurry? There's room for two in there."

His words startled and excited me at the same time. I stared at him, wondering if he was joking or serous.

"Sorry, I couldn't resist," he said, grinning. "Anyway, don't run off."

"I won't," I replied.

He disappeared into the bathroom and shut the door. Hearing the water turn on, and knowing that he was getting totally naked, made my mouth dry.

Heart pounding, I crawled out of bed and went over to the mini bar. I opened up the refrigerator and saw that there were cans of soda, water, and beer. There was also a small bottle of red wine. I grabbed the bottle, removed the cap and took a few sips until a new kind of heat began spreading through my veins. I took several more sips and then set the wine bottle down on the dresser. Taking a deep breath, I began removing my clothes. For once in my life, I was going to go after something I wanted, even if it scared the hell out of me.

FIFTY THREE

HOLLYWOOD

A FTER REMOVING THE rest of my clothing, I stepped into the shower and opened up the small bar of soap I'd found. As I began lathering up, I thought about the look on Ava's face when I asked her to join me. For a brief second, she almost looked like she was going to take me up on it. But then her eyes filled with panic.

It was such a shame.

A beautiful woman like Ava deserved a healthy and happy sex life. Obviously, it wasn't going to happen between us. I just hoped that one day soon, someone would help her overcome her fear and anxiety.

My mind went to earlier, when we'd argued before leaving for Tampa. Although, I'd been angrier than hell, I'd since had a chance to think things through. I now realized that Tarot was right. Ava had been desperate to find out what happened to Andrew, and if the roles had been reversed, I'd have probably done the same thing. I had to admit, the woman had balls.

She also had a nice fucking ass and lips that I wanted to taste again, but probably never would.

I closed my eyes and pictured her in the thong she'd worn during our inking session. All of the blood rushed to my cock as I imagined what was hiding underneath that sexy black lace. I wrapped my hand around my rod and was about to let my fantasies run wild, when I heard a noise. Startled, I opened my eyes and did a double-take.

"Uh, hi," Ava said softly, standing on the other side of the glass. She was naked except for the towel wrapped around her torso.

"What are you doing?" I asked, letting go of my erection.

She looked up at me from under her lashes. "I don't know. I just…"

My cock began to throb as I stared at the swell of her

269

breasts pushed up from the towel. I wanted to rip it off her and run my hands all over her body.

"This might have been a bad idea," she murmured, turning away.

"Wait." I opened up the shower door and held out my hand. "We don't have to do anything if you don't want to."

Ava turned back and I saw both fear and desperation in her eyes. "If I come in there, I want you to do something for me."

"Anything."

Her eyes traveled down my body. When she saw that I was rock hard, her face turned red. "Let me touch you first."

Thought of her hands on me got my body pumping hot. "Whatever you want."

She dropped the towel and I had to control myself. Soft, round breasts, a lean waist, and those tan, curvy hips I'd been fantasizing about. What made it even more erotic, was the tattoo. It was almost like I'd branded her with my art. It was sexier than all hell.

Bashfully, she walked in and I stepped out of the way. The fact that I was forbidden to touch her aroused me even more. She closed the door and then held out her hand. "The soap?"

Forgetting that I was still holding it, I handed the bar to her. She rubbed it between her hands and then began lathering herself with it. My pulse roared and every inch of my cock ached for release as I watched her hands move over her luscious curves.

"You sure you don't want help with that?" I asked, licking my lips and feeling like I was about to explode.

FIFTY FOUR

AVA

SEEING HIM STANDING in the shower, with the water dripping over his hard, muscular body, took my breath away. Then, when I glanced down at his thick, hard cock, I felt my core tighten and flutter with desire.

Damn, it was hard to breathe...

I finished lathering the soap on my body as he stared at me like a hungry wolf.

"You sure you don't want any help with that?" he asked.

I lowered the soap and began cleaning between my legs, where it was already wet and slick from being so turned on.

"You're punishing me, aren't you?" he growled, staring at my hand. "That's what this is. Fuck, I can't take it much longer, Ava."

I dropped the soap and let the water clean the remaining suds from my skin. I hadn't been trying to punish anyone. I just wanted to see if being in control could help me get over my frigidness. I'd never truly enjoyed sex and hadn't ever reached an orgasm—even by myself. But, by the way I was responding to Jayce, I felt like it could be different. Better. At that moment, my body was buzzing with so much excitement, I could barely stand.

"I want to take this slow," I murmured, moving closer to him. "Just, bear with me, okay?"

He nodded.

I pressed my hands against his chest and I felt him tighten under my fingertips. I began moving my palms over the hard ridges of his muscles and leaned up to kiss him.

Jayce's lips crashed over mine with the urgency of a starving animal finding food. His tongue plunged into my mouth and he growled in the back of his throat as our naked bodies came together. His raging hard-on pressed between us against my stomach, and I could feel it throbbing.

He tore his mouth away from mine. "Please, let me touch you..."

272

As much as I wanted to feel his hands on me, I knew it needed to be done my way. I had to be in control. "That's not what we agreed on," I said, moving my hand down his chiseled chest and tight abs. I went further, touching the soft nestle of curls just below his penis, and he released a hiss.

"Fuck, you're going to make me come and you haven't touched my cock yet."

Smiling, I cupped his balls. "Does this feel good?"

He stared down at me with a pained look on his face. "Are you trying to be cruel?"

"Sorry. Just a little longer," I said, wanting to touch him freely before he took over. I could tell by the way his body was coiled that our lovemaking was going to be primal and fast. Part of me ached for steady, hard thrusts. The other part wanted him to go slow.

I gripped his cock and it felt both hard and soft under my palm. I loved how I caused him to growl as my hand moved up and down his shaft. Suddenly, he grabbed my hand, stopping me.

"Ava. Let me touch you. Please. Let me make love to you."

"You won't be able to. Nobody can," I replied with a weak smile.

"Nobody has tried hard enough then," he said, rubbing his thumb on my wrist. "Now, open up to me. Please, give me a chance."

I nodded.

Before I could blink, Jayce had his hands around my waist and was kissing me again.

FIFTY FIVE

HOLLYWOOD

A VA'S BODY ARCHED into mine as our mouths moved together, the water raining down on our faces. Finally having permission to touch her, I squeezed her slick, wet breasts, growling in the back of my throat as I played with them. Her nipples were hard under my fingers and I broke away to taste one and then the other. I teased and nipped at her nubs, making her gasp in pleasure.

Panting, I broke away from the kiss, turned off the shower. I quickly dried us off with a towel, and then picked her up and carried her into the bedroom.

I set her down and was about to crawl between her legs and start exploring her pussy when I noticed the sudden look of panic in her eyes.

"How about we start off with a massage?" I said, eyeing a small bottle of hotel lotion on the dresser. It was obvious that I needed to ease into our lovemaking. Maybe even take her mind off of it for a while.

"Okay."

I grabbed the bottle and asked her to get on her stomach. After pouring some of the lotion into my palms, I rubbed them together, warming my hands up, and then got on the bed. I put more lotion on my hands and started to massage her shoulders and neck. She closed her eyes and I could feel her begin to relax as my hands moved to her back.

"You okay?" I murmured.

"Mmmm," she replied, a smile on her lips.

I spent several minutes on her back while she groaned in approval. When she was used to my hands touching her, I moved to her sexy heart-shaped ass, kneading her ample cheeks as I fantasized about sticking my cock deep inside of her.

Her breath hitched as my fingers moved to her thighs and began working the muscles all around.

275

Noticing that she was breathing heavier, I used my thumbs to brush the sides of her opening, which was slick with her juices. She mewled in pleasure as I slowly rubbed around the edges of her pussy.

"You're so wet." I slid my finger over her slit and a hot fire rolled through me.

She gasped and clenched the pillow.

I began strumming her slicken, silky, velvety pussy, making her whimper and moan. Slowly, I eased a finger inside of her and she sucked in her breath.

"Fuck, you're tight," I whispered, panting from my own desire to replace my finger with something else. I slid a second finger inside and began fucking her, imagining that it was my cock stretching her wide. "Does this feel good?"

"Yes," she said breathlessly.

Wanting her to feel even better, I pulled her hips up crawled between her thighs, and began strumming her slit with my tongue. She moaned as I dragged and wiggled my tongue over every sweet part of her. Soon her thighs were trembling and she moaning in pleasure.

She was so close. I could feel it.

I shoved my tongue deep inside of her and wiggled my head so that my nose brushed against her clit. Suddenly, she exploded, screaming and bucking against me as her cum coated my lips. Turned on, I stroked my cock, licking her through her orgasm until she collapsed off me.

I got up and kissed her fiercely, aching to feel her pussy clenching my cock as I drove in and out of her. She kissed me back and then pulled away.

"You… you made me cum. That was… fucking incredible."

I smiled, my ego bursting with pride. "We're not through yet."

FIFTY SIX

AVA

M Y BODY FELT as if I'd just gotten done running a marathon.

Jayce got out of bed and grabbed a condom from his wallet. He moved back over me on the bed and slid his hand through my hair. He kissed me wildly, his body shaking with desire.

Pulling away from my lips, he moved to my breasts, squeezing and teasing my nipples with his warm, wet mouth. Swirling his tongue around one of the nubs, he began to suck and nip at the sensitive area, sending an electric current all the way down to my core. I moaned and he slipped his fingers between my legs, rubbing my clit until I squirmed and begged him to fuck me.

Pulling away from me, he quickly rolled the condom on and slowly eased into me with his thick cock. We both groaned in pleasure as he stretched me wide.

"You okay?" he asked in a husky voice.

"Yes."

"Keep going?"

I nodded quickly.

Staring down at me with hunger, he pulled back, leaving the head just inside. Grabbing my thighs, he rocked his hips and then buried himself to the hilt in my heat with a low, guttural groan. He pulled back again and then started fucking me in deep powerful thrusts. After a few seconds, Jayce paused and pulled my legs over his shoulders. He started fucking me again and, because of the angle, hit me in pleasure places I didn't even know existed.

"Beautiful," he said as he plunged in and out of me. "So... fucking... beautiful."

We kissed and then his thumb found my clit again. He began rolling it under the pad of his finger as he drove in and out, faster and deeper, until I was screaming out in ecstasy. Just like last time, the orgasm was earth-shattering, leaving me trembling from its aftermath.

Jayce stared down at me with those gorgeous blue eyes of his, going balls-deep one last time before letting himself go. "Fuck," he gasped, panting as his cock pulsated inside of me as he came.

When he was spent, I pulled his face down to mine and kissed him, still in a state of bliss from the moment.

"You're right," he said, afterward.

"About what?"

"You just… can't orgasm. It's a shame because you have no idea what you're missing," he teased.

I slapped him playfully.

A grin tugged at his lips. "I'll be happy to keep trying with you, though. Eventually, we'll get it."

"You're crazy, you know that?"

He grabbed my hand and kissed my knuckles. "Crazy for you."

"Yeah, well I'm pretty crazy for you, too," I whispered shyly.

"That's kind of a problem, don't you think?" he said.

"How so?"

"We live so far away from each other."

"Let's not worry about that now," I replied. "Anyway, I'm used to traveling because of my job."

He sighed. "Yeah, I guess it's a little early for us to start talking about you moving to Minnesota."

"I'm sorry, but I will *never* move to Minnesota," I replied. "Not with the snow and the blizzards. Sorry. You should move here."

"With the alligators and bugs? Fuck, no. I'll take blizzards over those any day."

"You're scared of them? Most people never even get close to one."

"You know I can't leave my club," he replied. "They

should be patching me soon."

"I can't leave Millie," I replied.

"Bring her with."

I snorted. "Right. She'd never leave, either. And, I couldn't ask her to."

"You said so yourself, you travel a lot. Visit her every weekend."

"Who's going to pay for it?"

"Aren't you making the big bucks as a stuntwoman?"

My smile faded. "To be honest, I don't know what's going to happen with that. Not after my fallout with Hunter."

"He's not going to be a problem for you."

"He already is," I replied. "I was released early from my last job and he threatened to end my career."

"I'm taking care of it."

My eyes widened. "You?"

"Let me rephrase that—I know someone who knows someone who can take care of it."

The hair stood up on the back of my neck. "I don't understand."

"You don't have to. Just... trust me. He's not going to be a problem for you."

Oddly enough, even though Hunter was a powerful man, I had a feeling that Jayce's friends could intimidate the hell out of him if they wanted to.

Jayce leaned over and kissed me. "Let's get some sleep. We have a big day tomorrow."

"Trying to get into Blade's townhome?"

He closed his eyes and smiled. "*That*, I'm not worried about. I promised you orgasms. I'm going to deliver so many, you won't care where you're living. As long as I'm nearby."

From the wicked smirk, I knew he was dead serious.

FIFTY SEVEN

HOLLYWOOD

W E BOTH SLEPT in until ten, had another incredible round of mind-blowing sex, took showers, and checked out. After having worked up an appetite, we drove to a nearby diner. As soon as the waitress took our order, Tarot called me. I explained what we'd found at the townhome.

"So, someone is living there?" he replied.

"There was a big, fat cat, so I assume so," I replied.

Ava stood up and whispered that she was going to the ladies' room. I nodded.

"Maybe the bank took over the place and resold it?" Tank suggested.

"That could be."

"There'd be record of it, though. I had Peyton look in the database, and the same person has owned it for a few years."

"Maybe he had a roommate we don't know about?"

"Could be. Just be careful. If Ava's brother was murdered, the person living there now might have been involved."

"True."

"Call me when you find out what's going on."

"Okay. By the way, I was wondering if you could help out with something else."

"What is it?"

I told him about the trouble Ava had been having with Hunter Calloway.

"That doesn't surprise me. I've seen interviews with him on television. He's an arrogant ass-fuck."

"One who tries using sex to get what he wants, too," I replied. "I'd like to teach him a lesson myself, but I don't think I could get close enough to even speak to the fucker."

"No. I'm sure he has bodyguards and an impenetrable security system."

"What about the Judge paying him a visit?"

"We've already asked for too many favors. I highly doubt he'd get involved with this anyway."

"This asshole can't get away with intimidating women for sex," I replied.

"I agree." He sighed. "Why don't you call Tank and tell him about it? He might be able to bend the Judge's ear for another favor."

"What kind of payment would he want?"

"Your soul, *muahahaha*," he said in a devious voice.

"Maybe he'd settle for a tattoo?"

"Hey, you never know. Off the subject, how are you and Ava getting along?"

"Better."

"Good. You pick a date yet?"

I snorted.

"Seriously, though. I see good things for the both of you in the horizon. Together." He began singing some song from the seventies by Dr. Hook about spending the night together.

Grinning, I shook my head.

"Seriously, you two. Long haul. I see it."

I liked what he was saying, but it didn't sound like we had much of a chance unless one of us moved. I told him.

"Give it time. I have a feeling that both of you are going to be making sacrifices soon. But, they'll be worth it."

"What kind of sacrifices?"

"I don't know everything, Hollywood. You need to figure some of this stuff out yourself."

"Thanks," I said wryly.

He chuckled. "Patience, kid. Find that and you'll be good to go. Speaking of which, *I* gotta go. Keep in touch."

"Will do."

When Ava returned to the table, she wanted to know what Tarot thought about the townhome.

"He didn't sound like he knew much more than us

either."

"Isn't he psychic?" she mused.

"Yes, but he doesn't know everything, apparently," I replied with a smirk. "His words exactly."

She smiled. "Nobody should, though. Right?"

"Right." I reached over and grabbed her hand. "The only thing I know right now is that I'm glad we made up."

"Me, too."

She started apologizing for ghosting me and I cut in.

"It's over. You did what you thought was right."

"But, I was wrong," she replied.

"You didn't know. I just hope that when all of this is over, we have answers for you. About Andrew."

"I hope so, too," she said sadly. "I need closure."

"Whatever it takes, I'm going to help you find it."

She smiled.

AFTER WE FINISHED eating, we drove back over to the townhome in the rental car, leaving her SUV at the diner. When we arrived, there was a woman sitting on the front steps watching a little boy blow and chase bubbles. When she saw us approach, her eyebrows knotted together.

"Can I help you?" she asked in a guarded tone

"We're looking for Andrew Bordellini," Ava replied.

"You and me both," the woman said sadly. She pulled out a pack of cigarettes from her shirt pocket.

"We heard that he lives here," I said, wondering who she was. The woman looked to be in her thirties, had long, dark hair and glasses.

"He was. I haven't seen him in over three years, though. Joey, don't get too close to the road," she said to the little boy.

"So, he disappeared?" Ava asked.

She lit the cigarette, still staring at us with uncertainty. "Who are you and why are you looking for him?"

"I'm his sister," Ava answered.

The woman's mouth dropped open. "You're Ava?"

"Yes," she replied and smiled. "He told you about me?"

"Yes. My God, I can't believe you're here. He always talked about reuniting with you," she replied, her entire demeanor changing.

Ava's face lit up. "Really?"

"Yes. My name is Penny, by the way. That's Joey. Our son," she replied.

This time, it was Ava who looked shell-shocked. "What?"

"Joey is Andrew's son," she replied. "I guess that makes you his aunt."

FIFTY EIGHT

AVA

"**W**HAT?" I REPEATED, still trying to digest what she'd told me. I looked at Joey again and a knot formed in my throat as a flurry of emotions rushed through me. "Joey is my nephew?"

"It looks that way. I think it's why Andrew took off," Penny said dully. "It happened right after I told him I was pregnant."

"He wouldn't skip out on his unborn child," I said, trying to reassure her. "I don't know what kind of relationship you had, but Andrew wouldn't do that. We think that..." I looked at Joey and lowered my voice. "We think that a man named Blade might have *made* him disappear. Do you know who he is?"

"That's Felix. Everyone called him Blade because of his extensive knife collection," she replied.

"Yeah, we knew he was big on knives," Jayce said sarcastically.

She went on. "We've been renting from him. Of course, I haven't heard anything from the man in over a year. Seriously, though? You think Felix did something to Andrew?"

I looked at Jayce. "Could you tell her what we know? I'll keep Joey occupied."

"Sure," he replied.

I walked over to the little boy and asked if I could blow some bubbles.

"Okay," he said, handing me the small bottle. Looking down into his face, I could definitely see some kind of resemblance to my brother. Especially in the eyes and eyebrows.

I blew some of the bubbles out and watched as he went after them, laughing and giggling. He seemed like such a happy kid, which I hoped meant that Penny was a good mother.

"So, Felix died last year?" I heard Penny say. "I guess that explains why he stopped cashing the rent checks."

"Who pays the utility bills?" Jayce asked.

"I'm responsible for that. It's fine, though, because rent was reasonably low. Only five-hundred dollars a month, to be exact. Andrew and Blade were friends, though. Why would he kill him?"

"Who got killed, Mommy?" Joey asked.

"Nobody, baby," she replied and pointed to a large, yellow dump truck in the grass. "Why don't you play with that for a while?"

"No. I'm hungry," Joey said. "I want some ice cream."

"Lunch first… and then we'll talk about it." She turned back to us. "Look, why don't you two come in? I'll make him a sandwich and then we can talk some more," Penny said.

Jayce nodded. "Sounds good."

WHEN JOEY WAS seated in the kitchen with his peanut-butter and jelly sandwich, we went into the living room, for privacy.

"You know, we were going to get married," Penny said sadly. "We talked about it a few times."

"When was the last time you saw him?" I asked.

She sighed. "When he left with Felix. They went to Vegas for some kind of convention."

"Convention? For what?" I asked.

"Old cars. That's what they told me, at least. Andrew was into classic vehicles and had been talking about buying a GTO and restoring it," she replied.

"So, he never came back from Vegas?" Jayce asked.

"Nope."

"But Felix did? Was he alone?" Jayce asked.

"Yes. He told me Andrew had met some woman. Apparently, she was some showgirl. A real knockout, I guess. Anyway…" her eyes filled with tears, "they supposedly ran off together."

"And you believed him?" I said, the hair standing up on the back of my neck. I wasn't psychic, but I suddenly had a vision of Blade killing my brother and dropping his body off in the desert.

She shrugged. "I had no reason not to. Felix had always been really nice to me. I used to think that he wanted to be more than friends, if given the chance."

Jayce and I looked at each, an unspoken message passing between us.

If Blade wanted Penny, he probably wouldn't have thought twice about killing Andrew.

"Did Blade and Andrew look alike?" Ava asked.

"Yes. Especially after Andrew stayed away," she said, a troubled look appearing on her face. "Felix dyed his hair and started wearing it the same way as Andrew. I thought it was kind of weird, honestly. I guess deep down, I wondered if he did it because of me."

"To make you like him more?" I asked.

She nodded.

"Did you ever try calling Andrew when he didn't come home from Vegas?" I asked.

"Yes. Of course. He never answered my calls or texts," she replied. "Felix told me he'd spoken to Andrew a few times afterward, though. Apparently, he told Blade that he wanted 'space'."

"But, Andrew knew about the baby, right?" I said.

She nodded. "You probably think I'm a naïve idiot," she said, sniffling and wiping the tears under her eyes with the

289

back of her hand. "Maybe I was. It's just that I trusted Felix. He didn't seem like the kind of guy who'd kill anyone."

"When was the last time you spoke to him?"

"Felix? Last year. During the spring. He'd told me that he had some business to attend to in Minnesota and would be gone for a while. I guess that's why I didn't realize he'd actually 'disappeared'."

"Where did Felix live?" Jayce asked.

"Right next to us," she said. "He owns the entire building."

Jayce and I looked at each other again and then back to her.

"Do you have a key to his place?" he asked.

"No," she replied. "We weren't *that* good of friends."

"It's fine. I'll get us in there," Jayce said, looking at me.

SURE ENOUGH, JAYCE'S skills weren't just limited to the bedroom. He managed to pick the lock and we soon found ourselves in the living room, which consisted only of an oversized brown sofa, a matching chair, and a large, flat-screen television on the wall. Other than that, the place was void of pictures, plants, and anything else that might have made it homey.

"Oh, my God, what's that smell?" I gasped, my stomach heaving. The rancid smell was worse than a hot garbage dumpster that hadn't been emptied in months.

"Fuck. I think I know. Stay here while I search the place," Jayce said, covering his mouth and nose.

I opened the door to let some fresh air in, thankful that it was still daylight, since the power had been shut off.

Jayce appeared in the living room again, a grim expression on his face.

"Did you find anything?" I asked.

He nodded and from the look in his eyes, I knew it was

290

bad.

"What is it?" I asked, my heart leaping into my throat.

"I think I found him. Andrew," he said in a shaky voice.

"What?" I whispered in horror. "Where?"

"I don't think you should see 'where'. We need to call the police."

Tears filled my eyes. "You're saying that you actually *found* my brother's body?"

"I think so. It was…" He paused.

"Tell me," I said, openly sobbing now.

He walked over and put his arms around me. "I found someone stuffed in the freezer," he said in a regrettable voice.

My stomach heaved again as I realized what the horrible, horrible smell was in the apartment. I pushed him away right before I turned my head and threw up breakfast.

FIFTY NINE

HOLLYWOOD

I COULDN'T GET the image out of my head of the dead body in the downstairs freezer. I knew, even before I raised the lid, that I'd find something out of a horror movie. I only looked for a split second, too, but it had been long enough to provide me with plenty of future nightmares.

After Ava threw up, she demanded to see the body, but I talked her out of it. I wasn't a forensic specialist, but something told me that freezer had been working for quite a while before the electricity was shut off. Which was why it smelled so fucking bad and the corpse looked so ripe.

We called the police and told Penny about the body. She started crying and soon, both women were holding and comforting each other.

Two squad cars appeared a short time later, along with an ambulance. We were questioned by the police and then later, met with a couple of homicide detectives. Of course, they saw my cut and started giving me the third degree. Fortunately, Penny set them straight and told them everything she knew.

"These two had nothing to do with it," she said to them angrily.

They backed off, fortunately.

When everything was said and done, the police were able to identify the body as Andrew Bordellini. Obviously, this would re-open the other case, and we were pretty confident that Felix Doberly would finally be identified. We still didn't know why he'd taken Andrew's identity, but it was obvious, after looking at pictures, the resemblance between them was pretty similar.

"He'd changed his look again in Minnesota," I said, remembering the night I'd confronted him at Peyton's. He'd had the same hairstyle as Tarot and they were of similar build. But, up close, I had to agree that our V.P. was a much

293

better looking guy.

"I'm sorry," I said to Ava. "I know you wanted closure, but this was fucked up. Your brother didn't deserve the hand he was dealt."

"The cards dealt to the people in my family seem to never be in our favor."

"Maybe not before, but... now that I'm here, things are definitely going to change."

She smiled sadly and I knew from her expression that she didn't believe me. I was determined to prove her wrong, however. If she'd let me.

SIXTY

AVA

AFTER THE HARROWING ordeal, Jayce and I drove back to Miami and he stayed overnight at my place. After making love, he held me in his arms and we talked about Andrew, Penny, and Joey.

"One thing good that came out of this is that you found out about your nephew," he said, stroking my arm.

I smiled. "Yes. Penny and I are going to keep in touch. I was thinking about driving back to Tampa next week, actually."

"That's good. He seems like a sweet kid. You should really make a point to get to know him."

"I definitely will. Speaking of which, when are you going to visit your sister?"

"Hopefully sometime this month. You should fly back with me to Minnesota."

"I don't think I'll be going anywhere soon. I'm picking up Millie from the hospital tomorrow and driving her home. She had a mild heart attack. That's why I had to leave Minnesota so quickly."

His eyes widened in surprise. "Really? That's why you left? I thought it was to avoid me."

I slapped his forearm playfully. "Not everything is about you, you know."

"I'm a guy. We always want everything to be about us. Especially when it comes to our women."

"Sadly, that's not going to happen in this relationship," I said with a smirk.

His face turned serious. "I'm sorry to hear about Millie. How is she doing?"

"Okay, I guess. Tired and weak. She seemed in pretty good spirits, though."

"Is she going to need twenty-four-hour care?"

"It doesn't sound like it."

"That's good."

296

I asked him how long he was able to stay and he told me that he was leaving in a couple of days. It made my heart heavy.

"You've wrecked me," I told him.

"What?"

"I'm already missing you and you haven't even left yet," I pouted.

"I know the feeling," he said softly. "We'll just have to make the most of our time together then."

"Yes, we will."

His hand moved between my legs. "And I know just how to do it."

I started laughing, but then it quickly changed to mewling noises as he made good on his orgasm promises.

SIXTY ONE

ONE

HOLLYWOOD

THE NEXT DAY, I met Millie, who was surprised to see me, but also happy. She was a short, heavy-set woman with blonde hair, glasses, and a warm smile for everyone. From the way she interacted with the hospital staff and other patients, it was easy to see why Ava adored her. The woman didn't seem to have a mean bone in her body.

As we drove her home from the hospital, she asked how we'd met.

"When I was in Minnesota," Ava said quickly. "I stopped off at a tattoo parlor and he inked me."

"Inked you?" she repeated, looking amused. "Goodness… that sounds messy…"

We both laughed.

"I gave her a tattoo," I explained.

"Really? I can't wait to see it," she replied. "What is the tattoo of?"

Ava told her about the dragon. "It's not finished yet. I'll have to go back out to there, one of these days, so he can work on it again."

"Minnesota seems like such a nice place, especially with all of those lakes and trees. I hear that in the autumn it's just beautiful."

"It is. You should come up and visit, too," I said, grinning over at Ava. "Who knows, you might even decide to make Minnesota your home when you experience the beauty of all *four* seasons."

"Thank you, but unfortunately these old bones can't handle your blizzard season. I'd love to visit sometime, though, but it won't for some time, I'm afraid," she said. "The doctor said I need to take it easy for a while."

"Yes, you do," Ava said. "But, don't worry. I'll be around to help out, too."

"You don't have to go fussing over me," she said, waving

her hand. "I'm not going to break that easily. Besides, you need to get that tattoo finished, right?"

"She's right," I said. "But, I have to agree with Ava. You need your family around while you're recovering. Just in case. She has plenty of time for us to finish the dragon."

Ava smiled at me lovingly. "Yeah. What he said."

"You know, I've always thought about getting a tattoo. I'm too old now, though," Millie said.

"Bull. You're never too old," I said, looking back at her. "Don't let anyone else tell you otherwise."

"I'm sixty-two," she said. "You don't think that's too old?"

"Hell no. When you're feeling up to it, I'll come back down here and do the honors. If you'll let me," I said.

"That sounds like a plan." Millie reached forward and patted Ava's shoulder. "Dear, don't lose contact with Jayce. I've never been inked by a man before. I don't care how messy it is, I'm putting it on my bucket list."

We laughed.

SIXTY
TWO

AVA

WHEN JAYCE RETURNED to Minnesota, I felt lost. Our last few days together had been incredible, and when he got on that plane, I knew that my heart already belonged to him. I wasn't naïve enough to believe that he felt the same way, though. Guys who looked like Jayce, and lived the kind of lifestyle, where women were always throwing themselves at them, didn't fall in love at the drop of a hat. Besides all of that, I was pretty certain that a long-distance relationship with a biker would never last. Not when they weren't willing to abandon their club for a woman on the other side of the country. Of course, I couldn't abandon Millie either. Especially now.

Days turned into weeks, but we stayed in touch, either talking or texting each other whenever we had the chance. Eight weeks after he went back home, Jayce surprised me by making plans to come back out to Miami to stay for a week.

"When?" I asked, thrilled with the news.

"I'm hoping to come out next Friday. *If* I can take the time off of work," he replied. "By the way, did you get my text last night?"

"No," I replied. "I was wondering what happened to you."

He normally sent me messages every night, before turning in. I'd been so tired that I'd fallen asleep early, not noticing any missed texts.

He swore. "Sorry. We were at an underground club. It probably didn't go through. I've been having problems with my cell phone service anyway."

"So, you were at a club last night?"

"Yeah, we were celebrating. They finally patched me," he replied, a smile in his voice. "I'm now a full-fledged member of the Gold Vipers."

"That's great," I replied, wanting to be happy for him. This wasn't exactly thrilling news for me, however.

"What's wrong?" he asked.

"Nothing. I'm... I'm happy that you finally got what you've been wanting for so long."

"Thanks."

"So, what does that mean for you, besides getting new patches?"

"Basically, it means I've earned the respect of my brothers and have proved myself to be a loyal and worthy member."

"So, it's kind of like when you go through basic training in the military and finally graduate?"

"Well, it's more than that, but I guess you could say it's not the worst analogy."

"Is there any way they can kick you out?"

"I'd have to fuck up pretty badly, but I suppose. Anyway, being patched means I have more free-time. We can see each other more."

That, I liked.

"Good, because I miss you," I replied, a pout in my voice.

"I miss you, too."

I heard voices in the background, one of them a woman's.

"Where are you?" I asked.

"Across the street. *Danny V's*."

I rolled my eyes. "The strip club?"

"Yeah, the guys who couldn't show last night wanted to buy me a couple drinks to celebrate."

"And, they couldn't take you to a classier place?"

"What do you mean?" he said with a smile in his voice. "There's a lot of ass here."

"I said 'class'," I replied, annoyed.

Jayce laughed. "Relax. I'm just trying to rile you. I love it when steam starts coming out of your ears."

"So, you're not at the strip club?"

"No, we're here. I'm not interested in what's on stage,

though. This is more for my brothers than me. Strippers aren't my thing. I'm more into stuntwomen with long, beautiful legs, and a ba-donk-a-donk that I can play the drums on."

Jayce was obsessed with my ass. He was always trying to grab it, slap it, among… other things.

I smirked. "Okay."

"Hey," he said. "Trust me, okay?"

"I trust you," I said softly.

"Good. I've got to go. Can I call you tonight before I go to bed?"

"Yes. Definitely."

"Good. I'll talk to you then."

SIXTY THREE

HOLLYWOOD

I'D BEEN PLANNING on staying relatively sober, but my friends kept buying me drinks.

"So, tell us again about finding the body in the freezer?" Len said after buying me another rum and Coke.

I repeated the story.

"Smelled pretty fucking bad I bet?" he said.

"Fuck yeah. The worst smell ever. Even worse than when you take your boots off," I replied.

The other guys laughed.

"Ha-ha. Funny," he said with a growl, taking a drink of his beer.

I patted him on the back. "I'm just giving you shit."

"You know what I've noticed? That you only fuck with people when you're tense." He leered at the buxom stripper standing in front of us on the stage. "You need to get your dick waxed. That'll take the edge off."

"Tell me about," I said, thinking about Ava. I was already counting down the hours until I'd get to do exactly what he said. It made me hard just thinking about it.

"That one will blow you for a fifty," Len said, nodding toward the stripper.

"Maybe you," I teased. "She pays me twice that amount to blow my dick."

He chuckled and then his face went serious. "Really?"

I threw my head back and laughed. "Len, man. You've got to quit smoking so much ganja. It's making you about as gullible as a five-year-old."

We bantered back and forth until Tarot entered the club and walked over to us. He put a hand on my shoulder. "Can I talk to you alone?"

"Yeah," I said, wondering what was going on now. From his expression, I could tell whatever it was he had to say, was important.

306

We walked out of the club and stood outside together. It was just past seven and still light out.

"What's up?" I asked.

"Tank wanted me to tell you that the Judge talked to Hunter Calloway and set him straight."

My eyes widened. "No fucking way." I'd forgotten all about the call I'd made to Tank after returning from Miami. He'd told me that he couldn't make any promises, but would see what he could do. Apparently, he did something.

Tarot grinned. "Yeah. In fact, there's a new movie being filmed in Minneapolis soon. Ava Rhodes is going to be offered a stunt job, apparently paying pretty well, too. Complements of douchebag Calloway."

"How did he get him to bend?"

"From what I hear, he dug up some major shit on Calloway and threatened to expose it if he didn't stop fucking with Ava. It must have been pretty bad if Calloway is willing to try and get her hired for this movie, which is supposed to be a high-dollar production."

"No shit. That's great. I need to call Tank and thank him."

"You can do it next weekend. We're all riding down to Jensen for a barbecue he's having."

I groaned. "Next weekend?"

"Yeah, why?"

I told him about the plans I had to meet up with Ava.

"Invite her to the barbecue."

"She's been caring for her mother, and is afraid to leave her. I doubt she'll be able to go."

"Well, she's going to have to when they offer her that job in Minneapolis."

"Unless she refuses it," I replied. Remembering the disgust on her face when she'd talked about Calloway, I wasn't sure if Ava would want to work with him, no matter what the pay was.

307

"I guess there's always that. Look, if you want to see her so badly, talk to Phoenix. He might be able to give you this week off instead of next. I overheard him talking about how the weather was supposed to be shitty for the next few days anyway."

"Good idea," I said, relieved that I'd still get to see her.

"Just get your ass back in time for Tank's barbecue in Jensen."

"Don't worry. I'll be there."

SIXTY FOUR

AVA

AFTER HANGING UP with Jayce, I took a shower and then called Millie to see how she was. When she answered, her voice sounded merrier than usual.

"What are you so cheery about?" I asked.

"Oh, hello, Ava. I didn't even look at the caller I.D. I thought you were Charles."

My eyes widened. "Who's Charles?"

"I met him at church last weekend."

"Oh."

"We're going out for ice-cream tonight." She giggled.

Was it me, or did Millie sound like a teenager? "Are you able to even *eat* ice-cream?"

"As long as I don't overindulge. Anyway, I hate to cut you off, but I really have to go. I think he's here."

"Okay—"

"Bye," she said and hung up.

I stared at my phone in wonder.

Charles?

It had been a long time since Millie had dated. In fact, I couldn't even remember her going out with anyone in the last decade. I was happy for her, but also anxious about the idea.

What if she overdid it?

My phone began to ring. I looked at the number, but didn't recognize it.

"Hello?"

"Yes, may I speak to Ava Rhodes?" the woman asked.

"This is she."

Ten minutes later, I was left speechless again. The woman had just offered me a stunt gig for a big blockbuster movie being filmed in Minneapolis. They'd need me in two months, if I accepted the position. She was going to email me the information and a contract to sign if I was interested. What really blew my mind was the pay. It was more than anything I'd ever been offered before.

But, what about Millie?

My stomach tightened at the thought of leaving her. I had a week to accept the offer, however. I just wasn't sure if I could.

When Jayce called me a few hours later, I could tell he was three-sheets-to-the-wind. I told him about the job offer and he acted like he'd already known about it.

"Why doesn't this surprise you?" I asked.

"Remember when I told you not to worry about Hunter anymore?" he replied.

"Hold up. Are you telling me this job had something to do with Hunter Calloway?" I asked angrily.

"Yeah. The Judge found something on him and was able to convince old Calloway to not only leave you the fuck alone, but hook you up with a movie deal. Sweet, huh?"

"No," I said angrily. "Because that means he'll probably be on the set and I don't want to work with him again."

"If he gets out of hand, I'll fucking knock his block off," Jayce said sternly.

"He won't get out of hand because I'm not signing up for the damn movie. Thanks for trying to help, but you actually made things worse."

"How?" he asked, surprised.

"You just can't go around threatening people so they'll hire me," I said, frustrated.

"But, he threatened to end your career. What's the difference?"

"That's just it. I don't want to play those kind of games. I want to be hired because of my talent. Not because someone's hand was forced into it."

We argued some more and then I told him that I was tired and wanted to sleep.

"You're still coming week, aren't you?" I asked.

"About that..." Jayce told me that he couldn't because he

311

had to go to a club function in Jensen, Iowa.

"What kind of function?" I asked, disappointed.

He sighed. "A barbecue. Remember that guy I introduced you to at the party we had at the farm? The big guy named Tank?"

I pictured the friendly giant and nodded. "Yeah."

"He's invited our entire club. You're invited, too."

Obviously, I couldn't go. "Can't you get out of it?"

"No. Even if I could, I wouldn't. I owe Tank for helping with Calloway, among other things."

I growled under my breath.

"Why are you so pissed off tonight? Is it your period?"

"You really are clueless when it comes to women, aren't you?" I snapped, knowing that I was taking all of my frustration out on him, but unable to stop myself. "I mean, if you want to calm someone down, you don't blame their anger on being on the rag. Being on the rag *doesn't* make us angry. It just makes men's antics less tolerable."

"And you more emotional."

I growled again and then hung up. He tried calling me back, but I ignored him. A few seconds later, he sent me a text.

Jayce: *I'm sorry that I pissed you off. I really didn't mean to.*

I sat there staring at it and then messaged him back.

Me: *It's okay. I'm just tired. I may have overreacted.*

Jayce: *May have?*

I sent him an angry emoji face.

He sent me a heart and then: *I love you, Ava.*

This, of course, made me melt. I sent him the words back, my heart filled with joy.

Jayce: *Sweet Dreams.*

Me: *You, too.*

I put my phone down, pulled my knees to my chest, and smiled.

He loved me.

Nobody, besides Millie and Sheila, had ever said that to me before. I touched my lucky necklace and thought that sometimes good things came in threes, too.

SIXTY

FIVE

HOLLYWOOD

I WOKE UP late, a little hungover from partying the last couple of nights.

After texting Ava, I packed an overnight bag and pulled up the airline ticket I'd purchased the night before for Miami on my phone. I hadn't told Ava about it because I wanted it to be a surprise. I'd missed the hell out of her and was still determined to find a way to get her to move to Minnesota. I also hoped to change her mind about the movie so at least we'd get to see each other more. And if she did, I'd accompany her to the set and make sure that Calloway knew to stay the fuck away.

An hour later, Dover picked me up and gave me a ride to the airport. He'd also gotten patched the night before and so we were both now official Gold Vipers. It had been a proud moment for both of us after so much hard work. And a relief. No more grunt work and being available twenty-four hours a day when needed.

"Thanks," I said, when he dropped me off in front of the terminal.

"You need a ride when you get back, call me."

"Thank you. I appreciate it."

"No problem, *club* brother." He held out his fist and we bumped knuckles.

I ARRIVED IN Miami at just past three in the afternoon. Instead of renting a car, I verified that she was home by texting her, and then took a cab to her place. Fortunately, someone let me into the building so I was able to really surprise her.

"Oh, my God!" she squealed, jumping into my arms. "What are you doing here?"

I walked her back into the condo and kicked the door shut behind us. "I had to see you," I said, noticing the tears in

315

her eyes. It filled my heart with joy, knowing that she was so happy to see me.

We started kissing, and soon we were on her bed, making love. Afterward, she ordered some Asian food and had it delivered.

"You sure you can eat all that?" I asked, staring at the huge pile of fried rice and lo mein she was adding to her plate.

She smirked. "Just watch me."

Not only did she eat all of it, but she had an egg roll and some cream-cheese wontons, too.

"I'm impressed," I said, pushing my empty plate away. I had a hearty appetite, but this time, she'd eaten more than I'd been able to put down. "All of that and you're still sexy as all hell. You must not eat like this all the time."

"Lately, I've been pigging out," she replied. "I guess boredom will do that to you."

"*Bored*? Are you saying you're bored right now?" I teased.

She smiled "No. Of course not. Now that you're here, at least."

"Move to Minnesota and I'll make sure you're never bored again," I replied.

"You never quit, do you?" she replied laughing. Ava got up and started clearing away the plates.

I grabbed her waist and pulled her onto my lap. "I'm never going to quit because I want the woman I love with me all the time."

Her eyes filled with tears again. She wrapped her arms around my neck and hugged me tightly. "I love you, too, Jayce."

"You're crying," I said, pulling away. I stared into her eyes. "Is there something wrong?"

Looking embarrassed, she laughed. "Nothing. I've just been so emotional lately. And don't you dare ask me if I'm on the rag. You already know I'm not."

"I wasn't going to," I said, rubbing her back, concerned. "I shouldn't have given you any shit about your period. You were cursed with something we could never handle because we're wimps at heart. And to have to deal with it every month, too."

Her smile suddenly fell. "Oh, my God."

"What's wrong?"

She blinked. "I'm not on the rag."

"Yeah, we've established that," I said, chuckling. "Lucky timing."

"I haven't been for…" she began counting her fingers. Her face turned white and she put a hand over her mouth. "Oh, my God, it's been two months since I had my last period."

SIXTY SIX

AVA

*H*OW IN THE *world could I have missed that?*
I was *always* regular.
Never any surprises.
I just couldn't believe I'd gone through two months of no periods without noticing a damn thing.

Who does that?

"So, what are you saying?" Jayce asked.

I could barely get the words out. "I might be pregnant," I squeaked.

The look he gave me was almost comical. "But... we used condoms."

"Everyone knows there's still a risk with those damn things," I said, covering my eyes. "Oh shit, Jayce, what am I going to do if I'm pregnant? This is *horrible*."

He pulled my hand away. "If you are, we'll deal with it."

"I'm not getting an abortion," I said flatly.

His eyes burned into mine. "Babe, I would *never* ask that of you. If you're pregnant, we're going to do the responsible thing. We'll get married. You'll live in Minnesota. We'll buy a house with a yappy dog and a white picket fence..."

My eyes narrowed. "You did this to me on purpose so that I'd move to Minnesota, didn't you?"

He gave me a startled look. "What?"

I broke into a smile. "I'm *kidding*."

"I should hope so. That's nothing to joke about."

I got off -his lap. "We need to buy a pregnancy test. Maybe two, in case the first one is wrong," I said, heading toward the bedroom to get dressed.

He followed me. "Fuck the test. I'll ask Tarot. He can probably even tell us if you're having a girl or boy or, hell, twins."

I opened up my closet and with trembling hands, began searching for something to wear. "We both know that he's not one-hundred percent accurate. Anyway, I need scientific proof right now. This could change everything."

"Both of ours," he murmured.

I looked over at him. Thankfully, he seemed to be taking this better than me. The thought of being a mother scared the hell out of me. "We'll call Tarot after. Okay?"

He nodded.

AN HOUR LATER, I stared at the test result of the first kit.

"What does it say?" he asked, on the other side of the bathroom door.

I touched my stomach. "Um, it says I'm pregnant. I'm going to try the other one, in case it's wrong."

He gasped. "What? You're kidding, right?"

"No, it really says I'm pregnant," I replied, looking at the stick. I bit my lower lip. "But, I suppose it could be wrong. Right?"

He didn't say anything.

"Jayce?"

"Sorry, I'm calling Tarot."

Sighing, I opened up the other box, listening as Jayce began talking to Dom.

"Hey, brother. Guess what? I'm going to be a father," he said joyfully.

I froze.

He was happy?

Surprised that he was taking it so well, I opened the door and watched his face as Tarot spoke to him on the phone.

"What is he saying?" I whispered.

"That we could have saved the money on the test. He already knew."

My jaw dropped. "*No. Really?*"

Jayce looked at me again. "He wants to know if we'd like to know the sex."

Pursing my lips together, I grabbed the phone from Jayce. "Don't you dare say anything else, Tarot. If I am pregnant, I want the sex to be a surprise."

"You just took a test, right? You already know you're pregnant."

I gasped and laughed. "How in the hell do *you* know so much?"

"Hollywood told me about it," he replied, amused.

I sighed. "Yeah. I took the first one. It was positive. I'm taking the next one now. Just to make sure."

"Don't waste your money; return it. You're pregnant."

I touched my stomach again. "This is crazy," I said, not knowing whether to laugh or cry.

"Did he tell you what we're having?" Jayce asked.

I shook my head.

Having heard, Tarot spoke. "To be honest, I don't know if it's a boy or a girl. Not yet, anyway. I do know you're going to be good parents, though."

"I hope so," I replied in a shaky voice.

"The dedication you showed in regards to your brother proves how much family means to you. You're going to be a wonderful mom," Tarot said softly.

The idea of someone calling me "Mom" brought tears to my eyes again.

At least I knew why I'd been so emotional lately.

"Hey, are you about done?" Jayce grabbed the cell back. "Woman, don't you ever take a man's cell phone from him like that again," he teased.

"Blah, blah, blah," I said, walking back into the bathroom to take the other test.

"Did you tell her the sex?" Jayce asked Tarot on the phone. "Oh."

I turned around and looked at Jayce. "He doesn't know."

"I bet there's one thing he does now," Jayce said with a gleeful expression. "The date you're moving to Minnesota."

I groaned and shut the bathroom door.

AFTER THE SECOND test turned up positive, we made a doctor's appointment the following day. They also tested me and it turned out that I was almost two and a half months into my pregnancy.

"So, I imagine that means I can't do any stunts until after I have the baby?" I said to the doctor.

"I wouldn't recommend it," he replied, amused.

Although I'd been thinking about turning down the movie offer in Minnesota because of Hunter, I needed to make a living somehow.

"Don't worry. I actually make decent money," Jayce told me after we left the hospital. "Between slinging ink and roofing, we shouldn't have any financial issues."

"I can't expect you to pay for everything."

"It's just until you can work again," he replied. "Although, I wouldn't mind if you wanted to be a fulltime mother."

"Jayce, we don't even know where I'm going to be living."

"Minnesota," he replied firmly.

"I can't do that to Millie."

Jayce groaned. "Millie can take care of herself. She had a mild heart attack, and you said so yourself, she looks great and has a new spring in her step."

"I think that's because of Charles," I said, amused. They'd had two more dates since the weekend.

"You'd better call her and let her know you're pregnant," he told me after getting into my SUV. He started the engine. "I wonder how she'll take it?"

"Millie is the most understanding person I've ever met. She'll be happy for us."

I hadn't actually said anything yet to her. I'd wanted to know for sure.

Jayce nodded. "Hey, you hungry? Let's grab some food and bring it back to your place," he said as we left the hospital parking lot.

"Okay. Let me call her now and get it over with." I pulled out my phone and dialed her number.

"Oh, dear, I'm so glad you called," Millie said, sounding elated. "I have some exciting news that I wanted to share with you."

"Me, too. Tell me yours first."

"Charles and I are taking a twenty-nine day cruise with a small group from our church. We're going to the French Polynesia and New Zealand and Australia," she said breathlessly. "I'm so excited. It's going to be so much fun."

"Wow, are you sure it's wise in your condition?"

She sighed. "Ava, I'm fine. I just had a visit with the doctor and he said that I am doing very well. You need to quit worrying about me so much. I'm serious now. I know you care, but you worry way too much about me. As much as I appreciate it, sometimes it gets… annoying."

I snorted. "You're serious?"

"Yes. I was afraid to tell you because I knew you'd start giving me the third-degree. I feel like our relationship has turned around. It's almost like *I'm* the child and you're the adult. This can't go on, dear."

"I'm sorry. I'm actually very happy for you," I said, feeling as if a weight had been lifted off my shoulders. "It sounds like a wonderful trip. When are you leaving?"

"We leave next month already."

"Wow. When exactly are you going to introduce me to Charles?"

"We're planning on having a little dinner party for the family soon. He has children and grandchildren he wants me to meet."

"Sounds great."

"You said that you have some news for me?"

I swallowed. "Yeah, um…" I laughed nervously. "I guess I'll just spit it out; I'm pregnant."

She gasped. "What? When did this happen?"

"When Jayce was here last. I mean, he's here now. But, that's when, you know, I got pregnant."

She was silent for a few seconds and it was like I could hear the crickets chirping. Just when I thought my news had sent her into cardiac arrest, she spoke again. "My dear, I'm happy for you. You're going to be a wonderful, wonderful mother."

I sighed in relief. Her support meant everything. "Thank you."

"How does he feel about it?"

I looked over at Jayce, who was driving and trying to listen in. "I think he's okay with it."

He looked over at me. "Okay with what? The pregnancy?"

I nodded.

"I'm more than okay with it, Millie," he said loudly so she could hear. "I think it's fantastic. Now if I can just get her to marry me!"

My eyes widened.

"Did he just say what I think he said?" Millie asked, sounding amused.

"Uh, yeah," I said, swallowing the lump in my throat.

"Is that a 'yes'?" Jayce asked, grabbing my hand.

"If you love him, tell him 'yes'," Millie ordered over the phone. "You'd be a fool not to. It's obvious he loves you."

I looked at Jayce. "But he wants me to move to Minnesota," I told her.

"So? We make sacrifices for those we love. And don't you go saying that you can't leave Florida because of me. That's poppycock," she grumbled.

I snorted.

"What's it going to be, babe?" Jayce asked, bringing my hand up to his mouth. He kissed my knuckles.

"I guess you're getting what you wanted," I joked. "I'm... I'm moving to Minnesota, I guess."

He let out a loud "whoop!"

"Congratulations," Millie said. "Now, you two come to dinner tonight so we can talk more about this. Okay?"

"Okay."

"I love you, dear," she replied.

"I love you, too," I said softly before hanging up.

"So, she's fine with everything?" Jayce asked me.

I smiled and nodded. "She's going on a cruise with Charles next month." I told him about it. "Oh, and we're supposed to come over for dinner tonight."

"Sounds good."

Jayce suddenly turned into a mini mall parking lot.

"What are you doing? There's no food places over here," I said, my stomach rumbling already.

He drove up to a small jewelry store and parked the SUV. "We need to make our engagement official," he said, shutting off the engine. "I'm buying you a ring."

I was suddenly grinning from ear-to-ear. "Okay. If you want."

"I do want," Jayce said, looking at the necklace around my neck. "You mentioned that Millie gave you that."

I looked down at the cross and nodded. "For good luck."

"I think just being around it has given me good luck. Not only did I meet the girl of my dreams, but now she's going to be my wife," he said softly.

My eyes filled with tears.

He sighed. "I just want you to know that I appreciate the sacrifice you're willing to make for me. To move to Minnesota. I know it's not what you wanted."

"I want to be with you," I replied. "So, if it's Minnesota, then… I guess it's Minnesota."

"You know, there is a Gold Vipers chapter in Florida," he said.

My eyes widened. "Could you transfer?"

He shrugged. "Maybe. It would mean leaving my club brothers behind."

"Family is everything," I said, staring into his blue eyes. "I would never make you give them up just because of a location. Besides, I'm starting to really like Tarot and Peyton."

"What about Joey and Penny?"

"I'll come back and visit as much as possible. Along with Mille. I might be moving to Minnesota, but it's not like I can't hop on a plane and see them."

He grinned. "My little jet-setter."

"Get used to it, because after the baby is born, I'm eventually going back to work."

His face turned serious. "There's a lot of danger involved. You sure you want to do that?"

"There's danger in staying with your club. I'm not asking you to leave," I reminded him.

He smirked. "Point taken. We haven't had any club disputes for a while, though. I'm crossing my fingers that there'll be less drama in the future."

"God, I hope so, too. At least you won't have any more from me."

"What do you mean? I'm marrying you. Something tells me there'll be a lot of drama."

I scowled at him.

He grabbed my hand. "I wouldn't change it for the world, though. In fact, I think we should tattoo the word *Drama Queen* somewhere on your body. After we finish the dragon, of course."

We were going to wait until after the baby was born to finish that tattoo. We'd also decided to name our child Andrew if it was a boy, or Andrea if it was a girl.

"You keep that up and you're not touching any part of my skin again."

He laughed. "Have I told you how much I love the fire in your eyes when you get all feisty? It's so fucking sexy. Just like you, my little mama," He leaned over and kissed me.

"I won't be sexy in a few months," I pouted.

"Bullshit. I'm looking forward to seeing your stomach grow. I can't wait to see the changes and feel the baby move," he said softly. "I'm even thinking about getting a tattoo of you pregnant."

I didn't think I could love Jayce any more at that moment. "Stop it. Quit making me cry," I said, laughing through my tears.

He chuckled. "Let's put a ring on that finger," he said.

"Okay."

AS WE GOT out of the SUV and went into the shop, I thought about how much my life would be changing in the next several months. It was both scary and exhilarating, especially with the baby. Thankfully, I'd experienced both sides of parenting—the good and the bad. I didn't know what the future would bring, but I'd try to be the best damn mother I could be. Thanks to Millie, I ended up with a pretty good role model, too.

"Is this the one?" the jeweler asked me, thirty minutes later, after we'd looked at several rings.

Although I knew he was talking about the diamond solitaire on my finger, I looked at Jayce and nodded.

Yes, he was positively the one…

The End

CPSIA information can be obtained
at www.ICGtesting.com
Printed in the USA
LVHW010201170322
713569LV00015B/2055